THE MAYDAY

BOOKS BY BILL EIDSON

The Repo
One Bad Thing
Frames Per Second
Adrenaline
The Guardian
Dangerous Waters
The Little Brother

THE MAYDAY

A JACK MERCHANT AND
SARAH BALLARD NOVEL

BILL EIDSON

KATE'S MYSTERY BOOKS
JUSTIN, CHARLES & CO. PUBLISHERS
BOSTON

First edition 2005

This is a work of fiction. All characters and events portrayed in this work are either fictitious or are used fictitiously.

Library of Congress Cataloging-in-Publication is available.

ISBN 1-932112-33-2

Published in the United States by Kate's Mystery Books, an imprint of Justin, Charles & Co., Publishers
www.justincharlesbooks.com

Distributed by National Book Network, Lanham, Maryland
www.nbnbooks.com

10 9 8 7 6 5 4 3 2 1

PRINTED IN THE UNITED STATES OF AMERICA

FOR DONNA AND NICK

There are so many people I want to thank for their ongoing help in my career: my agent, Richard Parks; Frank Robinson, who has offered his years of experience and a keen editorial eye on each of my novels; Kate Mattes, who encouraged me to start a series. The folks at Justin, Charles: Stephen Hull, Carmen Mitchell, and Karen Connor, who do such a wonderful job of producing and publicizing my books. My advance readers: my sister, Catherine Sinkys, Nancy Childs, and Sibylle Barrasso. John Cole who welcomes me into the camaraderie of his office when I get too stir-crazy working out of the house. Richard Rabinowitz, with his generous help with contacts and publicity.

And I'd like to give special thanks to those who have helped specifically with this story: Chuck Geller for his knowledge of the diamond trade; Dr. Alex Bingham with advice for all things medical; Jim McNeil, my longtime friend and sailing buddy who's helped me keep a hand on the helm all of these many years.

Thank you all,

Bill Eidson

PROLOGUE

They were thirty-five nautical miles off the coast of Rhode Island.

It was a few hours before daybreak, and *Seagull,* a thirty-eight-foot sloop, was taking on thirty- to forty-knot gusts. She'd been doing it for the past ten hours, and although she seemed to be handling it well, her skipper was worried.

Matt figured he was still an hour away from rousing his wife, C.C., for her watch. Sean and Laurie, twelve and seven, were down there, too. They were all asleep the last he looked. If the wind got any stiffer, he'd have to bring C.C. up early. He didn't want to do that, though. They were both worn out with this weather.

He had the mainsail reefed down. He'd reefed the genoa to the size of a storm jib that morning, and had yet to need more sail.

They were on the way back from Florida.

Matt felt uneasy. He'd made the rounds earlier on his watch, hooking his safety harness on and moving quietly over the boat.

Everything had seemed fine.

They had to be careful of shipping traffic. He had a small

metal radar reflector up on the mast, and he checked his own radar regularly.

He was always a bit uneasy at night, with the possibility of ships looming out of the dark. But now there was something else, something he couldn't quite identify.

It was good that they were almost home. They'd make it through the Cape Cod Canal by the end of the day. Once through there, it was pretty much a straight tack to Boston.

Matt loved the boat. Sailing was his passion. And this trip was his dream. While C.C. and the kids were hardly just along for the ride, even little Laurie knew the trip was mainly for Daddy.

Yet he too was ready for land.

Tired, and ready for a break.

Matt jerked to full awake. He wasn't sure what had happened. There had been a banging sound. A vibration.

His first thought was they had hit something.

He turned to look in the boat's wake, but it was too dark to see if they'd hit a piece of driftwood. He cursed himself softly for falling asleep on watch.

Then he checked the depth gauge even though he knew the bottom was well over a hundred feet away.

It could've been simply a wave that they caught wrong.

He rubbed the back of his neck. Still angry with himself.

The boat shuddered again.

Damn.

Matt grabbed the flashlight and played it on the mast. He thought he saw the mast shift. He rubbed his eyes now and stared at the pole.

Seemed . . . fine. Matt wanted to say, It's fine, damn it.

But it was off.

He looked at the side stays, the cables on each side that held up the mast. He expected the two stays on the lee side to be a bit slack, with the windward side taking all the pressure.

But the lee shroud and side stay were more than slack. They were flopping around in the breeze.

His stomach dropped.

He looked on the windward side.

The chain plate had lifted. Fiberglass decking had been pulled up. The pressure of the sail was pulling the cable chain plate right through the deck.

Matt jumped back and disengaged the steering vane. He spun the wheel desperately, trying to tack around so the port side stays could take the pressure. Already he was running through a jury-rig plan in his mind. Get on a steady port tack . . . lower the sails . . . back up the stays with lines to the rub rail, and head straight for Newport under power . . .

But even as the bow started to come around, a gust — blowing maybe fifty knots — came along and finished the job.

The mast bent about five feet up from the cabin roof, the aluminum creasing like a cheap curtain rod. The boom slammed down across the deck, and the masthead crashed into the sea. The chain plate snagged on the coach handrails and then broke free, whipping across the deck into the cockpit. Matt put his arm up just in time and took the blow.

His arm hurt like a bastard, but that wasn't the worst news.

He put the flashlight to the lee. The sails filled with water. The white of the sail becoming gray-green.

Seagull began to list to port, broadside to the oncoming waves.

"Matt, what's happening?" C.C. was hanging on in the companionway. The kids behind her.

Twelve and seven, for God's sake.

He said, "Get their vests on, slickers, too. We just lost the mast."

"Oh my God . . ."

"Daddy, you've got blood," Laurie said. She pointed at his face.

He touched the side of his face and took away his hand wet with blood. His right arm was shaking, and when he felt his right forearm with his left hand, it came away with blood, too.

Then another wave swept across them broadside and he had more to worry about than lacerations.

"Hurry," he said.

C.C. turned immediately and began to hustle the kids back.

Seagull's broken mast made a shrieking metallic sound. Matt got to his feet and stumbled forward, seeing the aluminum tear further. The portion of the mast in the water twisted and worked, as if it too wanted to be free. Matt could see that when the break was complete, the mast would be a jagged-edged pole in the water — a pole that could puncture *Seagull's* hull.

He hurried back to the cockpit, opened the locker under the port bench, and pulled out a pair of red-handled cable cutters.

"What about the raft?" C.C. yelled from the cabin. Behind her the kids were snapping on their vests.

"We'll be all right if I can cut us free. But get our position, put out a Mayday. And, Sean, come up here with me and hold the flashlight." He hurried to the bow and went to work on the head stay.

His son was beside him in a minute, holding the flashlight steady. Matt glanced over, saw Sean had snapped a safety line to the base of one of the stanchions. Matt said, "Good boy. We'll get through this, buddy."

The metal was tough and it didn't give easily. It took him longer than he thought, hacking away at it. Blood poured down over his hand and made his grip on the cutters slippery. But at last the head stay gave.

"C'mon." They moved down to the port side stays.

He figured if he could get those off, he could let the mast stream out behind him. Then he'd have ample time to cut the backstay.

"It's going to be OK, Laurie," he called to his daughter. She was standing in the cockpit. "Scary, though, huh?"

She didn't answer, just stared back at him, her eyes wide.

He kept working on the stays. He didn't want to think about the position they were in. The position he'd put them all in.

He'd gotten through the first port side stay when Sean said, "Dad!"

Matt looked over his shoulder. He flashed the beam of light out to the water and they saw the biggest swell yet bearing down on them. He could hear C.C. below, saying, "Mayday, Mayday, Mayday," and then the wave hit.

The mast broke free from the remaining stump. Matt had to jump out of the way as it suddenly withdrew and then, still connected by the remaining side stays, plunged back against the cabin. The boat shuddered, then rocked away, and the mast slid down further, snagging on the stanchion lines briefly, then fell into the sea. Matt and Sean crawled back to the port stay and got back to cutting.

Matt started talking to himself. Hoping, praying, that the mast would slide alongside the hull.

But the sails on the mast held it in the water like a sea anchor. As the mast itself filled with water, it remained just what Matt had feared: a jagged spear sticking out of the water, attached to the boat by hardened steel cable.

The boat rocked in the next sea, and Matt had to give up on the stay when Sean played the beam onto the mast and yelled, "Dad, watch out, watch out!"

Matt rolled to his feet and pushed Sean ahead into the cockpit. They tangled in the safety lines as the broadside waves rocked the boat back toward the mast.

The mast was like a living, angry thing, gouging the deck where he had been kneeling. *Seagull* rocked away again, and the mast slipped out of view.

"Daddy," Laurie cried.

She was his baby, only seven for Christ's sakes.

"It's all right, it's all right." He hurried to the backstay with the cutters, but she clung to his leg.

"Give him room, Laurie," Sean said. "Let go."

"Shut up!"

"Don't worry about it," Matt said, trying for a calm tone. "She clings, I cut, and you hold the flashlight." He worked on the cable and was making good progress when *Seagull* was hit again. He staggered, and Laurie went down with him. He quickly regained his feet and went back to work on the cable. Sean braced himself and held the flashlight.

But Matt knew the bad situation had just become considerably worse.

Seagull seemed to lift slightly, and her motion in the water was different. There was a screeching again, metal against metal. Matt could hear the rush of water.

"What's that?" his son said.

Matt didn't answer. He took Laurie's hand and clutched his son by the shoulder and looked him in the eyes. He was terrified, but trying to keep it under control.

"Sean, take Laurie up on the starboard rail and the two of you huddle down behind the cabin. I'm counting on you to look after her. Can you do that for me?"

Sean nodded. He took his sister's hand. "C'mon, Laurie."

Matt lifted up the cover for the engine compartment and played the flashlight beam inside.

His worst fear was realized.

The compartment was half-full of water. The jagged end of the mast was visible, having punctured the hull. Only the engine block had kept it from moving straight through and puncturing the starboard side of the hull.

Matt turned to his wife. She was standing in the companionway, her face stark white. The microphone was in her hand.

"You get an answer to that Mayday?" he said.

"Nothing," she said. "It's not working!"

He swore under his breath and gestured to the sunken mast. "Of course not . . . the antenna. It's underwater right now." He hit his leg in frustration. He had to think.

"Grab the handheld radio and GPS. Get the flares, some food and water, while I get the raft. We'll have the EPIRB putting out a signal for us. Maybe with the handheld we can raise a passing ship. We need somebody. 'Cause we're going down."

THE MAYDAY

CHAPTER 1

It was good work.

Jack Merchant had been avoiding it for a long time, but the winch had finally frozen, leaving him no choice.

But now that he was into it, the parts spread out on an old beach towel, the problem found — he was enjoying himself. A little spring had come off the ratchet inside the winch. Without that little spring, the winch couldn't haul in the genoa sail. Without the genoa, there wasn't much reason even to take the boat from the dock. But Merchant had been lucky enough to get the spare part at the marina store. He had the tools, the knowledge, the time.

He took a moment to look out over the harbor. The sun was low enough that from his angle the water was a rich sea green. It was late afternoon, middle of the week. And Merchant was at home. Truly, his boat, *Lila,* was also his home in Boston Harbor.

He was wearing an old bathing suit and a T-shirt. His bare feet felt good on the warm fiberglass sole. A little trickle of sweat was going down his spine, but the faint breeze was keeping his brow dry.

No complaints.

He figured it'd take forty minutes or so to grease each part carefully, wipe off the excess, and put the winch back together. Maybe an hour.

Either way, there should be plenty of time for him to take a sail that afternoon. First, buy some groceries, get some beer. Then maybe he'd head out to one of the harbor islands, drop the hook. Spend the night. Maybe a couple of nights. He had enough money to not worry for the next month, maybe two.

He turned back to the winch.

It was good work.

"You're not going to leave all that grease, are you?" Sarah asked. "You've got to wipe off each part."

Merchant looked up. "You," he said.

He was surprised she'd managed to get so close without him noticing.

Her back was to the sun, but he could see she was grinning at him.

"Well?" she said. "Do I need to tell you everything?"

Standing there with her hands in her back jeans pockets.

"Apparently so."

"I'm not interrupting?"

"Course you are."

"Too bad." She climbed onboard and leaned down to kiss him. Their lips touched just lightly, and Merchant did his best not to convey how much the pleasures of fixing the winch had just paled.

Sarah was in her late twenties, dark hair, green eyes. The body of an athlete, which she was.

She said, "I've missed you the past couple of times you were down at the office."

"I noticed."

Sarah owned a marine repossession business down in New Bedford. Taking boats back from people who didn't make their payments. Since he'd come back to Boston a year ago, Merchant had helped her search and recover some of the tougher jobs. Helping her and keeping himself in dock fees and grocery money.

Merchant was fairly certain he was closer to Sarah than anyone on earth. And yet, he suspected she'd avoided him those last two times he'd been at her office.

Love, trust, intimacy.

Not always easy to get all three together.

"So," he said. "Seeing you does good things for my heart, as usual. To what do I owe the pleasure?"

"No explaining your heart, sweetie." She stepped down into his cabin and rummaged around through the icebox until she found an iced tea. "Want one?"

"Sure."

"I had to see somebody in town and figured I'd stop by."

"Glad you did."

She climbed back up the stairs and sat beside him. "So can I help you put your winch back together?"

"I've got an assistant now?"

"More like a supervisor," she said. She kicked off her boat shoes and leaned back against the cabin bulwark. They opened their iced teas, clinked them together, and drank.

"Hi, Jack," she said.

He said hi back. And refrained from asking her why she'd been avoiding him.

"So what have you got going on?" she asked.

He told her about some of the shooting he'd been doing. Back in his days as an undercover agent with the DEA, he had frequently posed as a pro photographer with a cocaine problem. Now that he was out, he'd been giving serious consideration to becoming a real photographer without the drug habit.

"Been working on the portfolio," he said. "Pretty soon I'm going to have enough of the marine stuff together, I'm going to make a submission to one of the stock houses. See how that flies."

"Gee, and the money will just roll in."

"Sarcasm isn't as attractive as you might think."

"Explains just one of my problems," she said. "So what else are you doing for real money?"

"Spending a little of it on beer and groceries." He told her about his plans to go out sailing for the afternoon. He didn't invite her, but the opening was there and she knew it.

"Sounds nice," she said. "But, you know the islands have been there for a long time and they'll probably still be there in a few days. Maybe even a week or so."

"You think?"

"Uh-huh."

"So what have you got for me?"

"A referral, maybe."

"Some boat you've got paper on?"

"No. This is different."

"Is it a boat?"

"Sort of."

"Uh-huh. Well, this is all clear to me now. Why do you have a guilty look on your face?"

"Don't want to take advantage of you. Don't want to take advantage of him."

"Who's him?"

"This client. This guy, really. He's in a spot, and he doesn't know what else to do. He came to me and I can't take the time out, and I'm really not sure anything can be done, and I don't want to take his money or lead him on and waste my own time for something that's hopeless."

"And so you thought of me."

She smiled quickly. "I think about you a lot. More than you'd know."

"Well, that's nice to hear. Be even better to see you some more."

"I know," she said. "Believe it or not, I'm working on it. But about this guy . . ."

"Yes, about this guy."

"He's lost a lot. Everything that matters. And he came to me to help him track down a boat."

"At least that sounds like familiar territory."

"Sounds it, but it's not." She checked her watch and looked up the dock. Merchant followed her eyes and saw a man walking toward them. He moved along slowly, as if he were tired.

"This him?" Merchant said. "You brought him here?"

"Listen to him," she said. "And be nice. He's lost his family."

"Lost them?"

She nodded.

"What do you mean, he lost them? And I'm supposed to help find them?"

"That's for you to decide."

"Did you say I could help him with that?"

"No. I said you'd listen. That I promised."

Merchant looked back at the man. Now he was right at the bow, just stepping on the finger pier to Merchant's boat. Even from there, Merchant could read the pain. The stiffness in his walk, the pallor under his sun-reddened skin.

Trouble, Merchant thought.

But he carefully folded the towel around the winch parts, and moved them aside.

Making room for the man.

CHAPTER 2

Sarah introduced Merchant to Matt Coulter.

"Come on up," Merchant said.

Coulter climbed up the three wooden steps slowly, but stepped into the cockpit without that tentative quality non-sailors sometimes displayed. He looked around the boat quickly, giving it an automatic appraisal in a way Merchant knew he did himself every time he climbed aboard someone else's boat.

Coulter was a sinewy-looking man. Middle height, sun-bleached hair, pale blue eyes. Mid-thirties. New-looking jeans, boat shoes, and a tan polo shirt. The clothes looked a trifle too big for him. There was a scar along his right temple and the back of his head where the hair had been shaved and was just beginning to grow back.

Surgery, it looked like.

Coulter saw him looking and seemed to wait, to let Merchant make his own judgments.

And then he said, "I'm patched up with baling twine, huh?"

"How are you doing?" Merchant said.

"Little better most days. Two weeks back I was in a hospital bed with tubes in my arms, so this is a move in the right direction. How much did Sarah tell you about my situation?"

"Not much," she said. "I thought he should hear it from you."

Coulter gave a faint smile. "Bad as that, is it?"

Merchant gestured for Coulter to sit, and offered him something to drink.

Coulter declined the drink, and they all sat down. Coulter said to Merchant, "Did you read about me and my family at all? *Seagull*?"

The boat name was faintly familiar.

"Almost a month back," Coulter said.

"The sinking," Merchant said. "A sailboat off the coast, dismasted, right?"

"That's right. That was my boat, my family."

Merchant glanced at Sarah.

Couldn't help it. He wanted to say, What-the-hell-did-you-bring-him-to-me-for? But Merchant had been brought up better than that.

The sinking had made the news for several days: a man bringing his boat home from Florida. Boat dismasted. Wife dead. Children lost at sea. He was the only survivor.

"I'm so sorry," Merchant said. "That's a terrible loss." He lifted his hands and dropped them, uselessly. Not knowing what else to say.

"It's worse than you think."

Merchant waited.

Coulter said, "It's worse because I believe my children are still alive and I can't get anyone to help me find them."

"I see."

"No, you don't," Coulter said. "But I see the way your face changes. I see it from everyone I talk to. The look of sympathy. The glance to my head, the scar. And, yes, I was out of it for weeks. And yes, things are screwed up in my head. I've lost big hunks of memory. But not about this. They're still alive. Or at least they were the last I saw them. They didn't drown at sea, I know that. And I want you to help me find them."

Merchant gestured to his boat. "This is it for me. A sailboat. Makes eight knots under the very best of circumstances. Figure four to five for an average. I'm not equipped for a search at sea. Really, the Coast Guard is your best option."

"I know all that. And they've done what they do. By now in their eyes I'm a desperate father, a nut, a sad case. Someone who doesn't know how to accept reality. And that's probably what you're thinking right about now."

Merchant didn't say anything.

Neither did Sarah.

"The difference," Coulter said, slowly, "is that I'm willing to pay you a substantial amount to help me look."

"Why me?"

"I've read about you. What happened with you and Sarah last year. The Baylors, that couple taking off in their boat, the trouble you ran into."

"I wouldn't see that as a reference," Merchant said. "Both Sarah and I got shot. People around us were killed. How's that a reference?"

"You found the boat," Coulter said. He leaned forward and touched Merchant's arm. "You found the damn boat."

Close up, Merchant could see the fatigue in Coulter's eyes even more clearly. Could feel the shakiness in his hand as he touched Merchant's arm.

"Isn't *Seagull* about a hundred feet underwater?" he said.

"I don't care about *Seagull*. If I had her on land I'd douse her in gasoline and throw the match. All you need to know about her is that the insurance company paid up. I've got money. So triple — quadruple — whatever you make repossessing a boat and I'll give it to you, if you help me find the boat that took them."

"I don't understand," Merchant said. "If *Seagull* —"

"Forget that! I'm not making myself clear. . . ." Coulter

passed a hand over his face. Trying to collect himself, it seemed. He said, "The boat I'm looking for is the one that took them away. The one that took Sean and Laurie."

Coulter's eyes filled, but he didn't stop. "That's the boat I want you to find. The one that took them away."

CHAPTER 3

Merchant said, "What do you mean, 'took them'?"

"Just that. They were our rescue."

"The rescue crew took your kids?" Merchant said. "Why?"

"I don't know," Coulter said.

"What's the name of this boat?"

"I don't know."

Merchant waited.

Sarah said, "He's had a lot of memory loss, Jack."

"I told you, huge gaps," Coulter said. "I have no problem with my long-term memory. I can tell you how I met C.C., tell you about the birth of both our children. Can tell you about the past twenty-five years. Can tell you most of what happened on our trip back. But after we got off the boat, into the raft, it's spotty. Doctors don't agree why. My surgeon says it's a result of the trauma to my head. The shrink says my psyche is defending me against the horror of what happened to my family — or, hey, maybe it was the knock on the head. Both doctors say the rest of it may come back soon, later, or never."

"I see," Merchant said.

"Yeah, you see," Coulter said.

Merchant could see the very act of being there was taking a lot out of the man. Merchant had suffered minor concussions twice in his DEA career, and he knew how the physical and mental weakness could hang on.

Sarah said, "Tell Jack about what you know. About the dismasting."

"Yeah. OK." Coulter seemed to gather his thoughts and told in a flat, unemotional voice how the mast had broken, his efforts to cut the stays, the puncture of his hull. "There was no choice but to abandon *Seagull*. C.C. worked with the kids while I got the raft in the water. She took the handheld radio and the GPS, so we could call out our position. We had an emergency kit in the raft with flares. We'd drilled all this plenty of times and it was paying off."

"Everyone wearing vests?"

"Absolutely. Which is one of the things I've been hammering to the Coast Guard. We were all wearing vests. They found me and C.C. If they found us out there, why didn't they find the kids?"

Merchant nodded. But he — and he suspected Coulter — knew the answer to that was brutally simple.

It was a big ocean.

No matter how well the Coast Guard searched, his children couldstill be out there. Subject to the horrors of the elements, scavengers, and time.

Merchant said, "Did your wife get through to anyone on the VHF?"

Coulter shook his head. "I don't know. It's here that my thinking gets convoluted. It's just flashes of memory. This boat comes out of the dark. We see the port lights. Red lights moving not too far from us. I remember the sound of big diesel engines."

Merchant waited, and then said, "And did something go wrong? Did they capsize you?"

Coulter shook his head. "I don't know. This is as far as I get."

"OK," Merchant said. "You remember what the boat looked like?"

Coulter shook his head. "It's like snapshots. Details, but nothing very cohesive. Big white cruiser sportfisherman. Maybe forty-five feet long. Getting closer and closer."

"Did you get onboard?"

"I don't know."

"That's it?" Merchant said.

"Just about. I've got impressions. Fear for my family, I know that. A huge sense that I had done something wrong."

"But that could just be the situation, that you had them out there at all."

"It could be. Because I certainly felt that. But this is something different. A different feeling, but without a specific reason, you know?"

"I guess. But from what you're saying, this boat might have just run over you."

"No," Coulter said. "No, that's not what happened. I don't know what did, but it wasn't that."

"How can you be sure?"

"I just am."

Merchant paused.

Coulter took a deep breath. Regained himself. He said, "The next thing I remember there's a tremendous white light overhead. Noise. And I was cold. Very cold. It must've been the Coast Guard helicopter, though I don't remember it exactly. They'd been following the EPIRB signal until it went silent, but they had a fix on the location."

"Why did it go silent?"

"I don't know. They couldn't find it."

"Those things don't just sink."

"I know. That's my point. Something had to happen to it to make it go silent."

"And the raft wasn't found?"

"No. I was very lucky. They'd found me on the first pass of their search grid. They put a diver in the water, and he got me into the basket. They found C.C. about a quarter-mile away."

He paused here. Tried to speak, then paused again. He rubbed his hands along his legs, as if attempting to get warm. Then he said, "The autopsy said she died from a blow to the head. But I don't really remember any of that. I was unconscious. A coma. It wasn't until almost a week and a half later that I came out of it. And then a couple of days of me going in and out, and asking for C.C., before I woke up to find a nurse beside my bed. I asked where my wife was. The way the nurse managed not to answer me, I just knew it was the worst news. If I could have, I would've crawled back inside my broken head and died."

"Tell me about the head wound," Merchant said.

"Blunt object. Consistent with a club or baseball bat, the doctor said. Also consistent with a swinging boom. And the same for C.C." Coulter touched his face, showing the scar along his right temple and cheek. "The police and Coast Guard latched on to this. I was cut from the side stay and chain plate when they broke free. The way they see it, I took some damage already, maybe I took some damage from the boom, too."

"Meaning you made everything else up?"

"They never say it like that. But that's what it comes down to."

"Did the Coast Guard see the boat?"

"No. But from my body temperature, they figured I'd been in the water about a half hour. The helicopter arrived ninety minutes after the EPIRB sent up a signal. And I think the boat that took my family was a fast boat. They could've been ten miles away by then."

"Anything to help identify the boat?"

Coulter paused. "One thing. The anchor plate. This boat

had a high bow. With the strobe light from our EPIRB, I could see the bow pretty well. So I've got a pretty good mental impression of the plate."

"You're talking about the plate the anchor rests against?"

"That's right. Two anchors, one on each side of the bow. And a plate to protect the hull."

"What about it?"

"The shape of the plate itself was unusual. Most of the time, they're just rectangles, you know. This one was unusual in that it wrapped around the entire bow. Top few feet anyhow. Gave the bow a very powerful look."

Merchant looked at Sarah, then went below for a moment and came back with a clipboard. "Here, draw it."

"I'm pretty terrible with this." Coulter took the pen and stared at the blank paper, then started. He quickly crossed out his first couple of attempts, then concentrated on the third. He handed it over to Merchant.

Coulter wasn't as terrible as he thought. The plate not only wrapped around the bow, but tapered back as it went.

"It looks like the Nike logo," Coulter said. "I'm not saying it is, but the shape is similar."

Merchant stared at the line drawing. Not knowing much else to say. Trying to read anything in the little sketch that would give him a direction to move.

Coulter said, "I can see it from your perspective. A boat that I can't identify takes my two children. The police and Coast Guard don't believe me. You're looking for a way to get this nut off your boat and go about fixing that winch."

"I don't think you're a nut," Merchant said. "I think you suffered the worst loss anyone can suffer. It's just that I'm not sure what I can do to help you."

"I've got money," Coulter said.

"And I can use money," Merchant said. "But I don't want to take your money if I can't help you. And I'm not a licensed private investigator."

Coulter waved that away. "I've talked to several of them. But the way I see it, it all starts with finding that boat, and no private cop I've talked to yet knows anything about boats and the sea. That's where I lost my family. That's where we have to start. Find me that boat."

Merchant paused. "Let me ask you . . . On the message your wife was putting out on the hand radio — did she also say that you had an EPIRB putting out a signal?"

"No. And no detective has asked me that question yet. But I've thought about it a lot. The people in this boat must have heard our message. Heard that we were out there, needing a rescue. Heard that we were out there, and had reason to think no one else was coming."

"Do you remember exactly what your wife said?"

"That's one thing I remember just fine. C.C. on the radio. 'Mayday, Mayday. This is the *Seagull*. Our boat is sinking. We have two young children onboard, we need immediate assistance. Help us please.'"

Coulter kept his eyes on Merchant as he said this.

And then he let the silence lengthen when he finished.

Merchant wanted to look away, but couldn't.

Whoever heard that message either decided they had no choice but to assist — or, infinitely worse — decided there was something in the distress call they liked.

When Coulter asked him straight out if he would help, Merchant said yes.

CHAPTER 4

Merchant saw Coulter's surprise and relief. His shoulders lifted slightly, his burden partially eased.

Merchant hated taking that away, but he had to be honest. "Listen. I don't want you to hold out a lot of hope here. This may be — this probably is — as simple and awful as your children were lost at sea and nobody has found them yet."

Coulter sat back.

Merchant continued. "All I can promise is that I'll help. I can help find the boat. I can chase up and down the marinas. I can chase down whatever information we get."

Coulter nodded.

"Money. I figure five hundred dollars a day, plus expenses. If I find the boat and if that leads to your family, you can pay me a bonus, how's that?"

"Make it fifty thousand if you get my children back. And I'm serious."

"Fine," Merchant said. "Now bear in mind, I don't have a PI license, I have no official status."

Sarah said, "You can do this under my company. You've got business cards. Doesn't mean anything legally, but sometimes a company name backing you up is all you'll need."

"I'll write a letter," Coulter said. "Stating that you're acting on my behalf searching for the boat that rescued my family. That my health prevents me from doing it myself. That's the truth."

"Deal." Merchant put his hand out, and they shook. Coulter definitely looked more relieved.

Merchant didn't.

While Coulter went to the marina restaurant, Merchant went below to change his clothes. He put on khakis, a light blue shirt, and boat shoes. When he came up, Sarah was waiting for him in the cockpit.

She said, "You think you've got a shot at helping him?"

"Just what I told him."

"So you think they're dead?"

"Don't you?"

"Why are you taking it then?"

"Maybe give him some . . . clarity." Merchant hated the word *closure*.

"And maybe it's the five hundred a day."

"My specialty," Merchant said. "Ripping off grieving fathers."

She smiled at him, but there was no happiness in it. "Sisters, too."

He and Sarah had met years ago, back when he was in the DEA. Her younger brother had been murdered along with the crew of a fishing boat down in New Bedford. Everyone assumed he was involved in running drugs, but Merchant kept digging until he could tell Sarah that her brother was guilty only of naïveté, nothing more.

"Your specialty is making a bad situation better," Sarah said. "So do it for him."

Merchant laid his hand against Sarah's cheek. For all her considerable toughness, he knew that she still keenly felt the loss of her parents and brother. And from what she'd gone through afterward with her former lover, Owen, she remained wary. Greater loss and pain could be just around the corner.

Coulter had walked into the right office looking for help.

"Maybe," Merchant said. "Only one way to find out." He leaned down and kissed her. "It would've been better if you had just gone sailing with me."

"Someday I'll learn."

"Keep promising," he said. "Someday I'll believe you."

Coulter was sitting by the window overlooking the docks. The sidelight etched the lines of fatigue in his face. Merchant waved to the waiter, and when he came over, they both ordered sandwiches and coffee.

While waiting for the order to arrive, Merchant opened his notebook. "How about you fill me in on some specifics?" He asked Coulter a number of questions. Not sure exactly if he needed the answers, but it was as good a place to start as any. Where had *Seagull* gone down? What were the coordinates for where the Coast Guard had picked up Coulter? Who headed up the helicopter crew? Who was the investigating officer with the Coast Guard? With the State Police? When had the Coulters last berthed and what was their destination?

Coulter was well organized. Most of the questions he could answer off the top of his head or he would consult a small pocket notepad. He gave Merchant the names and phone numbers of the police. He also took out his wallet, carefully removed pictures of his family, and handed them to Merchant.

Merchant put the photos on the tabletop and looked at them carefully. He was keenly aware of Coulter watching him.

C.C. was round faced, pretty in a smiling sort of way. Laugh lines about the eyes and mouth. Dark curly hair. Same with Laurie, the daughter. A grin that made you want to grin right back. In the current circumstances, her image made Merchant feel pressure behind his eyes, and an almost desperate sadness swept through him.

He could only imagine what Coulter was going through.

Coulter was clearly exhausted, but forcing himself to take things a step at a time.

"Beautiful family," Merchant said.

"Yes, they are. All of them."

Merchant looked at the boy last. About twelve years old. More solemn than the little girl. Sandy hair like his father. A direct look into the camera.

"He's my little man, Sean," Coulter said.

"Looks serious."

"He is. He had a lot of responsibility for a kid already."

"How so?"

"I was a drunk," Coulter said.

Merchant just waited, and Coulter continued. "I got it under control by the time Laurie was three, but Sean was around for too much of my nonsense."

"Huh. Begs a pretty obvious question."

"I realize it does." Coulter lifted his coffee cup. "And the answer is no — I wasn't drunk the night *Seagull* went down. Haven't had anything to drink in three years."

"You sure about that?"

"Positive."

"How about since?"

"What do you mean?"

"How's your sobriety holding up with what you're going through now?"

"Just fine," Coulter said.

A bit too quickly, Merchant thought.

"It's not easy," Coulter added. "Damn hard. But I've got it under control."

Merchant thought about how many addicts had said those last words to him.

About then their sandwiches arrived. Merchant ate his turkey club, and Coulter picked at his food for a few minutes, then pushed the plate aside.

Merchant let him just talk.

Talk about how he and C.C. had met. Where they lived. Where the kids had gone to school. What they were doing on the boat in the early morning hours.

When all was said, Merchant filed it in his head like this: Matt and Cecilia met while they were both at NYU. Computer science for him, art history for her. After they married, he started calling her C.C.

Coulter worked as a sales associate for a consumer electronics company right out of school until it went bust and learned while doing it that he enjoyed writing about the topic more than selling. He started working as an industry reporter for electronics trade magazines, and eventually opened up a small publishing firm with his friend Ben Pryor. The two worked well as partners and had a half-dozen technical and retail newsletters that earned them both decent incomes. And although Coulter had always been a bit of a drinker, he managed to keep it from interfering with his work life.

But he started hitting it harder around the time Sean was two and continued on until he was eight.

"What stopped you?"

"The kids. One day at the beach. I was supposed to take them while C.C. did the grocery shopping. I told her I wouldn't drink anything harder than Coke, but the truth was I had a small cooler in the car filled with a thermos of gin and tonic. I'd keep coming up with some excuse to head back to the car. I'd leave the kids under the umbrella, tell them I was going to get another towel, a beach ball, whatever. At first, it worked fine. Sean would watch Laurie. She was three. I'd come back and he'd be helping her with a sand castle or something. Easy as could be. During my third visit to the car I heard the whistle blowing. Thought nothing of it. I strolled back down to the beach and found a crowd of people around my kids. Lifeguard kneeling beside them. Sean had left Laurie alone for a few minutes to play Frisbee with a kid he knew from school, and she took off to go swimming. Went right into the surf and was pulled out. Sean saw her and went in after her. He's a good swimmer, but before they knew it, he was in over his head and she was pulling him down. Both of them nearly drowned. Would've if the lifeguard hadn't seen them. I'm standing there blinking in the sun, with gin on my breath. Sean's crying, telling me he's sorry he didn't watch her well enough."

Coulter looked into his coffee as he stirred it and then up at Merchant. "C.C. took them away for almost a year. The past three years have been the hardest and the best of my life, the best of my family's. The boat, the sailing . . . all of that was part of reclaiming my family. Last month, I sold off my half of the business to my partner, figuring that now was the time while the kids were still young to really put some time in traveling together. We were doing these coastal cruises, getting ready to do a transatlantic. "

"Why are you telling me about the drinking?"

"Because if you talk to people, you might hear things. I don't want you to get sidetracked. It all happened on the *Seagull* just like I told you."

"As far as you remember."

"This I know — we didn't have any alcohol onboard. I couldn't have been drunk."

"Got anything else you need to tell me?"

Coulter shook his head.

Merchant considered what he'd just heard. Looked down at the pictures on the table, and decided he'd still proceed. He told Coulter that he would.

Coulter seemed relieved, but he was also gray faced.

"You're about to crash," Merchant said.

"Don't worry about that. Maybe you can follow me to my old office in Newland. I called my partner, he's in. I'll write you that letter so you can get started." Coulter signaled the waiter for the bill.

There was an awkward silence while they waited, and then

Coulter said, "Were you ever a lifeguard, Merchant?"

"Two summers when I was a kid."

"Thought so," Coulter said. "I thought so."

He took out his checkbook and gave Merchant an advance on the first three days.

CHAPTER 5

Merchant followed Coulter about twelve miles west of Boston to Newland. Merchant's aging turbocharged Saab looked at home on the streets of Newland, as long as no one noticed the rust. Newland had once been a mill town, but those years were long past. It was now an upper-middle-class town complete with a fresh-painted look, lots of expensive cars on the road, and the feel of casual prosperity.

The office was located in a dark red wooden building just above a men's clothing store downtown. When Merchant got out of his car, the heat hit him. On the way over, he'd been thinking about his next steps, and wasn't coming up with anything particularly good.

"This way," Coulter said and led him through a doorway beside the clothing store.

The chill of a hardworking air conditioner was like an invisible wall. Merchant followed Coulter up the stairs, and they entered a small lobby. Coulter was moving slowly, resting on each step.

Once they reached the office, Merchant found the place airier and bigger than he'd expected. There were three offices along one wall and four or five cubicles across from them.

Framed posters of trade newsletters like *The VAR Report,* *CAD Corner, Retail Display Monthly,* and *Exhibit Week* adorned the walls. Merchant saw that most of the cubicles seemed to be occupied: there was an air about the place of quiet, efficient work being accomplished at a reasonable pace.

The receptionist looked up and said, "Matt!"

She came over and gave him a hug. "I'm so glad you called us."

"Thanks, Jeanne. I'll just need a moment with a computer to write a quick letter."

"Well, anything we can do to help, anything. I'll tell Ben you're here."

She had black hair streaked with white and an open, friendly face that grew guarded when she looked at Merchant. She went into the office to the right and said, "Matt's here."

Pryor came out immediately.

"Matt," he said. "You look half dead. Sit down."

"I'm all right."

"Oh yeah, you look it." He swung to Merchant. "So you're the PI?"

If the woman's look at Merchant had been guarded, Ben Pryor's was so protective it verged on hostile. Pryor was about fifty, with a strong sun-tanned face, receding hair, no more than medium height. Blazing white shirt, emerald silk tie, tailored black pants. He looked as if he put in at least a few visits to the gym each week.

Pryor spoke to Coulter. "So. You checked his references, Matt?"

"Ease off, Ben," Coulter said. "All I need is a computer for a few minutes."

"Sure. Isn't there one at the condo, though?"

"That's not mine."

"Suppose not," Pryor said. "But they're behind on their rent, so use it. Or if you're squeamish, I'll get a laptop over to you. We've got an extra kicking around here someplace." He looked over at the woman. "Jeanne, see if you can find that spare notebook PC for him, can you?"

"That's not necessary," Coulter said.

"Hell, don't worry about it. I think it was yours anyhow." Pryor tried to escort them to the conference room, but Coulter was having none of it. "Ben, stop managing us. Let me write that letter and I'll be out of your way."

Pryor smiled and said, "Sure, sure. Jeanne will set you up. I'll give your man here the grilling you're too tired to give him."

Coulter looked so exhausted that Merchant said to him, "That's fine. Just write me that note while I talk with Ben."

Coulter followed Jeanne into the office beside Pryor's.

"Jesus, looks like he's going to drop," Pryor said, quietly. Then he walked into the small conference room, waved Merchant in, and closed the door behind him. "Sit," he said.

He pulled out the chair at the head of the table and sat next to Merchant. "OK, I'll get right to it. That man in there's a friend of mine. He and I started a business together. Watched and helped each other grow it. Watched each other screw up and succeed in various ways. Our kids played together. Our wives were friends. And now I've seen him suffer the worst tragedy any man can stand, and I will not see him screwed over by some sharp bastard looking to make a few bucks by stringing him along."

"All right," Merchant said. "Let me ask you a question."

Merchant's mildness seemed to surprise Pryor. After a moment's hesitation, he said, "Ask it."

"How come you're so certain I'm leading him on?"

Pryor snorted. "His boat sank. His family may or may not have gotten into a little rubber raft at night with the wind blowing thirty to fifty. He and C.C. were found floating in their life jackets. It's sad and it's terrible, but it's no mystery what happened to them. The sooner he accepts that the sooner he gets back to a life."

"So you don't believe anything he's said about the boat

picking them up?"

"Do you?" Pryor didn't wait for an answer. "Look, people aren't exactly cruising around the high seas looking for kidnap victims. And if that's what it was, why hasn't Matt gotten a ransom note or anything? The police don't believe anything like that's happened, I don't know why I should."

"Matt told me about his drinking problem," Merchant said. "Any possibility in your mind that he was drunk?"

"Cops asked that, too. I don't think so. Matt turned that mess around, got his life back together. I can't imagine how he could hide drinking on a small boat like that — and C.C. wouldn't have put up with it if he did. You know, how they'd gotten back together. He'd sold his house, had me buy him out because he wanted to spend more time with the kids while they were young. This sailing trip was a dream of theirs, and frankly, life was pretty damn sweet. Why would he screw that up?"

Merchant's years in the DEA didn't like the sound of that question. If he'd learned anything about addictions — whether fueled by coke, heroin, alcohol, or the starting gate at the dog track — they frequently burned voraciously on nearly acquired dreams.

"Listen," Pryor said. "We held the funeral for C.C., and we want to hold a memorial service for the kids. We're trying to get Matt to move on. You giving him false hope, that's doing him no favors."

"I don't know it is false hope yet. That's what he's hired me to find out."

"And if you do?"

"Then I'll tell him."

"How long's that going to take?"

Merchant said he didn't know. But that all he had committed to so far was a three-day look.

Pryor looked at him silently for a moment, then said, "You seem like a good guy. Promise me that you'll let him off the hook if the facts make it clear."

"If the facts make it clear," Merchant said. "Nothing I haven't already said myself."

"Good." Pryor put out his hand to shake. "We're in agreement."

Merchant wasn't so sure about that. But he shook the man's hand anyway.

"I take it Ben mauled you a bit in there," Coulter said a few minutes later. They were standing on the street beside the cars.

"Nothing too terrible. Wants to make sure I'm not ripping you off."

"Yeah, he's a good friend, but not exactly subtle. He's been looking after me since I got out of the hospital. He owns some rental properties in town, and he's got me in a summer sublet for the next two months. Liz, his wife, keeps trying to force food on me. Both trying to make me face reality, as they see it."

"That's the gist of what he said. You know they may be right."

"Of course I know that." Coulter handed him the note. Merchant glanced at it.

To Whom It May Concern:

Jack Merchant is an employee of Ballard Marine Liquidation. Due to my poor health, I've asked him to act on my behalf in locating an approximately forty-five-foot motor yacht seen in the vicinity of the sinking of my sailboat, *Seagull*, on the night of July 22. Any help you can give him will be the same as helping me — and greatly appreciated.

Sincerely,

Matt Coulter

124 Newland Commons, Building 5
Newland, MA
(781) 924-3367

"Think it'll do the job?" Coulter said.

"I'll give it a try."

"Good." Matt opened the door and sank down behind the wheel of his car. His hands were trembling and the exhaustion was clearly upon him. He looked up at Merchant. "What are you going to do first?"

"Try to get a lead on that anchor plate."

"Got a way to do that?"

"Maybe. First let me drive you to your place."

"No. It's only a half-dozen blocks away. I can make it. You get started proving my realistic friends wrong. That's what you can do for me."

He put the car in gear and took off slowly down the street.

Merchant followed him until Coulter pulled into the driveway of a townhouse complex.

Then Merchant turned around and headed for the highway.

He figured if he gave her no warning, there was every chance Sarah would be in her office when he got there.

CHAPTER 6

Sarah's boatyard was on the waterfront near New Bedford's town center. Merchant walked through the open chain-link gate and waved to Manny and Richie, two of her new guys. Manny was in Sarah's black pickup truck, backing down someone's former dream machine: a ski boat with a big Merc on the transom. Richie was waiting with a Liquidation Sale sign to paste on the bow.

Nice business Sarah had.

The office itself was an old red-brick building, still in decent shape. Through an open window, he could hear her talking as he walked to the front door. Sounded like she was on the phone.

She was laughing and saying, "No, he actually said that?"

Merchant let himself into the office. As always, he was struck that it was a lot more pleasant than he'd expect a repo office to be. Exposed red-brick walls, sanded and varnished wood floors. A fair amount of decent marine photography up on the walls.

Two of the shots were damn good. His own, in fact, so he had to admit bias. They were black-and-white studies of a wooden Herreshoff S boat, the skyline of Boston in the background.

Merchant saw that Lenny, the office manager, was out. Which could be a problem. Merchant had hoped to get some help from him.

But having Lenny gone gave him a chance to test his theory. See how Sarah behaved when she didn't have any warning he was coming.

He walked past Lenny's desk to Sarah's open office door and knocked. But when she saw him, her smile was so genuine he wasn't sure his theory made sense at all.

She waved him to the chair in front of her desk as she finished off her conversation. She was leaning back, her feet up on a corner of the desk. She was wearing a navy blue cotton shirt, cutoff jeans, and boat shoes. Her thick black hair was pulled back into a loose ponytail.

She saw him looking at her legs and managed to shuffle off one shoe and flip it at his head without losing a beat in her conversation.

After she hung up, he tossed the shoe back to her, and she caught it deftly, and slipped it back on. She put her legs primly under her desk and said, "You're a pig."

"So you've mentioned," he said. "Business good?"

"Better every day. Just got a referral from North Carolina. Trawler puttering its way up here with unpaid bills just fluttering off the stern. Economy goes down, I get rich."

"How nice for you."

"I think so. What're you doing here?"

"Since this is supposedly a Ballard Marine repo job, I thought I'd put some of your resources to work."

"Huh. I make you a referral and you come back for more. What do you need?"

"That anchor plate. Pretty unusual shape the way he described it."

"Yeah, it was."

"I'm thinking that one of those B-to-B Web sites I've seen you guys use for ordering boat parts might give me something."

"Find the parts, find the boat? Better hope it's not Danforth or something popular like that."

"On the bigger yachts do the plates usually sell along with the anchors?"

"Don't know. I'd guess mostly not. Mostly I'd think the plates would be specced as part of the boat building. But we can look into it."

She swung around her desk, and he followed her out to Lenny's computer. She said, "He's the expert on this, and he just went out to get some munchies. When he gets back, have him help you. You figure out the money and he can work on it this afternoon and stay as late as he wants tonight."

Merchant sat down, and she leaned over him and quickly found the Web pages for three on-line boat parts brokers. She jotted down the account name and password for each of them. It was rather pleasant having her lean against him like that.

"There you go," she said. "Search away."

She mussed his hair and went back into her office.

It took him a while before he began to get the hang of it. Part of it was learning the shorthand. What he was looking for was an "Anch. Prt. Plt." For "Anchor Protection Plate." And then, even with the fast cable modem speeds, he found it took time to go through each iteration from each manufacturer. And judging a realistic photo against a hastily drawn line sketch was highly subjective. He quickly realized he could narrow it down, but Coulter would have to look himself.

Merchant kept at it.

Lenny drifted in about an hour and a half later.

He said, "What the fuck you doing at my computer?"

The way he spoke, it came out as "Whatthefuck-youdoin'atmycomputa?"

He was about twenty-five, narrow faced, narrow bodied,

skanky blond hair already receding at the forehead. Rattail down the back. Sleeveless shirt revealing pipe-stem arms and a concave chest. Maybe a dozen earrings jammed into his left ear, a stud in his right nostril and one in the middle of his lower lip. Which probably contributed to the way the lip sagged.

He was a whiner. He was lazy. But smart, quick, and just useful enough for Sarah not to fire him.

That's what she said, anyhow.

Merchant suspected Lenny was still around because he had gone to high school with Joel, Sarah's brother.

"Sarah and I made a deal," Merchant said. "I told her if I could finish your day's work in an hour, I'd take seventy-five percent of your pay and only be here one morning a week. We're still negotiating my drive time."

"Yeah, go screw yourself."

Merchant grinned. "Got a way with words, Lenny. How'd you like to make some extra money on company time?"

"She gonna bitch?" Lenny jerked his thumb at Sarah's door.

"Not about this."

"Get out of my chair and I'll think about it."

Merchant got up and let him sit in the rusty swivel chair. He brought a straight-backed chair from the waiting room, sat beside Lenny and explained what he was looking for. Lenny pulled at his lip stud thoughtfully while listening. "You say this boat's about forty-five feet?"

"That's right."

Lenny turned to the computer. His hands flew over the keyboard.

In a moment, he came up with the Web page for a popular yacht manufacturer. He found a forty-five-footer and zoomed in close to look at the anchors and their protective plates. Read the spec sheets and found the recommended anchor weights and blade sizes. He went back to one of the parts directories. He quickly found an anchor and plate that were matched and noted the size of the plate. "Yeah, OK. So ballpark, that's the size plate we're looking for. Got any idea of the age of the boat?"

"No."

"Course not." Lenny sighed. "'What a pain in the ass. Do this right, I'm gonna have to go to hard copy parts guides and thumb through for older boats." He pointed to three volumes on his bookshelf, each about six inches thick. "So what do you got?"

"For you?"

Lenny rolled his eyes. "For your mother. Yeah, me."

Merchant named a figure and Lenny doubled it and finally they split the difference.

"Anything reasonably close I'm going to want Coulter to see it," Merchant said.

"No shit, shithead."

Merchant didn't touch the kid.

Just looked at him directly for the first time that afternoon, and waited.

The kid winced.

Merchant was fairly certain that outside the office the kid suffered the consequences of overstepping his bounds all too often.

He said, "Now, Lenny, when Coulter is here tomorrow I want you to bear in mind what he's gone through. That means keep your sunny personality to yourself and be helpful, got it?"

"I'll be an angel," Lenny said. "A freakin' angel."

Merchant patted him on the shoulder. "What more could I ask?"

CHAPTER 7

Sarah found herself enjoying having Jack in the office even though he didn't spend much time with her. He kept his attention on the job at hand with Lenny.

But she was aware of having Jack in her space, and it was nice to find herself liking it. Midway through the afternoon, he poked his head in. "You up for dinner later?"

"Maybe," she said.

Then around six-thirty, she decided she'd put in enough calls to marinas looking for deadbeats. She leaned out of her office and saw Jack and Lenny going through hard copy catalogs. "I'm hungry, Jack. How about you?"

"Always."

"What about me?" Lenny said.

"I paid for your lunch yesterday," she said. "Besides, don't you have a freelance job right in front of you?"

Lenny scowled, genuinely pissed off.

She ignored him. She closed her office and they left Lenny feeling sorry for himself.

She took her truck and Merchant followed her in his car to the Stateroom, a fishermen's cinder-block dive on the waterfront. There was nothing inspired about the place except the food. And that was good enough to make it one of Sarah's restaurants of choice.

She and Merchant stood waiting while a busboy cleared a table for them. The owner called from the bar, "Hey, Sarah. You starting with the chowder?"

"Why change now?" she said.

She looked over at Merchant. "How was your afternoon working with my best employee?"

"How do you stand him?" he said.

"At one point there, I saw his face go white. You give him one of those looks you cops learn at an early age?"

"I figured buying you dinner would cover that," he said.

"We'll split it," she said.

He started to say something, but then let it go.

Jack was awfully good that way. He kept giving her the space she needed. Which may mean he found her so goddamn impossible that he wanted nothing to do with her.

But that didn't seem to be the case.

She said, "Truth is, I don't mind if you put a little pressure on Lenny. He can take it." She figured that Jack was so easy on the surface, it was just as well Lenny got a glimpse of what was really underneath.

The waiter waved them to their table.

Once they were seated Sarah said, "Since this is turning officially into a Ballard Marine repo job, how about you bring me up to speed?"

Merchant told her about meeting Ben Pryor, about Coulter's alcoholism. About his leaving the kids alone on the beach.

Sarah was disappointed, and that pissed her off. The business she was in, she should get it by now there were very few innocent victims. "Makes it different somehow," she said. "Coulter seemed such a . . . well, a tragic figure before. This complicates things, doesn't it?"

"Always does once you get close. Not many of us are pristine."

"Still, you're going to stick with him, aren't you?"

"What do you think?" He took out a set of photos and laid them on the table for her. "Coulter's family."

Sarah picked up each shot carefully, studying them.

"Yeah," she said, finally. "You'll stick with them." She felt tears beginning to well up in her eyes, and she looked away until she stopped. Goddamn emotional basket case tonight and she didn't know why. Those kids, the mother. Faces expecting a bright future.

She strove for a light tone and didn't quite make it. "Even us nonpristine types need help."

"Speaking of which . . ."

"Yes?"

"You know Lenny plays you because of your brother."

"People are always talking to me about Lenny and I'm sick of it. I know he's lazy and rude, I know that."

"So why don't you fire him?"

"Oh, c'mon."

"No, really."

Sarah paused as the waiter brought over two bowls of chowder and set up salads in little brown wooden bowls. She told him they'd order the meal in a few minutes. As she rearranged the silverware and place settings so that everything was lined up neatly, she said to Merchant, "You know what Lenny did for me."

"What?"

She looked up, surprised.

And realized that he truly didn't. It amazed her sometimes, the gaps there were between them. But it only made sense. Though they'd known each other upwards of seven years, Jack had sailed back into Boston little more than a year ago. For five of those seven years he had been out of her life, if not her thoughts. Five years between his assignment in Charlestown, then to the Virgin Islands, and his disastrous assignment in Miami.

So there was a lot he didn't know about her.

"Good old Owen," she said. "Stuck me for life with an office manager who's chronically late, rude, and not particularly neat . . . or even clean." Sarah tasted her clam chowder, closed her eyes for a moment. "I do not want to know what they do behind those kitchen doors. But it's *so* good."

The fact of the matter was it felt pretty damn good to be sitting across the table from Jack. Almost like a date. Except that she knew herself: before the meal was over, she'd demand the check be on her business tab and maybe at the car she'd be really bold and kiss him good-bye. And then manage to be out of the office the next time he came, unless he tricked her like today.

Which, again, had been nice.

He said, "*Owen* hired him?"

"Oh yeah, right. Owen *hated* him. And yet, scrawny little Lenny stood up to him. Stood up to him for me."

"I like Lenny better already."

"Not that Lenny challenged him to a fistfight or anything . . ."

Merchant waited. Interested.

So she continued: "Before everything turned totally crazy, Owen and I started arguing. One night, Owen got on my case right around quitting time. He wanted me to come and stay at his apartment and I didn't want to that night. It was one of the first times I'd told him flat out no to something he wanted. It wasn't pretty to see how angry he got. At first I was just pissed off too. But then I started getting scared. I realized he was inches away from hitting me — and then Lenny came into my office and asked if I could give him a ride home."

Sarah rested her hand on Merchant's arm. "You should've seen this. Owen is jabbing his finger at me and you could light fires with what was coming out of his eyes. And Lenny walks in with this 'Sarah, I need a ride, OK?' His voice is shaking, *he's* shaking.

"Naturally, Owen lights into him: 'What are you, deaf and

blind? Can't you see I'm talking to my lady?'

"It's obvious to me Lenny's trying to get me out of that room. He keeps repeating it, no matter what Owen says. 'Sarah, gimme a ride, willya?'

"I jump at it. 'You bet.' I grab my backpack, and out the door I go. Owen comes right after me and Lenny gets in between, just fumbles his way in front of Owen, who shoves him across the room . . . but by then I'm out the office door.

"Lenny comes running after me. And I guess Owen wasn't ready. Not that day. Not ready to lose it. He tries to laugh, like it was all a joke, and says, 'C'mon, babe. We just got out of hand there . . . ' And I laugh and Lenny laughs and we get in the truck and get the hell out of there.

"When we got around the corner I hugged Lenny and thanked him for what he'd done. And he just shrugged his shoulders and said, 'I just needed a ride home.' And that's how that boy got himself pretty much a job for life."

Sarah saw Merchant's face darken as she told the story. Though she kept the bullshitty light tone, inside, just relating the story, she felt the Buzz start.

It was with her so often, she'd given it a proper name.

The Buzz escalated her heartbeat. The Buzz gave her a slightly sick feeling in her stomach. The Buzz made her feel unsafe even sitting across the table from the man who was certainly the best friend she had and she hoped, if his patience held out, would someday be something more.

Not that she feared Jack Merchant.

Even though she'd seen what he was capable of doing, she knew — consciously anyhow — that he would never direct that side of himself at her. The blood pumping into his face just now had to do with what Owen had done to her. And that he hadn't been around to help.

But from her limited time with the shrink, she knew that when it came to the Buzz, the conscious had precious little sway over the unconscious.

It was Owen she feared.

That, and her own bad judgment for letting him get so close.

A good year or so before Jack came into her life, Owen had sailed into New Bedford in his trimaran.

He'd quickly signed on as one of her father's freelance skippers. And after her father died and Sarah took over the business, they had begun dating.

Owen was an ex-Marine. Big, weather-beaten. Thick black hair. They made a good-looking couple. It was easy to imagine sturdy children coming from the two of them. Sturdy children with thick black hair, playing boats by the sea.

But those fantasies had been very early in the relationship. After a time, what she'd taken as his self-assurance began to seem controlling. Plus, he appeared to be making assumptions about his role in her business that she didn't really like.

At lot of assumptions about her in general, not the least of which was a possessiveness that didn't jibe well at all with Sarah's view of herself.

But then the Colombians had killed her only brother, Joel.

Owen was a rock for her to cling to. *Made* himself a rock to cling to. Even to the extent that he felt he needed to run interference between her, the police, and DEA agents investigating Joel's death.

Jack Merchant had been one of those investigating officers. The first time she had seen him, he'd been one of several faceless cops standing around a crime scene in a waterfront warehouse. A crime scene that included five members of a local fishing crew and her brother. All of them slumped over in a warehouse. Their hands bound behind them with wire, clothesline cinched tight around their necks.

As the weeks passed, she very much began to recognize Jack Merchant. He did what no one else was willing to take the time to do — find out what Joel had been doing in that warehouse. Find out that Joel wasn't involved in the drug smuggling, that he had been trying to get a job on a fishing boat, no more.

Find out that her little brother was the innocent she believed him to be.

And so when Jack had bypassed Owen and asked Sarah to help by using her contacts in the fishing fleet to figure out who was spending money a little too freely, who seemed flush at a time when the catch was so bad . . . she jumped at the chance. And one of the fishing boats she suggested — the *Juju* — indeed turned out to be running drugs in from Colombia.

The upshot of it was that months later she and Owen were on a Coast Guard cutter off the coast of New York while Jack, his partner, and another DEA agent joined two SWAT team members a mile away on the *Juju*. Three Colombians came out in a cigarette boat to off-load a portion of the cache of cocaine and heroin.

She and Owen listened in on headphones, and heard everything go wrong when the captain of the boat broke down under the pressure and told the Colombians that the DEA was onboard.

Later, when they eventually let her on the *Juju*, Jack's leg was being bandaged. He looked pale and unhappy, and people were telling him he was a hero. Two of the Colombians were dead, the other wounded.

Meanwhile, Owen was telling everyone who would listen that he wished *he* could've been on that deck with a gun in hand.

But what really mattered to Sarah was that the surviving Colombian admitted they had been the ones to kill the fishing boat crew.

Jack had done for Sarah what he promised.

Found Joel's killers.

And though Sarah had come to see Jack as something more

than a cop, certainly as her friend, he was out of her life within weeks. He was promoted to his next assignment. Undercover in Charlestown. No more than an hour's drive away, but she barely saw him after that.

She couldn't know then if her reaction to him was more gratitude than anything else.

She just knew she wanted to find out.

As the months lengthened, she told herself that he probably felt it was inappropriate to hit on the sister of a victim. Maybe he was just being a gentleman and thought she was already committed to Owen.

Or maybe he was, in fact, simply not interested in a repo woman with a short temper and a highly opinionated view of the world.

Now that he was back, he had told her more than once it was the former of the two options. That he'd considered calling her dozens of times during his stint in Charlestown and always came down to the decision it wasn't right.

But back then, she was too proud to demand an answer. And so, about a week after Jack moved on to his next assignment in the Virgin Islands, she had finally accepted Owen's marriage proposal.

And with that decision, she felt the first tremors of the Buzz.

That engagement ring seemed to seal the deal in Owen's mind: she was his. Her business was his. All decisions relating to her were his.

In a matter of months, he went from controlling to jealous — to enraged. Enraged with Sarah's independence, her outside friendships, and her persistent attitude that she was in charge of her own life.

One night he took on one of her other freelance skippers, Raul. He was a short, powerful man of about forty-five. He had a wife and kids, an ugly goatee and a bald head. Sarah and he had been friends for years. Ever since her twenty-first birthday he would conclude whatever business they had with a plea that she sail away with him to Mexico.

"The sex would be spectacular," he'd say. "*Spectacular.* You call my wife right now and ask her. Go ahead, pick up the phone. Punch the buttons, dial it. . . ."

"She'd say anything to get rid of you," Sarah would say.

"Give me one night. I'll prove it to you."

"You know I never make wild, passionate love without references."

And so on . . .

It was a flirtatious routine, nothing more.

But Owen chose to take exception. He followed Raul out into the parking lot and shoved him. He probably expected it to end right there.

Except Raul shoved back. Owen was surprised. He tripped over the tongue of a trailer. Raul laughed and told him to stop being such an idiot. But when Owen got back to his feet, he had picked up a tire iron left by the flattened tire.

Sarah saw Owen wasn't going to stop no matter how much she yelled that it was a joke, a goddamn joke.

She ran into the office and dialed 911. And then she came back and tried to pull Owen off herself, but he knocked her to the ground with his forearm before turning back to Raul with the tire iron. By the time the police arrived, Raul was so badly beaten that he couldn't walk without crutches for months and his face would need reconstructive surgery.

When the cops arrived, Sarah pointed to Owen and told them he had started the fight.

Owen was stunned. "You can't," he said. "You're practically my wife, you can't do this to me."

"Watch me," she said. She went on to take out a restraining order and agreed to testify against him in court.

Over the next few weeks, Owen showed up at her boat,

pounding on the locked door. Called her late at night. Warning her that she better not testify. She told him she wouldn't back off.

The Buzz was a constant companion with her then. She bought Mace. Took self-defense courses. And started working out even harder than usual: swimming, cycling, running. She told herself that she could handle the situation.

And then one morning, Owen hunted her down.

She was out on her road bike when he swung his car in front of her. When she tried to take off, he knocked her over. Kicked her in the stomach. When she pulled the Mace from her back shirt pocket, he kicked it from her hand. Then stomped on her left wrist when she tried to grab it.

Then she tried to run.

But she was wearing bike shoes with cleats, and they made her slip and slide on the rocky beach. She was off balance anyhow, cradling her broken wrist.

He shoved her to the ground every time she almost made it to her feet. He kicked her in the ribs. And when he finally had her down for good, he put his boot on her head and cracked the bike helmet. "I could do that to your skull, Sarah," he said.

He knelt down to tell her that she was going to withdraw her restraining order. That she would change her testimony in court. He told her they would be married someday and put this all behind them.

And with her good hand, she hit him in the temple with a rock about the size of her fist. She did it again and the stone remained embedded there until the paramedics put him on the stretcher. But by then he had been dead for at least twenty minutes.

Unfortunately, the Buzz didn't go away after that. It nestled in deep and decided to become part of her.

Even with Jack Merchant sitting across from her. Maybe especially with Jack. Because the Buzz informed her on a daily basis that her judgment was for shit.

And as nice a guy as Jack was, she had seen what he could do.

Worse still, she had seen what she could do.

"Hey," she said. "Order anything you like. Dinner's going on the company tab."

CHAPTER 8

Merchant was just about to get onto Route 128 when his cell phone rang. He picked it up, and Lenny said, "No matter what you say she's not going to fire my ass."

"That's right, Lenny. All we've got to talk about is you. What have you got for me?"

"Shit if I know. But I've got it as far as I can go. Got three that look sort of like the plate. You want to bring your guy around tonight or do it in the morning?"

Merchant looked at his watch. It was just a little after eight-thirty. Traffic was light, and it'd only take him twenty minutes to head to Newland to pick up Coulter. Maybe another hour back. The man had been white with exhaustion, but Merchant knew he'd want to move on it as quickly as he could.

"Tonight," he said. "But it's going to be about an hour and a half before I can get him back."

"You keep paying me, that's no problem. I'll go out to dinner and I'll meet you back here. Dinner will be on you."

"OK," Merchant said. "Twenty-five-dollar limit."

"Thirty," Lenny said.

"Twenty."

There was a pause, and then Lenny said, "Twenty-five it is."

"See you soon," Merchant said and hung up.

Merchant reached Newland just before nine. He had Coulter's letter out on the seat, thinking he'd need it for the exact address in the small complex of townhouses.

But the lights drew him.

Flashing blue police lights.

Newland cops. And the red lights of an ambulance.

He glanced at the letter, watched the numbers on the town houses add up quickly: Building One, Building Two, Building Three.

Coulter's building was number five.

And that was where the police cars were.

Merchant pulled over and walked alongside the ambulance until he came to a small group of people. A polite, quiet crowd.

Looking ill, most of them.

But not the two in front of him. An older woman talking to an older man. Presumably her husband.

She looked excited. Eyes bright, tugging an old afghan sweater around her shoulders.

"I can't believe it," she said. "Here."

"Wish I'd talked to him," the old man said.

"Why? He was subletting the place, for God's sake. Who knows where those people come from? Besides, he had to be crazy. Mentally ill. A talk with a neighbor doesn't help that, Petey."

Merchant looked past them both at Matt Coulter. The paramedic was leaning over him. They had an oxygen mask over his face.

He was alive.

The old woman added, "Have to be crazy to try to kill yourself from the third floor." She pointed up to the small balcony. The door to the apartment was open, but the lights were off. "I mean, think about it. A fall like that might break your leg, break every bone in your body, but not do the job."

"Didn't have you to tell him," the old man said. "If he had you, he would've got it right, be dead right now."

"Shut up," she said.

"Oh yeah. Had you in the house, he would've got it right."

CHAPTER 9

Merchant slipped around the couple and started for Coulter. The EMT saw him coming and nodded to one of the uniformed cops.

"Just a minute, sir," the cop said. He was young, in his twenties probably. Short mustache and a careful way about him.

"I know him." Merchant gestured to Coulter.

The smell of bourbon was almost overpowering in the fresh air. The brown glass of a shattered bottle fanned out to the right of Coulter's outstretched arm.

The cop said, "OK, well he's not conscious anyhow and I need to let these guys do their job."

Merchant backed away a step. "What happened?"

The cop gestured to the open window above. "That's all I know. But I'm going to want you to talk with one of the detectives. What's your name?"

Merchant told him.

"All right, please wait right here."

They were lifting Coulter up at that point. His eyes were closed.

The uniformed cop came back. "Did you see him jump?"

"No."

"OK, Detective Lerner will talk with you." He pointed to a tall man with longish black hair standing by the townhouse doorway. "Where are you parked, by the way?"

"Over there." Merchant pointed to his car behind the ambulance.

"OK, they can get by. It'll be all right there. . . ." The cop looked at the detective and jerked his thumb at Merchant as if to say, "You ready?"

The detective nodded and waved Merchant to him.

Merchant passed by the ambulance as the paramedics slid Coulter into the back. He was dressed in the same clothes he had been wearing at the boat: polo shirt, jeans. One boat shoe was on, the other was still on the asphalt.

Without thinking about it much, Merchant picked up the shoe, stepped over to the ambulance, and put it on the floor.

"He going to be all right?" Merchant said to the EMT.

"You family?" the EMT said.

"No."

"Then I can't talk about it." The guy got in and slammed the back door shut while his partner got into the driver's seat. They took off.

Merchant continued on to the detective. He was holding a walkie-talkie. He didn't offer his hand but said politely, "Thanks for coming forward, Mr. Merchant."

Merchant nodded.

"Let's go over here."

They went to the townhouse landing, and Lerner put the radio in his sport jacket pocket so he'd be free to take notes. He was a tall man with hair that was a bit too long and a boyish look that Merchant suspected he cultivated. He looked like he was in his mid-twenties, but Merchant estimated he was at least ten years older.

The detective said, "So, Mr. Merchant, let's start with the basics. Who is he?"

"His name's Matt Coulter."

"That's not the name on the mailbox."

"No. He was subletting the place."

"Was he a friend of yours?"

"I didn't know him well," Merchant said. "Just met him today, in fact. But I felt bad for what he was going through."

"Which was?"

Merchant told him about Coulter's family.

"Yeah, OK, I read about that. That'd be reason enough right there to jump out a window."

He turned back to Merchant. "And what was your relationship to Coulter?"

As Lerner asked this, Merchant could see that the cop with the mustache was over by the Saab, running his hand across the hood.

Checking to see if it was hot, Merchant guessed. To see if his statement about just arriving was truthful.

If the detective noticed him watching, he didn't mention it. Instead he repeated himself, "And your relationship to Coulter?"

"He wanted me to help find the boat that he'd last seen near his family. If you want to call your man over there at my car, he can get a letter off the front seat that confirms what Coulter wanted me to do. Tell him to bring my notebook, too."

Lerner observed Merchant quietly for a moment and then, without comment, lifted his walkie-talkie and told the uniformed cop to look for the notebook and letter.

Lerner turned back to Merchant. "So let's get this straight. You met him when?"

"This morning."

"How?"

Merchant told him about Sarah. The cop took down her name and address.

"Then what?"

Merchant went through the day. His lunch with Coulter. Ben Pryor's office. Following Coulter back.

"So the last you saw of him was when?"

"Seeing him pull into the driveway."

"He seem despondent?"

"No. Upset. Depressed, certainly. But trying to do something. He felt sure his children were still alive."

"And you told him you could help him get them back?"

"No. I told him I would look for the boat. I made him no promises beyond that."

"You call in with any bad news?"

"No."

"Why were you here now? You owe him a report?"

Merchant told Lerner about the metal plates and how he was swinging by to pick up Coulter.

"But you didn't call first. What if he was asleep?"

"It's not that late. And I was close enough, so I just came by."

"Even though you said he was tired looking."

"He made it plain he wanted to move as fast as he could."

"And you think this —" Lerner looked at his notes — "this . . . anchor plate . . . you're describing might give you some link to his kids?"

"I was just trying to follow the details I could. You know how it works."

"Are you a private detective, Mr. Merchant?"

"No." Merchant took out his card for Sarah's business. Just then the uniform cop reached them and handed the detective Coulter's letter of introduction.

Lerner read them both and said, "All right. I think you may be on shaky ground, but I'm not interested in that right now." He looked at Merchant directly. "You seem awfully calm. You come across many bodies in marine repo?"

Merchant shook his head. "Seven years with the DEA."

"Figured something like that. You still in?"

"No."

"How come?"

"No simple answer," Merchant said.

"So tell me the complex one."

So Merchant told him the shortest version he'd derived for situations like this. That he'd interfered with a SWAT member to save a young boy's life. The SWAT member died. The DEA didn't charge Merchant or bring disciplinary action — but he knew his career was over.

"Give me some names on that. Somebody down in Miami."

"What's that got to do with this?"

"Damned if I know. But like you said, I follow the details."

Merchant could see the change in the cop. The coolness that came over him, the almost imperceptible distance in physical space. In the world of cops, the story was quite simple: Merchant had screwed up and someone had died.

Merchant gave him a name in Miami and one in Boston.

Lerner continued, "So you think Coulter's death has anything to do with drugs? Him taking them — or buying and selling?"

"Not a thing that I can see. As for him jumping, again, I wouldn't have expected it. He didn't seem to be in that frame of mind. He was trying to get his kids back."

"You think they're alive to be gotten back?"

"At this point, I've got no idea."

"You come across any evidence to believe they are?"

"No."

The cop grunted. "Maybe he came to the same conclusion." Lerner pulled open the door to the town house. "How about you come upstairs with me. Meet my partner. See if an ex-DEA agent can teach a couple of small-town cops a thing or two."

They walked through the town house on their way to the third floor. The first held a living room and bedroom. The second floor, a kitchen and dining room combination. The pictures on the wall were primarily of a good-looking older couple and their family. Children and grandchildren. The place was cheerfully decorated, if a bit overfilled. The couple seemed well traveled: from African masks on the wall to sculptures and wall hangings. Merchant got a sense of two people winding through a full life together.

The place must have been a little piece of hell for Matt Coulter.

Merchant followed Lerner up a narrow carpeted stairway to the third-floor master bedroom. His partner was sitting at a desk, apparently jotting down notes from what he was reading on the laptop computer screen. He pushed his reading glasses further down on his nose when he looked over at them, and Merchant realized he knew the man.

Petronelli.

Apparently, the recognition went both ways. He said, "What're you doing here, Merchant?"

Lerner said, "Wondered if you two would know each other."

Petronelli didn't smile or stand up. He said to Merchant, "Thought I heard you were canned."

"Not exactly," Merchant said. "But I'm out of the DEA."

"So, again, what're you doing here?"

"He was working for the jumper," Lerner said.

"Doing what?"

Merchant handed Petronelli his card.

The cop looked at it, squinted, and then laughed. "Repo. How the high and fucking mighty have fallen."

Merchant had seen Petronelli get fired back when they were both on the task force in Charlestown. Merchant with the DEA and Petronelli with the State Police. As he remembered, Petronelli wasn't crooked, just lazy and incompetent. Time hadn't been good to him: he had a potbelly, a fringe of gray hair, and bad teeth. The Newland Police Department was a far cry from the State Police.

Still, it was better than working repo.

Petronelli stared at him, seemed to arrive at the same conclusion, and came down on the side of being patronizing. "So, I hope you got paid in advance." He gestured with his thumb to the computer screen.

"May I?" Merchant said.

"Go ahead. You know the drill, just keep your hands off."

Merchant kept his hands on his hips as he bent forward to read the note that had been typed in.

> I'm sorry. It's just so hard. So damn
> hard. There's no place for me here. I'm go-
> ing to them.
> I'm sorry.
> Matt

Behind the laptop, the three pictures of his family were propped up against a couple of books. Coulter's wife and kids looked out at Merchant, those hopeful expressions frozen forever. Also on the table, already bagged and tagged, was a brown plastic pill bottle. Merchant looked close and saw it was a prescription for codeine made out to Matt Coulter. Sleeping pills.

It was empty.

"Was Coulter a drinker, Merchant?" Petronelli asked.

Merchant hesitated just slightly. Breaking a confidence. But it didn't matter now. He said, "He told me he'd had a problem with it until about three years ago. Said he kicked it. He said that drinking almost broke up his marriage."

If there had been any doubt before, this seemed to settle things for the detectives. Petronelli looked at Lerner and said, "Guy reforms and lives the straight and narrow, then loses it all anyhow. Pictures of his wife and kids staring at him. Decides he's just been conning himself, that they're all dead. Buys a bottle of bourbon and starts thinking, 'What's the use?' Pops some pills. Balcony is right there. Putting a leg over the railing looks like the quickest way to the family reunion."

"Maybe he's right," Lerner said. "Should've picked a building with a couple more floors though. All he's done now is busted his head."

Detective Petronelli snorted, looking at the message on the computer screen. "He thinks it's hard now, wait until he wakes up."

CHAPTER 10

Sean was playing Nintendo.

It was the James Bond game where you were just a hand holding a gun that traveled through hallways, deserted industrial sites, and ski slopes, shooting bad guys until they stayed down or until they got you. If they did get you, blood would suddenly cover the screen.

Then you started over again.

It was a game his parents wouldn't let him play at home. Too violent, they said. But here he could play it for hours.

He was bored beyond belief, but the game helped him be stupid.

And that was what he figured they wanted. Stupid.

Besides, there was nothing else to do at the cabin. Before he could at least walk out to the lake, go for a swim. They didn't let him do that anymore. Even if they did, the sun seemed too bright these days.

He had played with Laurie a lot in the beginning. She was scared and he was trying to keep her calm. But it was harder now because she would ask him questions he wanted to answer, but he figured they were listening. And he was pretty sure she was still herself, but he wasn't. He could feel whatever they'd been giving him buzzing in his system. Making his face feel numb. Laurie seemed too fast to him.

This cabin he was in was probably a nice enough place for a vacation. Big, for a vacation home. Three empty cabins around them. Ella said that it had once been a summer camp, that they should be happy to have a summer camp all to themselves.

He was pretty sure they were in Maine. It could have been New Hampshire, maybe Vermont. When he asked, Ella would say, "What does it matter?"

The lake wasn't busy, that he knew. Wherever it was, it was far away from any city. Back when they'd driven him up here, they'd stuck him with a needle, so he slept most of the way. Back then he had been screaming and trying to fight them, because of what they were saying about his mom and dad.

But he remembered seeing some signs. So he was pretty sure it was Maine.

There was a camera in his bedroom. It was one of those spy cams you could buy on the Web, and it was hidden behind a picture frame. He hadn't seen it at all for the first few days he was there. He could only see it from certain angles, and figured the same went for them. So he didn't touch it, just changed his clothes where they couldn't see him.

Laurie was one room down. She had cried a lot at first, but not so much now. He did too, at first. The tears would just come out of him, so hot on his face it was as if they burned him. But he kept coming back to his dad telling him that it was his job to look out for Laurie. That he was counting on him.

Ella made such a big deal about her, waking her up for breakfast with "how's my big girl?" and Laurie had started giggling over that. She still spent part of every day asking for their mom and dad, but not as much as she did in the beginning. At least that was the way it seemed to him.

Of course, he was sleeping so much now, maybe she was saying it but he wasn't hearing her. He slept more than he ever had in his life. He'd wake up to find Laurie standing by his bed. "C'mon, sleepy pig," she'd say. "You're a bed pig." She'd make her snorking noise, and then, when he'd roll over again, she'd say, "Don't you want to do anything?"

But he didn't.

They were putting something in his food. He thought he could taste something extra, a faint bitterness in the soup Ella would make for him most lunches. But he didn't say anything about it.

He didn't want them to know he knew.

Let them think he was stupid.

In the beginning, he'd made trouble.

Screamed at the door, said he wanted to be set free. He wanted to talk to his mom and dad.

Ella would say, "Honey, they're both gone. I know it's hard to accept, but you will over time."

He said he didn't. He yelled. He whined. Then he started smashing the furniture and calling Ella a bitch. Yelling that "Doctor" Weir was full of shit. She kept the door locked.

Finally, he smashed his bedroom window with his chair and tried to crawl out. Ella was waiting for him. Sean was big for his age, plenty strong, and she wasn't that much bigger. He tried to push by her.

But she twisted his arm behind his back, and it was all he could do not to cry as she made him walk back into the house begging her to let him go.

A couple days later, Sean tried to run from the beach. Ella had been watching him and this time he plain outran her. She started screaming for Weir, which surprised Sean, because he didn't think the doctor was there that day.

Weir caught him in the driveway and knocked him down. They dragged him back to the main cabin, and Weir gave him some sort of shot that made him so dopey he ended up peeing himself in his bed.

But still, Sean held it in his head that at the end of the long driveway, maybe a quarter-mile away, there was a paved road.

He also told himself that stupid was what they wanted. He decided to give it to them.

In the morning, he told Ella that he wouldn't try to run anymore.

"It's for your own good," she said. "I know it's hard for you to accept. Your parents alive one minute and gone the next. It's hard, it's horrible, but it's true." She used a voice that was supposed to be nice.

He guessed she was only in her twenties, but she acted like she was someone's mother. She was very pretty. Dark black hair and skin so smooth it was like she could've been in a movie. She always wore jeans and T-shirts, and kept her hair in a long ponytail.

If he'd seen her on the street back in Newland, he would've had a hard time not staring. She was like the girls on the Web sites he and Billy Pryor would check out on his computer in the basement. She was that good looking, but a little tough looking, too. She'd liked twisting his shoulder, he was sure of it.

Laurie was fooled, and that bothered him.

But he couldn't tell his sister the truth. She couldn't keep a secret, never could. And this was too big. If he was going to stay stupid in front of Ella and Weir, he figured that would have to be the way it was.

He was just so tired these days. But it was hard to sleep, too. He kept going back to the cabin of that boat, thinking they were saved, all of them were safe. And then he heard shouting. The other woman — the lady with the red hair — she and Weir came down and told him that his parents had just had an accident. That they were both "gone."

The woman held him and Laurie to her. She said it was a tragedy, but she would help them. Weir stood over them, his hands on his hips. Saying that he was a doctor and he would work everything out, they'd see.

And now he and Laurie were living with Ella. When Weir

came along he'd tell Sean that he was depressed, and who wouldn't be after what had happened to him and his family?

"Time," Ella had said yesterday. "It's just going to take time, Sean, and I'm here to give you that."

She tousled his hair.

He smiled at her.

It was the first time he'd done that, and it seemed to make her happy.

She must have thought he was really stupid.

CHAPTER 11

Sarah's phone rang just after midnight.

"Sarah," Lenny said. "You know what goddamn time it is?"

She looked at the ceiling. She'd been asleep for about a half hour. "That's my question, Lenny." Her voice was dangerously low.

But he didn't get it.

He was breathing hard. Had himself all worked up. He said, "Goddamn midnight, and they were supposed to be here more than two hours ago. Who the hell do they think they are? They're gonna pay. Every frigging second I've been sitting on my ass waiting for them to show up, they're gonna pay."

"Have you called Jack's cell phone?"

"I'm not an idiot, Sarah. He's got it turned off. Told me he'd be back with this guy and . . ."

She heard another call coming through on the office line.

"Just a second." Lenny put her on hold.

"Jesus," Sarah said. She slumped back. Damn, maybe she should just fire Lenny. God knows he'd made her pay what she owed about a dozen times over. But the truth was, no matter what she told Jack, she could remember Lenny showing up to walk to school with Joel. Lenny was already a skinny little creep she didn't like. A bad influence on her brother.

Ragged him every damn day.

But jumped to his defense more than once, too. Took on bigger kids and won. Took on bigger kids and lost.

Joel was always glad to see him.

Still, the more she woke up, the more pissed she was.

"Hey," Lenny said now. His voice was surprisingly subdued.

"You really are an asshole," she said. "Calling me like this."

"He jumped."

"What?"

For a moment she thought he meant Jack.

"What?" she said, again.

Lenny told her that Merchant had just called to say he wouldn't be down that night. Coulter had taken a header out the window.

Not Jack's words. "Taken a header" was Lenny's word choice, she was sure of it.

Her heart was pounding. Bitter adrenaline taste in her mouth. She'd thought he'd been saying Jack was dead.

"Jack's all right?" she said.

"Course he's all right," Lenny said. "*Coulter's* pretty messed up. And you tell Jack he still owes me the overtime. Dinner, too."

"Yeah," she said. Not thinking. "So Jack's OK?"

"I'm gonna be late tomorrow," Lenny said. "You tell your boyfriend he should be a little choosier picking his clients. Wasted my goddamn time."

She drove up to Charlestown. It was a little past one when she got down to his boat.

The dock lights were on low and the air was quite still.

Even though there were a few people still awake and sitting in the cockpits of their boats, their voices were muted.

Merchant's boat was entirely dark.

But he was there anyhow.

Sitting out on the bow, his back against the mast. Looking at the harbor. She walked down the little finger pier to stand beside him. She could see him just faintly in the dark.

"Hey there," she said.

He said, "I take it Lenny called you."

"Uh-huh. How come you didn't?"

"I don't know."

She said, "Can I come onboard?"

"Sure."

He stood up and offered her his hand.

Not that she needed it. She spent every day of the week clambering up on boats. But she took his hand anyhow.

She sat beside him in the bow. "Tough day, huh?"

"Turned out that way."

"Wouldn't have figured it for him."

"Me neither. And that's what I've been sitting here thinking about."

"We hardly knew him well enough to know."

"Course not. But that's not it. If it was just a matter of my poor judgment, I could let it go. Not the first example I've run into."

"I'm sorry," she said.

"That you referred him? C'mon."

"What are the cops thinking?"

"Damned if I know. They tell me no witness saw anyone enter the building. But, on the other hand, none of the neighbors said they were outside anywhere within a half hour of Coulter jumping. The guy who shares the other half of the town house is out of town, too. So, someone could've come and gone and no one would know."

"That's what you say or that's what the cops say?"

"What cops say in front of me and what they believe are not necessarily the same thing. But I know one of the cops, and he's nobody's idea of bright." He told her about Petronelli.

"So this will be treated just as a suicide attempt?"

"In theory, they're supposed to treat a suicide like a homicide until proven differently. But Coulter's still alive, so the easy thing to do is wait until he comes out of it and ask him what happened — and with Petronelli leading things, I'd bet on the easy way."

"Do you think it's attempted murder?"

"Who gets anything out of Coulter being dead?"

"I don't know," she said. "That wasn't my question."

"I've got no evidence to suggest it was anything but a suicide attempt. But that still doesn't answer your question, does it?"

"Not even close. And that's why you're sitting here at" — she looked at her watch — "one-thirty in the morning."

"Uh-huh. Thinking things like why didn't he address his suicide note to anyone?"

"Tell me what it said."

Merchant told her. "That's pretty much verbatim," he said.

"Huh. Sounds sort of . . . generic, doesn't it?"

"Yep. Like anybody who was in a low spot could've written that. And since his friend Ben Pryor owned the building and Coulter was there at Ben's hospitality, don't you think the apology might go to him? The mess basically being left for him to clean up?"

"I'd think," Sarah said. "But a guy leaping from the balcony doesn't necessarily consult Miss Manners."

"Maybe," Merchant said. "But you find there's a protocol for most everything, and by and large, people follow it. Drug dealers act like the drug dealers they see on TV. Street punks come up with a language and a look and stick to it. Minor variations. Even somebody about to jump out the window knows leaving a note is part of the gig. Usually they've got someone in mind when they write it. Somebody they want to blame and say, 'Look what you made me do.' That note Coulter left sounds damn close to 'Good-bye, cruel world.'"

"And you don't buy it."

"I guess I don't."

"So where does that leave you?"

Merchant paused, looking out at the dark harbor. "Well, I've been holding on to this." He took a piece of paper from his pocket.

She held it up to the light and saw that it was a check.

He said, "Coulter paid me for three days' work, and I've only done one."

"Then you better get your rest," she said.

CHAPTER 12

They went to bed, but not together. He opened up the double bed in the main cabin, and she went off into the bow.

It bothered him, but he let it go.

Coulter alone on that hard asphalt. That pathetic note upstairs. His family lost, probably dead.

Merchant wanted Sarah in his bed, but life had worse to offer than loneliness. Or so he told himself.

Merchant couldn't fall asleep.

Instead, he thought about the boy. Not Coulter's boy but Carlos Gacha's.

The boy was eight at the time. His father had been the target of a DEA investigation. He was the cousin of one of the most notorious Colombian cartel leaders.

Soon after Merchant had been transferred from the Virgin Islands to Miami, he'd been assigned to work undercover, posing as the pro photographer for a book Gacha had commissioned about his life story.

Over a period of months Merchant had been out to Gacha's house many times. Gacha's two children, Robert and Justine, liked and trusted him.

The day came when the DEA thought they had enough evidence to arrest Gacha and put some real pressure on him. Merchant set up an appointment to take some photos of Gacha in his home office. His assignment was to disarm Gacha and his bodyguard before the SWAT assault began. He was also charged with making sure the children were out of the way.

Merchant casually asked Gacha where the children were and was told they were upstairs playing video games. He checked out the office and bathroom where he and the SWAT team thought the arrest should be made.

Then he gave the signal, "I've got to switch lenses."

And reached into his bag and came out with his gun and a badge.

But Gacha's bodyguard started to pull a gun.

And even though Merchant had contained the situation, when the SWAT leader, Bobby Lee Randall, came through the door, he apparently decided the situation was still out of control.

He shot the bodyguard.

He shot Gacha.

And then little Robert jumped out from his hiding place. His favorite game was hide-and-seek, and apparently he had been hiding behind the bathroom door.

Merchant had missed him.

Robert started screaming, and Bobby Lee swung his automatic weapon onto him. Merchant wrestled with the SWAT leader and knocked the gun barrel up to the ceiling.

It was all just a matter of seconds.

But that gave the wounded Gacha time to grab the bodyguard's gun from the floor and shoot.

Bobby Lee Randall had cursed Merchant as the blood flowed amazingly fast out of his body and his face turned sheet white.

He died before he reached the hospital, his femoral artery severed.

Not the stuff of sweet dreams.

Merchant threw off his covers, figuring he'd go on deck and pass the night there if need be.

But Sarah slipped out of the forward cabin and knelt beside him. "Can't sleep?" she whispered.

"No."

He could barely see her face in the darkness, just the silhouette of her. She said, "I should have come to bed with you."

"Taking mercy on me?"

"On both of us," she said. She slipped off her T-shirt and dropped it onto the cabin floor.

He took her by the hands and pulled her forward until she lost her balance and collapsed onto his chest, the very heat of her body making him gasp.

"Explain something to me," he said. His voice was hoarse.

"What?"

"Why aren't we doing this every night? Every goddamn night, why aren't you in my bed?"

"Because I'm an idiot." She covered his mouth with hers.

Afterward, they both slept just fine.

Merchant awoke just before six. Sarah had coffee on and was dressed. She looked sleepy and a little smug at the same time.

He felt the same way.

He said, "What time does Lenny get to work?"

"Normally, hours from now. But today, you can set his schedule."

"You know where he lives?"

"Course I do."

"All right then." Merchant swung his feet to the cabin sole and stood and stretched. Pulled on some jeans and a shirt, shuffled into his boat shoes. She poured coffee for him in a travel mug, and they left.

They were outside Lenny's by seven. A sagging two-family

with asbestos shingles surrounded by an asphalt yard and a rusty chain-link fence.

"Nice," Merchant said. He pounded on Lenny's door until he opened it. It took about five minutes, all told.

Lenny looked out at them through the screen. He was wearing gray underwear and a tank top that matched.

Both, presumably, were white at one time.

"Rise and shine, sweetie," Sarah said.

Lenny said, "You got a clue what time it is?"

"Now where have I heard that before?" Sarah opened the screen door and handed him a bag. "Coffee and three glazed donuts. Get dressed and come with us to the office."

"And if I don't?"

Sarah seemed perfectly sincere when she said, "Actually, I'm kind of hoping you don't. Because I told myself this morning that if you drag your ass or give us a hard time, I'll consider all debts between us paid. And from then on you'll be judged solely on your merits as an employee."

Lenny bit into a donut and chewed it thoughtfully.

Merchant would've believed Sarah if she'd said it to him.

Lenny sipped the coffee, then spit a thin stream of it back over his shoulder. Onto his own floor.

"This coffee sucks," he said. "We stop at the Starbucks on the way in and get something that won't peel paint if I spill it."

Sarah said, "We'll be waiting in the car."

"All right, this is what I've got," Lenny said about a half hour later. He was sitting in front of his computer, Merchant and Sarah looking over his shoulders at the monitor. He said, "And it's not my damn fault if your jumper can't draw worth shit. All I can say is, to me, these three look sort of like what your guy drew."

Merchant looked closely at the three plates Lenny had selected. And looked at Coulter's sketch.

Any one of them could have been right.

There was a resemblance in the shape. The anchor plate Coulter had drawn was swept back from the bow and had an odd swoopy look, like the Nike logo.

And all three plates had that to a degree.

"Show me some of the ones you rejected."

Lenny scrolled through a half dozen other selections he'd bookmarked. Indeed, Merchant wouldn't have picked any of them.

"Looks like you did a good job," Merchant said.

"Yeah. You gonna pay me a bonus?"

Merchant dropped his hand on Lenny's shoulder. "I'll thank you for your cheerful support."

Lenny shrugged so Merchant's hand fell away. "I'm billing you for waking me up, too."

Merchant took the company names and addresses Lenny gave him. Sarah brought him into her office and handed him the telephone.

"They're not going to care," Merchant said.

"Give them the chance."

He took the card Detective Lerner gave him and dialed. He was put on hold for a few minutes before the detective picked up the phone.

Merchant identified himself, and the cop said, "Yeah, what's up?"

Merchant told him about the plates.

Lerner was quiet for a moment, then said, "Don't mean to be daft here, Merchant, but tell me again why I should care?"

Merchant went through it patiently. About the anchor plates as the one detail of the boat Coulter had been able to remember. The only link toward finding it and, by extension, what had happened to his family.

Lerner said, "Look, when Matt Coulter comes out of his coma, he can tell us why he was so despondent that he jumped. But I made some calls, and the Coast Guard and State Police both see this as a sad situation but nothing too complicated. Coulter himself maintained his sailboat went down on his watch after he lost the . . . ah . . . the mast. Neither the Coast Guard or the State Police are looking for a mystery motor yacht."

"So you don't want me to send this information to you?"

"Of course I do," Lerner said. "I'll put it in the file so if anything changes, I have it. Now, Merchant, just so we're clear on this. Petronelli tells me you once had some chops, but you are out of the game now. No status whatsoever. You keep your nose out of business that's not yours. You got any further thoughts, just call me."

"Got it," Merchant said. "So I'll fax you this stuff."

"As long as we understand each other."

"Sure we do." Merchant confirmed the fax number was the same as the one on the detective's card and hung up.

Sarah said, "So what's the story?"

"He said chase it to my heart's content. That they'd appreciate all the help I can give them."

"Yeah," she said. "Told you so."

Merchant headed back to his boat. Took a shower, put on clean khakis, then walked into town. He brought his briefcase holding the Web page printouts and Coulter's drawing of the plate. The day was overcast but hot, and he was ready for another shower before he found the address on Commercial Street.

He took the elevator to the investigative offices of the Coast Guard. A young man was behind the desk, in uniform. Merchant gave his name, said he wanted to speak to Lieutenant Reed.

"I'll see if he's available, sir. May I ask your business with him?"

"My name is Jack Merchant, and I'm here on behalf of Matt Coulter."

"Yes, sir."

Merchant waited in the lobby for about ten minutes. Lots of boat pictures to look at. None the quality of his photography, he decided.

Besides, all of them were Coast Guard cutters or rescue craft.

Finally, a tall sandy-haired man in uniform came out of the office. "Mr. Merchant?" he said. "I understand that you represent Mr. Coulter. In what capacity, may I ask?"

Reed had pale blue eyes and deeply reddened skin.

"Mainly as a friend at this point," Merchant said. "Did you hear about his suicide attempt?"

"Yes, I heard from the Newland Police. I was very sad to hear it. Mr. Coulter certainly has gone through a terrible time. He was here to discuss our investigation frequently, and we did our best to satisfy his questions. I'm not sure what I can do to help you."

Merchant nodded and mentally translated Lieutenant Reed's words as: Coulter bugged the hell out of us for something we could do nothing about. Now what the hell do you want?

Merchant tapped his briefcase. "I've got something here. Too thin to call evidence, but maybe a lead."

Reed looked skeptical, but he waved his hand to his office.

Merchant followed him in and sat down in the chair across from Lieutenant Reed's desk.

"Let's see what you've got."

Merchant took out the pictures of the plates and went through the story as he had with Lerner.

Got about the same reaction. Whatever interest he'd seen before in the man's eyes — feigned or otherwise — went away.

"Too thin is right," said Reed. "You know how many boats that could eventually lead me to? I've got limited resources here. And no proof that any of what Matt Coulter believed happened was true. As I understand it, he didn't come up with this memory about a boat picking up his family until a week into his recovery. We found his sailboat and sent divers down and they found the hull with the broken mast, no bodies onboard. We did a grid search by aircraft for three days afterwards. We did what we could. I don't know if you know anything about the sea yourself, Mr. Merchant, but tragic though it may be, two children lost in the ocean are very, very hard to find. Let me show you something." He pulled out a chart pack, flipped through it until he got to the Rhode Island coast. He talked about prevailing wind, about currents, about the size of the deep blue Atlantic.

Pretty much the same speech Merchant had given Coulter himself.

He didn't like hearing it. Made him think how Coulter must've felt.

"So you're not even going to chase these?"

"Of course I will," Reed said. He drew the papers together, shuffled them neatly, and slipped them into a manila file folder. "I'm going to look into this. But I don't have high expectations, and I have other investigations requiring my immediate attention."

Merchant could translate that answer just fine as well.

CHAPTER 13

Back at the boat, Merchant took out his copies of the Web page printouts and spread a road map on his nav station desktop. He matched the locations of the three metal fabrication companies Lenny had selected.

Southern New Hampshire. Upstate New York. And the third on the coast of Connecticut.

Luckily, they were all within driving distance. He printed out specific directions from the Web and packed clothes, binoculars, and a small digital camera. He got dressed for his road trip and was on his way within the hour.

It was midafternoon before he reached the machine shop just south of Portsmouth, New Hampshire. It was located in an old red-brick factory about three miles from the waterfront.

Merchant parked the Saab in the lot and headed for the open door to what he presumed was the machine shop. Although the cloud cover had lifted and it was now a bright day, the lights inside were blazing as if to keep up.

The shrieking of metal on metal was bad enough out in the parking lot. Inside, it was an appalling wall of noise.

He saw four men, each with his own bench. The one in the front was grinding the edges of a large piece of stainless steel, apparently for what looked to be the centerboard of a sailboat.

Sparks flew, and the noise dominated everything.

Merchant felt a tug on his arm and turned to see a big red-headed man beside him. The guy cupped his hand and yelled, "What's up?"

Merchant tried to speak, and the grinder spun to life again.

The redheaded guy put his thumb over his shoulder, and he and Merchant went out into the parking lot. "Forget about talking in there, mister. What can I do you for?"

Merchant took out his Ballard Marine Liquidation card and gave it to the man.

"Repo?" The guy had pale blue eyes, and the card seemed to worry him. "What's this about?"

"You the owner?"

"Yeah. Carl Beggy." He put out his hand, and Merchant shook it. The palm was hard and callused.

"We're doing an insurance job. Trying to track down a boat that may've had a plate like this on the bow."

"Why?"

"There was a collision."

Merchant showed him Coulter's drawing and the Web page printout showing the plate that Beggy's company made.

Beggy said, "No one's complaining about the anchor plate, right? I mean, it's just a little protective metal on the bow. Keep the anchor from scratching the fiberglass. What people do with that bow is the operator of the boat's business, not mine, right?"

"Sure. There's no issue there."

"OK." Beggy looked more closely at the plate and the drawing. "I can't tell for sure it's ours looking at this. I mean, who knows? I guess it could be. So you want to know which boat manufacturers we sold to?"

"That's right."

"C'mon."

Together, they went into the office. It was small, holding

just one desk, a fax, computer, and answering machine. A picture on the wall of Beggy holding a marlin up, grinning ear to ear.

"Most of your work go into boats?"

"Nah. Good thirty percent, though. My dad was into it, that's how I got into it. . . ." Beggy got to his desk and perched awkwardly on the chair. Then began tentatively working with the mouse, scrolling his way through various files. "This thing," he said of the computer. "It still bosses me around. My wife's brother, he put it in for us. I can tell you where we sold everything, how I'm doing for stock, everything. It's supposed to make my job easier. Doesn't though, because I always have to keep entering the shit. My brother-in-law said I should throw the plates and a bunch of other one-offs I've done up onto a marine Web site. Said if I made it once, maybe I can sell it again."

"Makes some sense. Was this plate a one-off?" Merchant tried to keep his voice casual. Wouldn't it be nice if was.

"Nah. Didn't sell that many, though. It's for a big boat." Beggy swiveled the monitor around.

There was a list of four boat builders. Beside each was a part number, quantity number, shipping date, invoice number, and price. Beggy said, "My sales history of nine-two-six-three C, Anchor Plate — SS."

"'SS' for?"

"Stainless steel. That shit is hard to work with, tough as nails when you're done." That seemed to make him think, and he said, "Hey, how'd they do?"

"Who's that?"

"You said there was a collision. How'd it work out with the people who got hit?"

"Not well," Merchant said. "Not well at all."

Merchant headed up toward Concord and got onto Route 202 toward Albany. The drive passed slowly, but he didn't mind.

He expected that he'd get there after the building was closed, and he was right.

He drove around the parking lot of the second metal fabrication shop, FabRite. It was a much bigger facility than Beggy's. A big beige one-story building with concrete walls. Part of a small industrial park. Enough room in the parking lot for a couple hundred cars.

Merchant spent the night in a chain motel that was so aggressively sterile he dreamed he had a new job that involved lots of travel, rayon suits, and a well-practiced sincere smile.

In the morning, rather than sitting down to the plastic-wrapped "continental breakfast" served off the lobby, he made his way to a truck stop just down the road. Eggs, bacon, home fries, and no attempt to hold the grease.

He pulled into the parking lot of FabRite just after eight-thirty and went into the main reception area. A middle-aged woman with wire-rim glasses looked at him and smiled in a perfunctory way. "How may I help you?"

Merchant gave her the same insurance job version he'd told Beggy.

"Boat," she repeated. "You'll want our marine product manager, Randy Sikes."

Merchant waited on the black vinyl sofa in the lobby. There was a surprising number of trade magazines devoted to metal fabrication.

Merchant thumbed through some of them, and the scope of his task began to swell even further. There were so many ways that plate of metal could have been made for a boat which may or may not have existed.

When Randy Sikes came out, he quickly came to the same conclusion. He was a balding man with a blazing white shirt and silk tie. He stared at the drawing and Web page printout. "Jesus, could be anybody who made this. Now, why do you want this again?"

Merchant told him. Trying to find a boat that had been involved in a collision. This plate was the only identifier.

Sikes looked at the card Merchant had given him. His brow wrinkled.

"If you'd like to call my office," Merchant said, "you're welcome to check with the owner. Her name is Sarah Ballard."

That seemed to tip it. Too much trouble.

"Hell, I don't care," Sikes said. He turned to the receptionist. "Get Barry in to help this gentleman, will you?"

Sikes took off for a meeting.

Barry was about twenty-five, and he clearly thought whatever the boss told him to do was stupid.

With great forbearance, he tried to help Merchant.

"If this is the plate I think it is . . . you could be looking at a production boat. You follow that logic along . . ." He tapped in the print command, and the laser printer began to run a depressingly long list. When it was done, Merchant flipped through. He saw the actual number of manufacturers wasn't that great, but one of them, Sun Coast Trawlers, had ordered fifty-eight plates in lots of about ten at a time.

"Yep," Barry said, looking over Merchant's shoulder. "Production boat. Their forty-five-footer was quite a hit. Based in South Carolina, and people take them all over the world. If the boat you're looking for is one of them, good freaking luck."

He stacked the sheaf of papers quickly and handed it off to Merchant. Glad he was done with this little task and glad it wasn't his responsibility to do a damn thing with it afterward.

Foster, Connecticut.

Foster Metal Fabrication.

Big name, tiny operation. Made Carl Beggy's shop look like a medium-size corporation and FabRite look like U.S. Steel.

The shop was in the garage of an old white colonial. When

Merchant pulled into the driveway, a mean-looking mutt with a lot of German shepherd in the mix put his paws up on the window and barked repeatedly through the glass until his owner came out and kicked him.

The dog yelped and then backed off. From about ten feet away, he growled warnings. The man ignored his advice.

Merchant rolled the window down, and the man looked in at him. He and the dog were clearly related. Blue bandanna pulled tight against his skull, faded blue eyes, stubble of beard going white in places. Probably mid-forties. Strong looking in a wiry sort of way. "You looking for me?"

"Think so."

Merchant told him the insurance story and saw the crafty look he expected.

"Tommy Caldwell," the guy said by way of introduction. "I got to tell you, I'm busy with paying jobs right now."

Merchant sighed. It felt barely worth the effort. He had over a dozen manufacturers to check out now, and if the plates represented boats sold, which they probably did, there were over eighty-five possibilities out there he already knew about. Tracking down each of those boats to see if it could have been in the area a month back would be a monumental task.

What did he need with a few more?

But he said, "Listen, I can throw a couple bucks your way if you can help. But my client's on a shoestring unless we find this boat."

Caldwell seemed to consider it and yelled for the growling dog to shut the hell up and go into the house. The dog didn't want to, but after Caldwell advanced on him, he slunk away.

Merchant got out of the car and showed the man the picture.

"Yeah, looks like one of mine," the guy said.

They spent a few minutes haggling over what constituted a shoestring budget. They settled at seventy-five dollars. Then Merchant followed Caldwell back into his shop. It had the same hot smell as the other shops, that of ground metal and acetylene gas. Caldwell opened up an ancient floor file cabinet and thumbed through a few manila folders before pulling out a slim one.

"I'm not a big operation," he said, with an entirely straight face. "I do real solid work though. You ask anybody, they'll tell you. Most of the boat shit I do, it's for three yards right here on the coast."

"These yards make power yachts the size that could use this plate?"

"One of them does. Foster Marine. Thing about me compared to a lot of the other fabricators out there, I go out and measure the boat, install the fittings myself. Everything's damn near custom. Anchor plate's no big deal, but the way I do it, can be a work of art, really add something to the look of the boat, you know?"

"Sure."

Caldwell thumbed through a thin sheaf of pink order forms. "How far you want to go back? Six, seven years, like that?"

"Far as you got."

Caldwell shrugged and fanned the sheets out. Unlike the other two fabricators, these order slips were headed by the names of the boats as well as the boat builders.

"So you were actually on each boat?"

"Yeah, like I said, I installed each plate myself."

"Got any idea which of these boats are still in the area?"

"Maybe." Caldwell turned the pink slips to himself again and looked at them closely. He set aside one to the left, then another. And then took the third and pushed it off to the side. He went through the rest of the slips, finally selected one more and set it with the stack of two. "That's all I can tell you. These three, I'm pretty sure you'll still find them chugging up and down the coast. It'd take me a little time to figure exactly which marinas." He rubbed his thumb and forefinger together as he said this, making clear that time was money.

"The others you don't know?"

"Nah. The others, I got no idea. Foster Marine, they'd probably know, but I don't think they'd tell you if the sun was shining. They're a tight-assed bunch."

"And this one?" Merchant said, pointing to the one slip off on its own.

"That one, don't waste your time."

"How come?"

"*Isabella* I know for a fact you're not gonna be able to chase her."

"How come?"

"Blew up," he said. "Blew up at her slip about three weeks ago. Took out the skipper. That plate, I'd guess she flew along with the rest of the bow, damn near sunk the sloop across the dock."

He grinned. "Like I said, I do solid work."

CHAPTER 14

The computer screen was suddenly covered with blood again.

Sean was surprised. He must have drifted off. He had practiced so much in the past . . . four weeks, he guessed . . . that he'd pretty much mastered the game.

He started the game over. Chose his weapon. A big knife this time.

Outside, he heard the Jeep pull in.

He got up and looked out through the blinds. He squinted against the light.

He saw Weir get out, walk in the way he did, as if he'd like to be out climbing mountains.

Sean heard him walking through the cabin, heard him and Ella talking for a minute. But their voices were too low to understand what was being said.

Then steps down the hall and a knock on the door.

Weir stuck his head in. "Sean Boy. Got a few minutes for me?"

Sean stared at the screen. "I was just playing," he said. Mumbling.

"I won't be long." Weir closed the door behind him. He looked over Sean's shoulder and said, "James and Sean. Is Bond your alter ego?"

Sean shrugged.

Weir looked more like an athlete than a doctor — and Sean really didn't think he was a doctor, anyhow. Weir was somewhere in his thirties, probably. Blond hair with some silver in it. Tanned. Strong, too. Sean knew that the hard way.

Sean sneaked a glance at him, saw that Weir was waiting for him, patiently. Sean let his face go dumb. Just let his muscles slack, put his eyes down. That was what they wanted, that was what they'd get.

Stupid.

Weir said, "So how's it been for you, Sean?"

"I want to see Mr. Pryor."

Weir made a face. "Yes, I wanted to talk with you about him. I want to see you back into a normal life when you're ready."

"Then send us to the Pryors."

Weir didn't say anything for a moment. Then he said, quietly, "I just want you to know we're doing everything for you and Laurie we can."

Sean yawned, in spite of himself. The drugs.

"Tired?"

He nodded.

"Well, like I've told you, that's a symptom of depression, which is certainly understandable given the upheavals you've been through."

Weir tapped a manila envelope against his leg. The same kind that had the newspaper article about Sean's father's body being found at sea. Dead from exposure.

Weir sat on the sofa beside the computer table and leaned back. He was dressed a little better than usual today, in khaki pants and a dress shirt. "Mind if I hide out with you here for a while?" he asked. "I'm supposed to be doing rounds at the clinic, but you're technically a patient."

That was the story they'd told him. That Weir was a psychiatrist at a clinic just a few miles from the cabin. That since he happened to be on the boat when Sean's parents had their "accident at sea," he had arranged to take care of them.

Like Ella, Weir seemed to think Sean was really stupid.

Sean didn't know exactly what was going on, but he didn't believe a word the man said. He noticed that Weir had positioned himself so they were in line with that hidden camera. Like maybe he was making sure he could be seen.

By who, Sean could only wonder.

Weir kept smiling for a little bit, then made a face as if he'd just bit into something rotten. "Like I said, I've got something to discuss with you."

Sean started trembling.

Whenever Weir began with this, the news was bad.

Weir said, "Under the circumstances, you made a good point about guardianship, so I pursued it on your behalf."

"Did you talk to him?"

"Several times."

"You talked to Ben," Sean said. He tried not to sound too excited. Whatever they were giving him kept him down, but still, his heart started beating fast. He knew that Ben Pryor was supposed to be their guardian if anything ever happened to his parents.

He kept the tears back. Seeing Ben would be as close to seeing his dad as was possible. Being back in Newland, being close to his home.

Still, Sean kept his face slack. Keep stupid until he and Laurie were out of this cabin forever.

Weir tapped the yellow envelope. "I called him, met with him, and even had our attorneys meet with him. We've had conversations with a judge. I'm afraid things haven't worked out as you or I would've expected. But the thing I want you to take to heart — and this is as true for your sister as it is for you — this isn't your fault. These are issues that come up between adults. And while I wish more adults would behave like adults . . ." He sighed. "I have this letter from him."

Weir reached into the manila folder and passed over the letter. Sean recognized the logo at the top instantly. He'd seen it most of his life. The logo of his dad's company. His dad's and Ben's.

The letter in his hands was a copy.

He focused on what Ben had written to him.

Dear Sean and Laurie,

I've been following with great interest the reports that Dr. Weir has sent me. I'm glad to hear that you're both in good health after this terrible tragedy.

Kids, there's no simple way to say this. It pains me and Mrs. Pryor to let you know that we've come to a decision about you living with us. While it's not your fault, I've come to realize that your father, who I always thought was my friend, had cheated on me in important business matters.

I can't expect you to understand the details of this. Nor do I hold you responsible. However, it's simply no longer appropriate for us to have you come live with us. I've explained the situation to Billy. Though he's sad, he understands.

Your father did a terrible thing, and for that reason I must tell you that I do not wish to have any further communication with either of you — meaning no telephone calls, visits, e-mails, or anything else. I don't want you contacting Billy. Quite honestly, I recommend the same for

anyone else you might know here in Newland. We are "off limits."

I suggest you listen well to Dr. Weir. He
clearly has your best interests in mind
and will help reestablish you elsewhere
with a new family. Most likely you will be
in a different part of the country where
no one will know what your father did.

Kids, take advantage of this new opportunity. Your father's transgressions don't
have to ruin your lives.

Best of luck to you both.

Benjamin Pryor

Sean read the letter two times.

Bullshit, he thought. Bullshit, bullshit.

But the problem was he couldn't really be sure. Part of him
could see Ben sitting behind the computer in his office, typing
away, his face serious and sort of angry.

It could all be true. Maybe his mom and dad did get
crushed under the powerboat during their rescue. The red-
haired woman had hustled him and Laurie down into the cabin
while his parents were still in the life raft. Sean hadn't actually
seen what happened.

But why hadn't they rescued their bodies? Or why hadn't
he talked to any policemen? He'd watched enough television at
least to know that should have happened.

Early on, Weir had answered those kinds of questions by
saying, "This isn't television, Sean. This is real life. And in real
life you can lose people you love suddenly and without explanation. And it's not fair, but that's the way it is."

Now Sean was so tired and his thoughts weren't clear. He

didn't want Weir to tell him that again. What he wanted was to punch Weir right in the face.

But he didn't. Instead, he retreated back into stupid. He put a whine into his voice. "He's not taking us?"

"I'm afraid not," Weir said. "I know it's a shock. And I've double-checked for family on both sides of your parents. It's as you said. Your father was an only child, and your mother's older brother passed away. Cancer. I'm sorry."

Tears began to roll down Sean's face. "My dad wasn't a cheat," he said. His lower lip was quivering. He hated it, but it wasn't hard to fake. It was what he felt.

"You said before he had a drinking problem," Weir said. "Sometimes adults get into trouble with alcohol and financial matters."

Sean's face flushed. When they had first arrived at the cabin, he'd said something to Weir about his dad drinking. He was trying to make sense of it all. He said his dad wasn't drinking, he knew boats, and he wouldn't just let the powerboat come down on him and Mom. He knew what he was doing.

But Weir kept bringing it up. Like it explained everything, like it was all his dad's fault. Now Sean felt like a traitor for having said anything.

"My dad's not a cheat," he repeated.

"I wouldn't know anything about that," Weir said.

Sean kept trying. "There's other kids I know. You could talk with their parents."

But already Weir was shaking his head. "You mentioned some names before, and I've had some preliminary conversations with Peter Gallagher's family, and Nicholas Fraser's. Apparently, Mr. Pryor has been talking to others in town, and they share in his decision."

"That's not fair."

"Of course it's not. Unfortunately, very few things in life are. We have to focus upon what we can do, not what's fair or unfair." He patted Sean on the arm and then held on to him a bit. "You and Laurie are strong, and I know you'll pull yourself out of this and go on with your lives. Ella and I are here to help you do just that."

Sean may've been wrong, but he was pretty sure Weir had raised his voice slightly. For the camera maybe?

"Answer me," Weir said. "You understand, right? Your parents are gone. But Ella and I will take care of you until we get you situated with another family. You understand?"

"Another family?" Sean said. "When?"

"We'll see. I just need to see that you accept that your parents are gone and that it's time for you to move on. Can you do that?"

Sean hesitated. He could see from Weir's face that he wanted him to say yes. Sean tried desperately to think through the haze they'd put him in. Living with some other family. Probably in a different part of the country — that was what Ben's letter said. The letter that Sean was pretty sure Ben had never written.

Sean knew they wanted stupid.

But he was pretty sure that if he said yes, the next time Weir came in with one of those manila envelopes it would be to say that he and Laurie were to be sent off to another place to live.

Maybe separately.

He'd never find her then.

"I want to talk to Ben," he said. "Let me at least talk to him on the phone."

Weir shook his head, annoyed. He stood up. "That's your past, Sean. I'm here to help you forget it. Let's talk about it later."

Sean wanted to argue, but he didn't. He was just about stupid enough for them now. He was stupid enough so that he could start doing something about it.

CHAPTER 15

The next morning Sarah went to her boatyard early, hitched up a solid but beat-looking Boston Whaler with a Repo Sale sign on the bow, and drove down to meet Merchant at Foster Marine. He was waiting in the parking lot in his car. When she pulled in beside him, he got out and came and leaned in against the open window.

"Nice to see you."

"Ditto," she said, leaning out to kiss him hello.

"You didn't have to come all the way down," he said.

"Did too if you want to get anything from Alden," she said. "Besides, it turns out he needs a new workboat. Figured I'd mix business with business."

"New workboat just a coincidence with the explosion?"

"Not hardly. Old one was docked right beside *Isabella* and it went down too." She jerked her thumb toward the Whaler. "I've been trying to off-load this ugly puppy for six months. Let me do the talking."

"You would anyhow."

"Oh, shut up," she said. "You're lucky to have me."

Sarah led Merchant through the crushed shell parking lot up the wooden outer stairway of the small marine gray building. The stairs led to a porch overlooking a spectacular view of the Foster Bay harbor. The wind was up now, and a burgee snapped on a flagpole above her head. They paused for a moment, looking down at a set of three floating docks. There was a noticeable difference in the condition of the end of the far right dock: it looked brand new. New pilings, the decking unpainted.

"Must be where *Isabella* blew," she said.

"Surprised they got the hull out already. Couldn't have been easy clearing out a forty-five-foot hulk."

"Hmmm. And just think how bad for business it'd be. Alden's trying to build and sell new boats and one of his own is sitting there half sunk."

The door opened behind them.

Sarah turned and smiled. "Alden."

Typical response. Pale blue eyes giving nothing away. White shock of hair, white eyebrows, and a sun- and wind-reddened face. Vague look of disapproval. He said, "Sarah."

She introduced Jack. Alden glanced at her curiously, then shook Merchant's hand. Apparently Alden figured him for one of her yardmen and didn't know why he was expected to be polite.

Sarah could see Merchant was more amused than insulted, which was good. This was the way Alden behaved with anyone who wasn't about to buy a boat. Then, the change was remarkable. Those blue eyes could twinkle and he could call up an old-salt charm at will.

Still, she sort of liked Alden, and he seemed to feel the same about her.

"That it?" he said, gesturing with his chin toward her truck and the Whaler. "Looks like a piece of shit, Sarah."

"You said you wanted cheap and solid, and she's both. The outboard's a ninety, and I had it rebuilt."

He made a face, then sighed. "I dunno. I've got another workboat, and we've been scraping by without the second one.

Maybe I should just keep on until sales perk up."

Sarah didn't even bother replying to that. He'd asked her to bring the damn boat down. She said, "Jack's not here about the Whaler. I was wondering if you could maybe help us with some questions."

Alden frowned. "About what?"

"About *Isabella*."

"How's that your concern?" he said.

Merchant spoke up. Laid it out quickly for Alden that they'd been hired to find a boat that may have been near the scene of a sinking sailboat. He didn't mention Matt Coulter's attempted suicide.

Alden's brow furrowed. "I don't get it. Why not just ask whoever was rescued?"

"They may've been taken off. My client is trying to reach them."

"And you think Captain McNaughton rescued them?"

"It's possible," Merchant said.

"Based on what?"

Sarah had Merchant show Alden the drawing of the plate and described how he'd made his way to Foster Marine.

"Jesus Christ," Alden said. "It looks like the plate, but it's not like Captain McNaughton is around to fill in the blanks. You can ask his brother, but what he carries around in his head's not worth much."

"We would like to talk with him," Merchant said. "What happened exactly?"

"'Exactly' I don't know. *Isabella* blew about two in the morning. Must've been a hell of a flash." He pointed to the new dock. "Propane explosion. She was bow in. The whole front quarter just lifted, landed right onto the dock, and top-pled onto the Peabodys' ketch on the other side. Broke their bow stay, and so their mast came down. Wooden workboat I been using the past few years, it went right down along with the dock."

"What a mess," Sarah said.

"Queen of the understatement, Sarah. Insurance company had a salvage crew working pretty much round the clock. They got the hulk filled with foam, refloated it. Meanwhile, I got two fifty-five-footers just about finished, and now I got the owners running around peep-peep-peeping about how maybe my boats don't have the ventilation they need."

Alden stared at the drawing some more. He cleared his throat. "Well, come on. Put that ugly Whaler in the water, let's see what she can do. Might as well go take a look."

"Go where?" Sarah said.

Alden seemed surprised. "You didn't know? We've still got the bow."

They walked down to the Whaler. Alden took his time looking at it, commenting and scowling over every scratch. But the price she was asking was dirt cheap, and for the way he'd end up beating on the boat, she knew the cosmetics were meaningless.

Finally, he pointed to the ramp and said, "Do the honors, Sarah."

She got into the truck and backed the boat down into the water. Merchant stood on the trailer, shoved the Whaler off, and swung himself aboard. He lowered the outboard, started it up on the second try, and puttered to the end of the dock.

After Sarah parked the truck, she and Alden walked together through the parking lot toward the dock.

"This guy been with you long?" Alden asked.

"I've known him for years. He's not exactly an employee, but he's helping me on this one."

Alden looked at her. "Not your typical kind of job, Sarah. You branching out your business, or just with this guy?"

She decided not to give him an answer, and he didn't seem to expect one.

* * *

Alden visibly brightened once the outboard was growling and he was behind the wheel. He puttered along out to the black can and then gave the boat some gas. The bow rose, and the boat planed off easily. It was the first time Sarah had been out in it herself, and the boat ran more smoothly than anyone had a right to expect for the price she was offering.

"You're getting a deal, Alden," she yelled.

"Haven't taken it yet," he said back.

She felt like socking him in the arm just to get him to lighten up. But he wasn't that kind of guy.

Up ahead, she could see the bow of the big powerboat on the sandbar. Alden went straight to it, the Whaler topping out around forty.

The high white bow was awash in the shallow water of the bar. Alden slowed the boat to a crawl as the green of the deeper water gave way to the gold of the sandy bottom.

Even in its current state, a huge piece of charred and partially melted fiberglass, Sarah could feel the power of the hull. The high flaring bow, the still-brilliant stainless steel anchor plate. She saw Merchant looking up at the bow, perhaps, like she was, envisioning what this would've looked like coming out of darkness in stormy seas. What this would have looked like to a man with two children and a wife in a partially swamped inflatable raft.

Salvation, maybe.

Potential destruction, certainly.

Merchant looked at Sarah. Held up the piece of paper. Matt Coulter's little illustration of the plate looked exactly the same.

"I think we found it," he said.

CHAPTER 16

Merchant kept looking back and forth at the plate and the drawing. He pulled the little digital camera from his pocket and took a few shots. The whole time he felt a fast-growing sense of excitement mingled with dismay.

Up to this moment, he had been fulfilling an obligation. Searching for a boat that he was willing to believe never existed.

But maybe it did exist.

And if that were true, just maybe the rest was true.

Merchant said, "Had to be quite a propane leak for an explosion of this magnitude."

"It wasn't a leak," Alden said. "It was a screwup. A drunk's screwup, and the integrity of my work is being impugned."

Merchant looked at Sarah. He turned back to Alden. "He was drunk?"

"The alcohol in his blood confirmed that. The knob on one of the propane burners was wide open. Like he turned it so fast it didn't have a chance to light and he was too drunk to know the difference. Maybe he lit a match, he turned on a light, I don't know, the boat blew. And I've got to hear this peep-peep-peep now from the other customers."

"Are the police saying suicide?"

"They're not saying anything. But it's not the fault of my boat."

Sarah said to Merchant, "Two drunk men killing themselves?"

"Who's the other man?" Alden asked.

"Different states," Merchant said. "The other guy's not dead, but it looks like attempted suicide." He looked at Matt Coulter's little drawing. Then back at the stainless steel plate. "Different police forces. Who's going to make a connection?"

"We did," Sarah said.

Merchant turned to Alden. "What kind of guy was Captain McNaughton? Did you know him to be a drunk?"

"I've seen him put back a few."

"So that's a yes? He had a problem?"

Alden made a face. "Can't say that. Let me put it this way, McNaughton and I weren't exactly friends. He was a tough guy, ex-Navy. He came along about six years ago, when his boat was in the works. The original owner had gone bankrupt, and I was left holding a boat that was ninety percent done and there was no way I was going to get paid. So McNaughton bought her at a fire sale price. And then demanded the sky making her perfect."

Merchant looked back at the bow of the boat. "Fire sale or not, this had to cost some serious money. What did he do to afford it?"

Alden lifted his shoulders. "I think he took every dime he'd saved in the Navy and the bank gave him his loan. That's all I asked. He had me finish the boat for charter work. Then he hustled pretty hard with fishing trips, diving trips, coastal cruises, whatever kept the boat going. He wasn't an easy guy, but I'll say this: he loved the boat, he knew what he was doing.

He worked the customers, found the fish, knew the dive spots . . . knew when to tell the Navy stories and when to shut up. He kept the boat spotless."

"Still," Sarah said. "You should see how often I show up with paper on spotless boats run by hardworking skippers. Do you think he was doing something illegal? Running drugs maybe?"

"It didn't exactly come up in conversation."

"But your impressions?" Merchant said.

"I have none." Alden's voice had gone flat. "And I hardly need any rumors about drug running out of my marina."

"Got it," Merchant said. "How about this? Do you know who McNaughton's last charter guests were?"

"I don't pay attention to that kind of thing, and even if I did, I was out of town the week before his boat blew. Police asked me this already. I'll tell you what I told them: you want that kind of detail, go talk to McNaughton's brother, Ronnie. He crewed for him sometimes."

"I'd like to talk with him," Merchant said.

"And I'd like to get back to work." Alden shoved the throttle down and they roared back into the marina. He ignored the No Wake signs that his employees had probably tacked up.

Once they were close to the docks, he spun the boat around and backed in.

"You like?" Sarah said.

"Depends what you can do with that god-awful price."

As they walked up the ramp to the main deck, Alden gave Merchant directions to McNaughton's house.

"You got that?" Sarah said to Merchant.

"I'll muddle through," he said.

"Good. Because I can see Alden and I have to talk money."

"I damn well better get a discount for playing twenty questions," Alden said.

"You get a discount just for being you," Sarah said.

That seemed to please him. "C'mon up to my office and put that in writing."

Merchant got into his Saab and drove along the waterfront street past a lobster pound, a couple of decent looking restaurants, and a couple that smelled of long-dead fish before he took a right up the steep hill, kept climbing three blocks, and turned left. He had expected something pretty rough, but McNaughton's house was a small cape, neatly painted white with green shutters. However, the front yard was overgrown. A rusting red pickup truck was parked with one wheel up over the curb on the sidewalk.

Merchant noticed that all the shades were drawn as he went up to the front door. He knocked, waited, knocked again. From inside, he could hear the faint sound of a radio playing.

He was about to knock again when the door opened. A guy who appeared to be about forty years old looked out at him through the screen. "Yeah?" he said.

"Ronnie McNaughton?" Merchant said.

"Uh-huh. Who're you?"

Merchant gave his name.

"Yeah, so what's up?"

"I was sorry to learn about the loss of your brother. I have some questions, can I come in?"

"Questions about what?"

Ronnie crossed his arms. He was a big guy, over six feet tall. Fairly strong looking. Two- or three-day growth of wispy beard. Black hair shot with gray. He looked hungover. From the outwardly neat home, Merchant could smell the stale odor of beer and sweat.

"Well, about your brother. And some people he may have come in contact with during a rescue at sea."

"What rescue?"

"It'd be the week before your brother's accident."

"Yeah, well, if something like that happened, my brother would've mentioned it."

"Were you on his last charter?"

"No. I had a day job then. I haven't been working for him the last three months, anyhow, except for some weekends."

"Still, could I come in for a minute?"

"Why?"

Merchant took out his Ballard Marine Liquidation card. "Don't let the repo part throw you. I've been hired to find your brother's boat, but not for repossession."

Ronnie opened the screen door to take the card. "Repo, huh? Well, the boat's blown to bits."

"Again, that's not why I'm here."

Ronnie's brow furrowed.

"I've just got some questions for you. Nothing that's going to cost you money."

"You're sure?"

"Positive."

"You're not screwing with me, are you?"

"I'm not."

"I mean maybe I can buy a smaller boat with the insurance. Nothing like Greg's. But, you know, I don't have a captain's license."

Merchant wasn't sure if Ronnie was slow or if he was drunk. He said, "I just want to talk with you about some guests your brother may have had onboard." He stepped a little closer to the screen. "Can I come in?"

Now he could smell the beer on Ronnie's breath.

"Well, how do I know who you are? How'd you find your way here?"

"Alden Cabot told me how to find you."

"Cabot sent you?" Ronnie didn't look as if he and Alden were members of each other's fan clubs. But the familiar name seemed to have the right effect: he opened the door and said, "We can talk out back."

He led them through the small house. The air was stale, and when Merchant glanced around he saw the windows were closed. There was an open overnight bag near the entrance to the kitchen, and Merchant could see a tangle of dirty clothes inside.

"You just back from a trip?"

Ronnie looked at him. "Yeah. Took some time. You know, to forget."

He waved Merchant to one of the two Adirondack chairs on the back deck and sat in the other. The chairs were separated by a lobster pot used as a table. On the table, there was an open beer, a pack of cigarettes, and a lighter. Ronnie sighed heavily, took a deep drink from his bottle, belched behind his hand, and then slowly tapped out a cigarette.

He offered one to Merchant.

"No thanks."

Ronnie held up Merchant's business card, read it slowly, and then said, "So, Mr. Jack Merchant of Ballard Marine Liquidation, tell me why you were looking for my boat again?"

Merchant took out the pictures of Coulter's family and the letter from Coulter. "I'm trying to locate some people," he said. "And there's a chance that your brother and his charter guests may have either helped them or seen someone else help them during a rescue at sea the week before your brother's death. So, first of all, have you seen these two kids?"

Ronnie took a look at the pictures, flipped them over to see if there was anything on the back, then looked at them more carefully. "Nah," he said. "Never saw them."

"You ever hear the name Matt Coulter? Sean or Laurie Coulter?"

"No."

"How about records? Your brother was probably an organized guy, right?"

Ronnie laughed. "Christ, yes. List for every goddamn thing."

"So did he have a calendar with the charter guests' names, maybe? Billing addresses?"

"Dunno, maybe. That was his department. When I went

out with him, I was just crew: cooking, gutting the fish, setting up the tanks, that sort of thing."

"Well, where would you think he'd have it? Does he have an office?"

"Sure. Mine now."

"I see. Can I look in it?"

Ronnie seemed surprised. "You want to look in my office? That's private, man."

Merchant waited, looking at Ronnie.

The guy didn't let it slide. "I mean, hey, I come around asking to look into your office? C'mon."

Merchant tried a different tack. "How was your brother after his last charter?"

Ronnie shrugged. "He never was Mr. Personality, you know."

"Was he upset about something?"

Ronnie snorted. "He wasn't that kind of guy. You know, he had twenty years in the Navy and he was just a hard-ass from way back, even when we were kids. He was only a year older than me, but you'd think it was ten."

"Difficult guy to have for a brother?"

Ronnie drew deep on his cigarette and exhaled. "With Greg, there was his way and the wrong way. If you were going to be around him, it had to be his way. Period."

"Let me ask you something. If he heard a Mayday on the radio, would he respond?"

Ronnie gave a short laugh. "That would be the right thing to do, right? So he'd do it. But if he did, I'd know about it."

"So he did talk about some things."

"Yeah, sure. Just not what he was thinking or feeling about something. None of that shit. But, yeah, if he rescued somebody, he'd tell me. And he didn't say anything like that."

"But you weren't on the last charter trips?"

"Nah." Ronnie's eyes shifted, as if he was embarrassed.

"How come?"

He shrugged.

Merchant waited.

Then Ronnie said, "Look, money's tight. Real tight. I kind of screwed up."

"How?"

"By being stupid."

"What's that mean?"

"I got a problem."

"What kind? Drugs?"

"Naw. Gambling. Horses, the dogs. I got behind and he bailed me out. He was always breaking his ass to keep the boat, but I really put him behind. It was that or they'd bust me up. He was pissed, and he told me he wanted me off the boat. I got a dishwashing job at the Ninety-nine."

"Was he broke after that?"

"I don't think so. The money I owed was a lot to me — seven thousand. But I think he could handle it. Besides, he wouldn't tell me what was bothering him, we weren't those kinds of brothers."

"So he was upset after the last charter?"

"Nah. There was nothing like that. But he's like me in one way: neither of us needs an excuse to tie one on."

"He was a drinker?"

"Not all the time. But when he was, he was serious about it. Must've been plenty loaded to turn the knob on the gas and forget to light it."

"So you think that's all that happened? He got drunk and blew the boat up?"

Ronnie shrugged. "Got no idea, really. Not like I can ask him."

"So what are you going to do now?"

Ronnie drew deeply on his cigarette and blew out a cloud of smoke. Merchant thought he wasn't going to answer the question, but then he said, "Got no idea about that, either."

CHAPTER 17

The truck felt lighter now that it was no longer towing the Whaler. And that made Sarah's heart feel lighter, knowing she didn't have to look at the ugly thing sitting in her the boatyard every morning when she drove in.

Alden got a good price and she moved stock, so everyone was happy. And there was every chance she and Jack would have dinner that night, and she was pleased to find she was looking forward to that, too.

Progress.

She missed the last turn to Captain McNaughton's house, realized it immediately after, pulled a U-turn, and then turned down his street. Jack's Saab was parked out front of a nice little house.

She parked the truck, waited a second, debating whether or not she should go in or just wait for Jack to finish. She decided on the former and hurried up the sidewalk. She rang the bell.

She could hear voices in the background, and in the gloom of the house she could see a man, Ronnie McNaughton, she assumed, coming into the living room. Merchant was right behind him.

"Hi there," she said. "I hope I'm not — "

Ronnie's reaction stunned her.

He whirled around, shoved Merchant against the wall, and then reached into a bag on the floor.

Merchant said, "What's your problem?"

And Ronnie pulled out a gun.

He held it in both hands, a big blue steel revolver, and he swung it around to Merchant. But Merchant swept the gun off to the right and twisted it away.

The guy lunged across him, trying to get the revolver back.

Sarah finally stopped standing there like her feet were nailed into the steps and opened the screen door. There was a fireplace to her left. She snatched up the poker, planted her legs, and swung a hard backhand across his lower back.

It put him right down. The guy clutched at his back, his mouth open wide. He scuttled back up against the wall and started saying, "Jesus, Jesus, Jesus," then he covered his head as if she was about to split it with the poker.

When Merchant reached over to take it away from her, she realized that she did have it poised over her own head, ready to bring it crashing down.

"Easy," he said. "You've got him."

She handed Merchant the poker. She kicked the guy in the legs, making him scramble back even further. "I just about punched your ticket, you moron."

She stepped away to the other corner, breathing hard. She was shaking.

Merchant tossed the poker away and held the gun by his leg. "Just what the hell was that all about, Ronnie?"

His voice was quiet in the sudden silence.

Ronnie was breathing hard, clearly winded. He looked at Sarah more closely, then back at Merchant.

He shook his head. "Ah, shit."

"What?" Sarah said.

"I'm sorry, lady, I thought you were someone else. Then I thought maybe he was just screwing with me all along."

Merchant gestured to the big easy chair in the room. "How about you have a seat. Can I count on you not to pull any more of that nonsense?"

"Yeah. Just a misunderstanding." The guy sat down. He looked at Sarah. "I'm sorry, lady."

"You should be. Dipshit."

"Yeah, OK."

"Ronnie," Merchant said. "Are there any more guns in the house?"

Ronnie shook his head.

"Whose is this?" Merchant held up the revolver.

"Greg's."

"Why'd he have it?"

Ronnie shrugged. "Just said it was a tool."

"He ever use it?"

"I don't know. Can I get up now?"

"No," Merchant said. "He ever take this gun on his boat?"

Ronnie shrugged.

"What's that mean?" Merchant said.

"Sometimes, I guess."

"Why?"

"Like I told you before, he didn't tell me everything."

"You go fishing, he'd take the gun?"

"No."

"Then when?" Sarah said. "Would you be on the trips when he took the gun?"

"I don't know. I haven't been working with him, I've been doing the dishwashing job."

"So why'd you run for the gun now?"

Ronnie crossed his arms. "How about you two just get out of my house?"

"How about I call the police and say you're running around waving a gun?"

"You're not going to do that," Ronnie said, his voice striving for angry but coming across as petulant and confused.

"Why wouldn't we?" Merchant said.

Ronnie shook his head. "Look, I made a mistake, all right? I thought this lady was someone different, so maybe you were someone different."

"Who'd you think I was?" Sarah asked.

He looked up at her. "I don't know her name. She's got dark hair, like you and, you know" — he waved his hand at Sarah's body — "she's skinny like you."

Sarah suddenly felt the urge to laugh. Because Ronnie was blushing now.

But she worked at keeping her face calm, ignoring that twitching feeling, the slightly breathless quality, like when she'd have a laughing fit in church with Joel when they were little kids. "OK," she said. "So what's this skinny woman's name?"

Ronnie shook his head.

"Why the gun?" Merchant said. "Why would seeing her send you running for the gun?"

"That's what Greg did."

"Your brother saw this woman and he got his gun?"

"Pretty much. We were at the bank. And when we came out he saw this woman walking across the street. He saw her and got mad — I said I'd like to have a woman like her look at me. He said to just shut up and get in the truck. Then he got the gun from under the seat. I didn't even know he was carrying it in the truck then."

"When was this?" Merchant said.

"About three weeks ago, a month," Ronnie said.

"This is after his last charter?"

"Yeah."

"So he saw her the week he got killed?"

"Yeah, the day before."

"Is that why you pulled the gun when you saw Sarah in the doorway?"

"I got suspicious. All of a sudden, I thought you were tricking me and trying to get into the office — "

He shut up abruptly.

"What's in the office that you're worried about me seeing?" Merchant said.

"None of your damn business," Ronnie said. "That's my office now."

"Uh-huh. Well, you lost some of those privileges when you put a gun in my face," Merchant said. "Come on and show me what's so important in here."

"You can't do that," Ronnie said.

"Sure he can," Sarah said. "You put a gun on both of us, you've got to show what you were hiding. Or else we call the cops."

Ronnie swore. Said it was none of their goddamn business. But both Sarah and Merchant remained implacable.

Finally, he gave in and followed them into the office. He tried to get them to leave, but it didn't take long for them to find what he'd been hiding — the right-hand desk drawer held a bag just about half full of cash.

Sarah counted it. Fifteen thousand dollars. Thirty packets of twenties wrapped with a paper bank strip. Each packet worth five hundred dollars.

It was a lot of money to find in a bag, but even more disconcerting were all the empty wrappers. They were ripped open and littered the bottom of the bag. Sarah quickly counted them up: twenty in all. Ten thousand dollars.

Meanwhile, Merchant was talking with Ronnie. "Where'd you get this?"

"I inherited it."

"How?"

"My brother died, that's how," Ronnie said. "His lawyer said everything was mine, the house, and the insurance on the boat. Everything. So this would be, too."

"You found the cash in the house?"

"That's right."

"No," Sarah said, looking at another piece of paper in the bag. "This is a sign-in receipt from the safety deposit box. Did you go in there after your brother got killed and clean out his box?"

"So what?" Ronnie said. "I inherited everything from him, the lawyer said so. Maybe I didn't wait for everything to get signed nice and neat, but I figured why should I? What's his is mine, and I knew where he kept the bank key and his driver's license. We've always looked alike. It wasn't a crime."

"Actually, it probably was," Merchant said. "Banks don't look kindly on identity theft these days."

"I inherited everything!" Ronnie said.

"So, OK. You find your brother's dead, and besides being all broke up, you go and clean out his safety deposit box. And then you spent ten thousand dollars," Merchant said. "On what?"

"Took a trip," Ronnie said. "Give myself a chance to forget everything."

"Where'd you go?" Merchant asked.

"Atlantic City, if it's any of your goddamn business."

"How long were you there?"

"Few weeks. Got a buddy down there, stayed at his place. I made it work. Just did the slots, a little poker. I was up fifteen K at one point."

"But now you're down ten thousand," Sarah said.

He shrugged. "I know people who lose that in a night. I was careful. I can get more."

"'More'? How?" Merchant asked.

"I mean I can win it back."

"You said, 'I can get more,'" Sarah said.

"I know what I said."

Merchant moved to another topic. "So you've been out of state. You've been back now how long?"

"Since last night."

"And seeing Sarah made you run for a gun. You thought she was that woman outside the bank. Exactly who are you afraid of?"

"I've been thinking about that," Ronnie said. "And it's not you. So you two can get out of my house right now before I call the cops."

"Ronnie, you pulled the gun on us —" Merchant began, but Ronnie cut him off.

"Yeah, you had me going on that. But so what? You're in my house and I want you to leave. If I call the cops and tell them two people from Ballard Marine Liquidation won't leave my house after I told them to, you're gonna have trouble of your own." He picked up the telephone and started to dial 911.

He got to the second digit before Sarah ripped the phone cord from the wall. "Oops," she said. "We've gotta go."

She and Merchant left.

CHAPTER 18

Kathleen knew she was better than this.

Slot machines, one-armed bandits, were strictly for the pink-collar girls. Hairdressers, flight attendants, cosmetic counter girls.

And Kathleen Gardner. Sitting inside the revamped jai alai center in Newport, full now of hundreds of slot machines, a lot of cigarette smoke, and a lot of losers. An old lady in a wheelchair was to her right, and a cigar-smoking fat guy wearing a cowboy hat to her left.

Losers.

Not that she would classify herself that way. Not on a good day, anyhow. Not with her three-thousand-dollar Donna Karan suit, coiffed auburn hair, and cheekbones matched to her husband's portfolio. Thirty-eight years old, but she could pass for ten years younger, easily. Everyone told her so.

She pulled on that mechanical arm, felt the slight catch in the system. The whirring colors, the mismatched symbols provided her with that little stab of disappointment that was almost as addictive as the occasional win.

It got her blood pumping, yet it soothed her, too.

Took away her problems for a little while.

God knows, she had problems. Caused most of them herself, of which she was well aware. That only made the tug on that arm all the more appealing. She wondered if it was a phallic thing, fondling that chrome arm. Lately, she liked playing with it more than her husband's phallic thing.

Her husband, David. Good old Dave. Davy to his buddies, Mr. Gardner to his employees.

In this day and age, making his employees call him by his formal name, that was her husband. One of his theories about being professional.

She once loved him, or thought she might. Now, for the life of her, she couldn't remember why.

She pulled the arm again. Turtle, duck, turtle, donkey, monkey.

Fed another token from her plastic container.

Turkey, turtle, turtle, donkey, monkey.

The plastic container was getting light, and that was a problem.

It had been years since she actually needed more money than she had, but that was definitely the case now.

She pulled the lever, let the sound ratchet to a stop in front of her. Then opened her eyes.

Turtle, turtle, pig, horse, cow.

Son. Of. A. Bitch.

She took her time, figuring that every pull she missed was money saved. Who said she couldn't control her gambling?

Well, besides Dave.

"You've got a serious problem, honey," he said, putting on his sincere and concerned look. "You know how that would look in the trade."

That was what he'd said before the robbery. Since then he was too distracted to give a damn what she did. Not distracted, scared.

A couple of weeks ago, Kathleen took a trip up to Maine,

ostensibly to relax at their vacation home. In truth, she just wanted an excuse to go across the lake to see the children. In addition to the little camera, they had drilled holes in the wall to check in on the kids.

The little girl was so adorable. Kathleen wished she could just take her home. And the boy was such a solid citizen. She could see it in the way he looked after his sister.

But, of course, Kathleen couldn't let them see her. After they had gone to sleep, she had driven away in her Mercedes, the tears just pouring down her face. Thirty-eight years old, two miscarriages, and the only children she had any influence over were kidnapped. And while she was keeping them alive, the fact that they had been abducted at all was partially her fault.

She had bypassed her home in Boston, where Dave had probably been either pacing nervously about the condo or trying to act like a man with his girlfriend. Kathleen drove on to their Newport house and hit the slot machines and the tables for the next few days, tossing down over seven thousand dollars and recouping just three.

Then she went back to the Boston condo for Dave and tried to make love with him. He wasn't really interested, which maybe was because of the pressure he was under, but it may have been because he was with his lover that day. Kathleen wasn't supposed to know about either one, and so she said something meant to tweak him a little bit, but he got mad, and then she got mad, and the upshot of it was that she had spent most of the past week back at the Newport house. Telling herself she had to go slow.

Kathleen sighed. It would be so much easier to focus her attention on the problems at hand if she wasn't also battling an obsessive-compulsive desire to gamble.

She pulled the arm again.

She wondered what the kids were doing right now.

Duck, horse, turtle, monkey, cow.

Damn.

Still, that tiny loss took precedence over her other problems for a few seconds. For those few seconds, she felt as if those other problems didn't even belong to her.

Of course, when she got home that night the videotape would still be there. The tape where he was acting like he was a doctor. She couldn't tell if they believed him or not. Laurie seemed to, but Sean had acted suspicious before. Now he seemed different. Kathleen couldn't be sure, because the tape quality wasn't all that good and the sound was awful. But Sean seemed dumber somehow. Maybe he was just bored all the time there.

God knows, she couldn't blame him. They'd had him there for almost a month.

Kathleen hesitated. Her hand on the lever. Sometimes it became so clear to her. How her every movement, her every breath was wrong. And while she knew it, she didn't seem to be able to stop herself.

Those children didn't even know her name, but they needed her. Needed her as much as any child needed a mother. Needed her to do the right thing.

And yet, here she sat. The very contraction of her biceps to pull that lever was wrong. She needed money, and she was smart enough to know that gambling was many, many more times likely to break her than to make her rich. Yet here she sat.

Compulsive, out of control, untrustworthy.

Add to that, if Dave saw her like this again and told the Colombians, they'd be visiting her next. And where would that leave those poor children?

Still, she yanked the arm back.

Suddenly she couldn't see the symbols so well. Her eyes were blurred.

She was crying and she couldn't see.

Then there was ringing and she felt tokens falling onto her lap. She scrubbed the tears away long enough to see that she was winning.

Her afternoon and the six hundred dollars she'd pumped into the machine were paying off — or she was at least recouping some of her losses.

She laughed, and wiped the tears from her face. The old lady in the wheelchair smiled at her, but it was a jealous smile. Kathleen scooped out a handful of tokens and gave them to the old lady. "For luck," she said.

"Could use it," the woman said, and shoved one of Kathleen's tokens into her machine, and pulled the lever.

It didn't pay off, and the woman glared at her as if she had been cheated.

Kathleen was able to almost fill her container with her winnings. She started over to the window to cash out and then noticed a young blond woman leaving her machine on the other side of the room. Kathleen had watched her pump money into it for almost two hours without pulling out a thing.

She was a loser.

Kathleen went over to the young woman's machine and sat down.

Her head and heart were telling her that she had far more important things to do. But her compulsion told her to stay.

When she pulled the lever, Kathleen almost began to weep again.

Because she knew she was better than this.

CHAPTER 19

"You get me into trouble," Sarah said. "I hang with you and I'm almost getting shot at and having to hit people with pokers."

She wasn't smiling.

They had stopped for coffee at a diner just south of Providence. They were on their way back home, and Merchant could see that they would not be sharing a bed that night.

"I could point out that you introduced me to Coulter," he said. "That maybe you're putting me in the way of getting shot. And am I complaining?"

"You should be complaining. The fact that you're not means you like this kind of thing in some way, and so it's ultimately more your fault because I hate having to get guns away from people and hit them with a poker."

"I see."

"Yeah." She sipped her coffee. "You know I'm right."

Actually, he did.

"You even left him with the gun," she added.

"Without bullets. And if I took it from him and a cop stopped me with it under the seat, I could go to jail for a year."

She didn't answer that one. Looked sullen, and sipped her coffee.

He took out his notepad. "Listen, can we do something here rather than bitch at each other?"

"I like bitching sometimes."

"I noticed. But right now, can we figure out what we know and don't?"

She didn't answer.

For a moment, he thought that was all there was to it, and he started to get a little pissed himself.

But she stood up, came around to his side of the booth, and sat beside him. She pulled her coffee cup over, and he slid the notepad and pen between them. She leaned against his shoulder. "I suppose I did say this was a Ballard Marine Liquidation job, didn't I?"

"You did. But it doesn't have to be from now on. I would appreciate a little thinking from you though. Then you can go home."

"I can do a little thinking," she said. "Gimme some paper. You do yours, I'll do mine."

He wrote her name on the top of a sheet of paper and handed it to her. He wrote his own name on the top of another sheet. She took a pen from her breast pocket and bent over her sheet as if she were doing a test in school that she didn't want him to copy. He started on his own. They worked companionably for a few minutes, her leg warm against his.

Finally, she said, "Ladies first," and put her list down.

SARAH

Coulter — drunk and/or suicide attempt??

Captain McNaughton — drunk??

We found bow plate (maybe)

Boat / skipper explosion
Ronnie — $25K — even though skipper was supposedly broke
Ronnie — said black-haired woman following brother
Skipper witnessed what? Kidnapping of Coulter's
        family? Why?
Ronnie — gone for past few weeks in Atlantic City
Skipper didn't want Ronnie along for last charters.
        Doing illegal stuff to save his boat?
Someone paid skipper off and then killed him?
Who?
Matt Coulter — if he recovers, will he remember?

JACK

Found bow plate
Captain McNaughton dead
Skipper's brother — cash & gun
Coulter's suicide attempt — I don't believe
Skipper sees woman with black hair — he starts carrying gun
Skipper needed money for boat — but now has $25K.
        Blackmail?
Skipper — explosion accident or murder?
If so, why? Abduction of Coulter family? Why? Coulter never
        contacted for ransom
If they are dead, where are bodies? If alive, why haven't they
        contacted Coulter?
What happened on last charter worth killing for?
Matt Coulter — What did he see on that boat?

Merchant and Sarah looked at each other's lists.

"Are you getting the feeling there's someone we haven't met?" Sarah said.

"Woman with black hair," Merchant said. "With a skinny body like yours."

"That was a compliment, you know."

"I know. From a forty-year-old guy with the mental age of about fifteen."

"Take it where I can get it," she said.

They pored over both lists again, and Sarah pointed to the last line of each. "Matt's still the key. Who knows, maybe the second concussion will shake something free."

"Assuming he ever wakes up," Merchant said. "I'll stop by on the way home. See how he's doing."

"Good idea," she said. "And I'm going home. Pretend that you didn't make me smack somebody with a poker."

He gave her a gentle push out of the booth. "Give it a rest, Ballard."

CHAPTER 20

No rest for the Weiry, he thought as he bent over Matt Coulter's comatose body.

The guy was barely alive. Still, that wasn't as good as dead. Who knew when he might wake up and remember?

Weir — he'd come to think of himself with that name — was just about to stick the syringe into the IV bag when there was a knock on the door. He palmed the syringe and slipped it into his sport jacket pocket as a tall, weather-beaten man came into the room.

Weir hesitated. He'd lied his way in, saying he was a visiting friend. This guy didn't look like a doctor; if anything, he looked like a cop. Tall, strong without being bulked up. Similar to Weir's own body type, and he knew what he was capable of doing. Weir realized he still had on the latex gloves — for fingerprints — but they worked with his doctor gig, too. "Can I help you?" he said with a friendly but slightly impatient tone. The busy doctor.

The guy paused, then said, "You're his doctor?"

Weir pulled the stethoscope from his left pocket and fit it around his neck. "So they tell me." He'd studied medicine several lifetimes ago, and technically, he was a doctor. So he knew the tone, knew the attitude: get lost and let the professional work.

The tall guy didn't seem to get it. Or chose not to. "How's he doing?"

"Still in a coma. And are you family or friend?" Knowing that there wasn't any family left, so he should be able to boot him out posthaste.

"Friend," the man said. "I didn't get your name, Doctor."

Weir thought fast. He could lie, but this guy didn't seem like the type to vanish with a little pressure. If it got down to asking for his card, "Weir" was the only one he had on him. Besides, it was just a name he made up for Kathleen anyway. "Dr. Weir," he said. "And yours?"

"Jack Merchant."

"Pleased to meet you. Now if you wouldn't mind, I need to finish this exam. . . ."

"Sure." Merchant opened the door. "Do you have any way of knowing if he'll come out of this?"

Weir shook his head, impatient. "Sorry."

"I'd like to talk with you before you leave," Merchant said. "I'll be waiting in the hall."

Weir shook his head firmly. "Afraid not with the schedule I have today."

"I'll keep it short."

"No. Just leave me your card and let me finish my exam — "

Bad timing, that.

The word *exam* was just out when the nurse walked in. Not just any nurse, but the one he'd snowed on the way in. He hadn't been a doctor then. He'd been Matt Coulter's college roommate, Rob Weir.

And she was the head nurse, no shrinking violet.

She took in the stethoscope, paused for two beats, and then said, "What did you say about an exam? Are you a physician, Mr. Weir?"

Weir sighed. "Let me catch up with you outside," he said

to Merchant as if this was a minor matter that needed to be re-solved among professionals.

But Merchant didn't move.

Yet the door remained open behind him.

Weir stood, looped the stethoscope over his neck, and walked around the bed toward them. "I'm sorry, I should have mentioned it. I'm here as his friend, but I thought I'd take a look at him while I'm here."

"I understand," she said. "But could I see some ID?"

If Weir could read her right — and he was pretty good at that — she was being more officious than suspicious. But this Jack Merchant wasn't going out in the hall to wait. Goddamn it.

"Sure," he said. He reached into his trousers pocket for a business card, handed that to her, and then took the stetho-scope from around his neck. He was conscious that he still had his gloves on and that it would've been natural by now to have taken them off.

She looked at the card, hesitated, and then said, "Well, I mean an ID, Doctor Weir. This is just a card."

The bitch. Still not that suspicious, but getting there.

Merchant, on the other hand, had gone still. He noticed the gloves.

Weir reached into his pants pockets, then made a face. "Sure . . . well . . . actually it looks as if I left my Mass General ID down in the car. Is this really necessary?"

"You're with Mass General?" she asked.

"I have privileges there, yes, as well as my private practice. Now as I mentioned to Mr. Merchant here, I have a very busy schedule today, so is there anything else?"

He didn't wait for an answer but tried to move past them.

She got out of his way.

Merchant didn't. He said, "How about a driver's license?"

"What?"

But Weir knew then what he had to do. This guy wasn't going to be blustered, and from here came hospital security, police, and real trouble.

"How about a driver's license?" Merchant repeated.

Weir chuckled ruefully. "OK, Officer. I didn't know I was speeding, but if you insist."

He reached into his sport jacket pocket as if for a wallet and got his hand around the syringe. Put his thumb on the plunger. There was a big enough dose of Lantus, a long-acting insulin, to kill Coulter. Maybe enough for this nosy bastard.

"Here you go," he said, and with the speed that was his primary gift, he reached out, slammed the syringe into Merchant's chest, and shoved his thumb all the way down.

CHAPTER 21

Merchant was being very inefficient.

Not that he normally worried about such things. But here he was trying to do simple things in some sort of reasonable fashion, and things kept going wrong. He was trying to leave his boat to go up and meet Sarah, but then just as he was walking away, he would realize *Lila* was untied from the dock.

The wind was pushing her away. So he'd stop, tie the bow line, the stern line, and then the spring. And then he'd do it on the other side of the boat. Altogether, it would take him a few minutes. Then he was free to go up the dock. This time to meet Coulter and his family. They were waiting at the restaurant where he and Coulter had first had lunch.

Except that when Merchant was finally finished with the lines, he would realize they were free again. And it was all his own fault because he hadn't tied them properly in the first place.

Merchant's mild annoyance was becoming more acute. He simply couldn't move with anything close to normal speed. And suddenly it became appallingly clear to him that he must get up that dock, he must go see Sarah and the Coulters because something terrible was about to happen to them unless he got there.

But he could barely move. It took all his effort to walk away from his boat. Especially since the lines had fallen into the water and the boat was out of the slip altogether. This time he was forcing himself to ignore her.

He was furious that he couldn't seem to cleat the boat down. He was also ashamed. Because he knew that one of the reasons he was moving so slowly was that he was suffering a terrible hangover. He couldn't remember being a drunk.

That was his father, not him. A drunk sitting in front of the television day in, day out.

But nevertheless, Merchant knew a hangover when he felt it, and this was it.

That hangover was no longer just part of the dream.

Because he was coming to realize it *was* a dream. *Lila* and those slipping lines. He was in bed and he was enormously thirsty. Plus what little fluid that was in him wanted out. And it wanted out now.

He woke up vomiting.

"Oh Jesus," Sarah said. She was holding one of those trays under his mouth. She had her arm around his shoulder helping him sit up, and that was a good thing because he didn't think he could have done it himself.

He didn't bring up much, but that didn't stop him from trying.

Finally, he croaked, "OK," and she let him back onto his pillow. His heart was pounding and he could smell his own sweat and stink. He was in a hospital bed. Through the windows he could see it was dark outside.

She wiped his face and mouth with a damp cloth. He could feel the rasp of his beard on the cloth. His face hurt, his ribs hurt. Everything hurt, just some places more than others. She said, "You just talked. Can you understand me? Do you know who I am?"

He tried to focus his thoughts, couldn't, but said her name.

That seemed to make her happy. She laughed even. "Oh, thank God."

She was calling for a nurse when he fell back to sleep.

When he awoke again the sun was up.

He wished it weren't. He covered his face and rolled over onto his side. He found that there was an IV tube going into his right forearm and he had to be careful the way he rolled.

He also found Sarah sitting in the chair beside him.

He watched her sleeping for a while and then joined her.

The sun was just going down when he awoke the third time. He opened his eyes, lay still. No one was in the room with him. He blinked a few times, licked his lips, and made a slow mental assessment. Arms moved, legs moved, hands worked. He sat up. Felt dizzy as hell at first, but he could do it. Saw a plastic pitcher on the try beside him, reached out with a shaky arm, and poured himself a glass of water.

Damn.

The water was the best thing he'd ever drunk in his life.

He finished the first cup and then had another.

Dribbled a little water onto his palm and wiped his face down. His beard felt at least a day old, maybe more.

Sarah walked in.

She was holding what looked like a cup of coffee, and she stopped when she saw him sitting up. She looked almost frightened, waiting for what he had to say. Probably wanted to know if he was some sort of mental vegetable now.

He remembered what had happened. That doctor jamming something into his chest. Merchant knew it was possible his brain was permanently fried. He nodded to the coffee. "That mine?"

And felt pleased. Not only because that made Sarah laugh but because she walked over, put an arm around his shoulder, and lifted the coffee to his lips.

Sure cure for a hangover.

CHAPTER 22

An hour later, Detectives Lerner and Petronelli came into Merchant's room.

Sarah was sitting up in the bed beside him, eating most of his dinner. He was just finishing the soup.

"Look who's up and about," said Lerner. "Even has company."

"I'd be feeling better," Detective Petronelli said, putting a smirk into it.

Merchant knew Sarah wouldn't like that, but she wouldn't give them the pleasure of seeing it. She just smiled coolly.

Lerner said to Merchant, "We've got some questions for you."

Sarah slipped out of the bed and took the tray away. "I'd hope so. He's tired, though, so let's keep it short, OK?"

Petronelli grunted but made no promises. He gestured for her to sit in the chair beside the bed. He turned his attention to Merchant. "Now tell me about the assault."

Merchant went through it slowly, telling how he'd come in to find the blond man standing over Coulter. Both detectives listened quietly as he told them about the attack.

"How about afterwards?"

"I don't remember much about that."

"No? Maybe this will help." Lerner took a videotape from his briefcase and slipped it into the VCR. A grainy black-and-white image of an empty stairwell appeared. "Security camera," he said.

For a moment, the stairwell was empty. There was no sound.

Then the door slammed open and a blond man — the guy from the room — came running through. He started down the stairs. Immediately after, Merchant saw himself.

His movements were awkward. Even in the poor-quality images, that was obvious. The blond man was three steps ahead of him and moving faster. But Merchant threw himself down the stairwell onto the man's back. The two of them fell the remaining stairs onto the landing. They both got up about as fast, and Merchant landed several solid shots, putting the other guy up against the wall.

But then his legs began to buckle.

Lerner said, "You can see the drug's really kicking in. You're beginning to convulse."

Merchant collapsed.

"Jesus Christ," Sarah whispered. She went over to the window, her back to the television.

The man kicked Merchant three times hard in the chest and stomach, then turned and ran down the stairs. The tape was edited to show what the remaining cameras in the stairwell revealed: a blond man in a sport jacket running, his hand and forearm partially covering his face.

"You're lucky," Petronelli said. "The doctor told us you kept going in and out. The guy took the syringe with him, so the doctors had to scramble figuring out was in it. Ultimately figured it was some kind of heavy dose of insulin."

Lerner said, "Matt Coulter's pretty lucky too that you came along when you did."

"Have you got security on him?" Merchant said.

"Yeah, Merchant," Petronelli said. "We take attempted murder inside the hospital pretty seriously. So you know who this guy is?"

"Not really. But I'll tell you what I do know."

With Sarah's help, he told them about the search for the plate, McNaughton's boat exploding, about the twenty-five thousand dollars Ronnie had taken from his brother's safety deposit box and no explanation for how his brother could have earned that money.

The two partners looked at each other, then back at Merchant. Petronelli said, "Well, you tell me what usually fits in just fine with boats, large sums of cash, and attempted murder."

Merchant said, "I know."

Drugs.

It could fit.

"Say Mr. Coulter wasn't being entirely straight with you," Petronelli said, jerking his thumb to the room next door.

"Which I'm sure you've had happen," said Lerner said.

"Say he was transporting something in that sloop of his," Petronelli continued. "It sinks. He can't make his delivery. The people at the end of these deals aren't the kind to forgive him over boat trouble. Even if that includes his whole family drowning."

"Some of them would drown a family just to make a point," Lerner added. "I don't have to tell you how much Colombian coke and heroin comes into New England by boat."

"I don't think that's it," Merchant said.

"Yeah? What do you think when you hear about a home invasion in Roxbury or South Boston?" Lerner said.

"I know," Merchant said. And he did. The cop in him knew that the most obvious answer was usually the right one. Someone tries to murder a man in a hospital bed, it's only natural for a cop to wonder what the man in the hospital bed did first.

In his gut, though, he just didn't believe that Coulter would have involved his family in something like that. But his gut had been wrong before. And Coulter was an alcoholic, an addictive personality.

Anything was possible.

He said, "Did the doctors do a blood test on Coulter?"

"Yeah," Petronelli said. "Just like it looked, an overdose of codeine mixed with bourbon."

" 'Mixed,' " Sarah said. "Does that mean the pills were mixed directly in the bottle or that he swallowed the pills and drank the bourbon?"

"We had some of the bigger shards from the broken bottle tested, and it looks like he put the pills into the bottle first."

"What about his stomach contents?" Merchant asked.

Lerner said, "We had that done. Cereal, orange juice, bourbon, and way too much codeine."

"Jesus, that doesn't sound right," Merchant said. "Was there codeine in the milk or orange juice container?"

"Don't know," Lerner said. "They were washed out, put in the trash. Dishes were done."

Merchant said, "He does the dishes, even washes out the milk and juice containers and *then* he gets drunk and tries to commit suicide? That sounds strange. This Weir guy likes to use drugs, maybe he put codeine into Matt's food and then came up after he was incapacitated."

"That's a theory and maybe it fits," Petronelli said. "But I've got no evidence to support it. As for tidying up before committing suicide, that's not even close to unusual."

Merchant closed his eyes, tried to pull together enough brainpower to see Coulter for who he was. But he didn't know him well enough to be sure. Finally, he said, "How about this guy who attacked me? Have you got anything to get hold of him?"

"You saw the video," Petronelli said. "No clear shots of his face. Had gloves on the whole time, so there were no prints. He even snatched that business card back from the nurse after jabbing you. So we were kind of hoping you could tell us more."

Sarah turned from the window.

Here it comes, Merchant thought. He said, "I've told you what I know."

How many times had he heard someone say that?

"You know, I'd heard rumors about what you did in Miami," Petronelli said. "But since you're in this thing, I called down, got some details. Talked with Special Agent Cruz."

"Uh-huh."

"He's not your biggest fan." Petronelli smiled as he said this. Merchant had been in the room when Petronelli's commander told him his career with the state cops was "fucking over."

Petronelli was enjoying this.

"Cruz is an asshole," Merchant said.

Lerner said, "Look at it from our point of view. We see a crime that has all the earmarks of a drug deal gone sour . . . and who's sitting in front of us but an ex-DEA agent who's short on cash and trying to maintain a lifestyle beyond his reach."

Petronelli said, "Makes me wonder, finding you've got your boat docked in Charlestown. You have some friends there none of us knew about back then?"

Merchant felt tired. Even without his background with Petronelli, he knew that they were doing what most cops would do in the circumstances. The sort of thing he'd done hundreds of times before. But he was so tired. And in spite of understanding it all, he was getting angry.

"Hell, I'd like a nice boat, too," Lerner said. "I can't afford it and I go to work every day and pull in a salary. How do you do it?"

Merchant tried to sit up. Tried to gear up for the cops so they could get past this stage.

But Sarah stepped in. She pushed Merchant back down, not quite gently. He decided to stay there.

He closed his eyes and let the exhaustion sweep over him. His arms and legs felt leaden.

She said to Lerner, "Then you won't mind coming back tomorrow."

"What?"

"One way or another, you're getting paid. So you might as well do it tomorrow. Because today's interview is over."

"Bullshit, lady," Petronelli said.

They all argued some more after that, but Merchant wasn't awake to hear them.

CHAPTER 23

"Eat your soup, Sean," Ella said.

They were at the kitchen table. The three of them. Her, Sean, Laurie. She'd taken to feeding them around the table now, instead of alone in each of their rooms.

"I ate my soup, Ella," Laurie said.

"I see that, Laurie. You're such a good girl."

Sean was truly hungry.

He took a spoonful, hoping this was a clean bowl of soup. Sometimes she did that, gave him a bowl with no drugs in it.

But this one had it. A bitterness that the chicken and noodles couldn't quite hide.

"I just want to lay on the couch," he said. "I'm so tired."

"You need to keep up your strength," Ella said. She was dressed in cutoffs and a bright yellow T-shirt. She looked like someone's pretty mom on television, only mean.

Laurie was wearing cutoffs, too. When they first got there, Ella had bought them both some clothes: jeans and shorts and T-shirts. But yesterday Laurie said she wanted cutoffs like Ella's. They spent hours sewing on little hearts and flowers out of a curtain in Laurie's room.

It was weird. On the one hand, he couldn't imagine any other adult just cutting up a curtain like that — one still hanging on the window. On the other hand, it made Laurie happy and it seemed like Ella was enjoying it too. But it was hard for Sean to tell if she really liked Laurie or not.

As for Laurie, she kept trying to make Ella love her. So if Ella wore cutoffs, she wanted to wear cutoffs. . . .

Ella repeated herself, and he snapped back into the moment. She said, "Did you hear me, Sean? Eat your soup."

"Yeah," he said. "I'm just tired is all."

She nodded. He noticed she didn't mind when he acted distracted. That was probably all she wanted to do with the drugs, anyhow. Make him want to sit still. Between the drugs he was getting down and the lack of food, that was pretty much what he felt. But he also felt a nervousness in his belly. Because he had something to do. It made him scared inside.

Ella was only a few inches taller than he was, but she was strong and he knew — just knew — that there were lots of things she would do that he couldn't.

He took a sip of his soup. There was the medicine taste, but it was barely noticeable.

"Ella, aren't we just like a family?" Laurie said. "You know, sitting at the table? We used to do that with my mom and dad."

"I'm sure you did, honey."

"Got my shorts," Laurie said. "See?"

"I sure do."

"Can we watch TV after?"

"Yes, you can. But your brother needs to eat his soup if he expects to watch television."

Laurie looked at him, her eyes hopeful. She whispered, "Sean, eat it."

Ella smiled at her.

And then she looked at him and the smile faded pretty fast.

He wasn't sure if she was suspicious or if it was that she just didn't like him. He'd been dumping most of the soup she'd given him in his room into the toilet. Making do with whatever else came along for food. Sometimes she gave him soup and a sandwich, and then he was just fine. But lately, she was making cans of instant soup and that was it. He'd eat just a little and throw the rest away.

God, he was hungry.

He said, "Can I have some crackers?"

Ella looked at him. It seemed like she was trying to figure out if he was faking or not.

Finally, she said, "Get them yourself. Crunch them up in your soup."

He got up and went to the cabinet. There was a window right by the cabinet, and this was a good excuse to look out. Other times if she saw him staring out this window, she might put him in his room for hours.

He looked up the dirt driveway as far as he could see.

"You got them?" Ella said.

He realized he was fading in and out. Forgetting why he was really doing this. "Yeah," he said. He took the saltines off the second shelf.

It was the third shelf he was really interested in. The third shelf behind the cabinet door to his left — he could see a brown plastic bottle.

He was pretty sure that held the drugs she was giving him.

"C'mon," she said. "Sit down."

He realized he'd been out of it again. He came back and sat down to eat the crackers.

"Don't you want them in your soup?" she said.

He thought about saying no and decided against it in an instant. "Yeah, I do." He quickly popped another cracker into his mouth, then crushed the rest onto his soup. The crackers softened immediately, and with the drugs already in his system, the look of the sopping crackers almost made him puke.

He closed his eyes, but that made him feel worse. The room began to spin.

"You OK, Sean?" Laurie said. She patted his arm.

He opened his eyes. Saw that she was patting him the way she did with her stuffed animals, like she was the mom. Which was kind of cute. Made him feel bad for what he was about to do.

"Stop it," he said, brushing her hand away, like the cranky older brother he could be.

She pushed back. "Hey!"

"Quit it!" Ella said.

It took everything he had to ignore her. She wasn't like his mom or any other adult he knew. When she lost her temper it was scary.

He pushed Laurie again.

"Hey!" she yelled, top of her lungs. "You're a jerko!" And tried to hit him.

He returned the favor, only this time he made sure to knock his soup off the table and onto her lap.

She shrieked.

He knew it wasn't that hot, so he wasn't so worried about that.

It was Ella.

"Goddamn it!" she said. She stood so fast that her chair crashed to the floor.

"I'm sorry, I'm sorry," he said.

She hit him. Across the face and then with the back of her hand. He buried his face into his arms and felt her hit him twice more, and then she was done. She jerked Laurie by the arm and pulled her from the table. "Come on," she said. "I'll wash you off."

"My shorts," Laurie cried. "He ruined my shorts."

She looked back at her brother, outraged.

"Oh, he'll pay," Ella said, throwing a look over her shoulder of such hate that Sean's stomach clenched. "He'll pay, the little bastard."

And then they were in the bathroom.

Sean sat there, breathing hard. Wondering what he'd done.

Knowing he had a reason, but he was so out of it from the drugs and being scared that he could barely remember.

Then he did.

He got out of his chair and hurried over to the cabinet. He opened the door and tried to reach the top shelf.

Couldn't, by just a couple of inches.

He got Ella's chair, lifted it so that it wouldn't make a dragging noise. And he put it underneath the cabinet, got up onto it, and took the medicine bottle down. Knowing that she could come around the corner any second.

He tried to open it by twisting the bottle cap but couldn't. He tried harder. Then realized it was a childproof cap. He forced himself to slow down. To read the top of the bottle. He had to press both sides.

He did that. Felt a little give in the bottle cap. Then he twisted the cap and it opened. The bottle was half full of little pink pills. He wondered how many he could take without her noticing. Wondered how many he would need.

Then he heard Laurie saying, "Now I'm all wet!"

And he poured a bunch of pills into one hand and put the cap back on. Shut the cabinet door, got off the chair, and picked it up to put it back where it had been.

He started putting the rest of the chairs back as if he were trying to clean up after the mess he'd made. And then he saw from the corner of his eye that Ella was now standing in the hallway. Watching him.

He almost vomited.

But told himself to keep moving. He didn't turn his head. Didn't let her see that he knew she was there. He put Ella's chair down away from the table. And then moved Laurie's away from the table, the soup dribbling off the seat of the chair onto the floor.

"What are you doing?" she said.

It wasn't hard to act scared when he turned around.

"Cleaning up," he said. His voice squeaked. "Really, I'm sorry, I'm cleaning up the mess. It won't even be here when you get back."

She stared at him a moment longer. He had to fight off the sudden urge to pee. "It better not be," she said.

And then she turned toward Laurie's room. Probably to get some dry clothes.

Laurie stepped out of the bathroom. Her lower lip stuck out. He was so revved up, it almost made him laugh, but he knew better. If Laurie got any more upset at him, Ella might decide to hit him again.

"You jerko," Laurie yelled. "You ruined my shorts. You big, fat, stinky jerko!"

"Sorry," he said, turning so she wouldn't see him slip the pills into his pocket.

"Say it!" she said.

"What?"

"Say you're a jerko." She pointed at him dramatically. "Say it."

He looked down the hall. Saw Ella coming up behind his sister. Her eyes on him.

So he said it. "I'm a jerko."

It seemed to satisfy Laurie.

He didn't think it would be good enough for Ella.

CHAPTER 24

In the past, Kathleen could have relied on the sex.

And she still used it. She had stayed with him in the Boston condo the night before, and when the alarm went off at seven she teased Dave into staying in bed. Starting him with a massage, telling him that she knew the pressure he was under, that she wanted to help.

Pretty much doing everything for him after that and pretending to enjoy herself immensely.

She let him sleep after, but he still woke up in a mood, looking to pick a fight.

This was no way to get what she needed.

He pushed aside the late breakfast she'd served him. "Look, I've got to get out of here."

She was still in her bathrobe, a silk one that brought out the green in her eyes. She could remember the way he used to look when she walked into the room wearing that robe.

Now, he didn't seem to notice.

He went into the bathroom, brushed his teeth quickly, and came back to get dressed. She sat on the bed, watching him. He had begun to gain a little weight around the middle. Still, he was a good-looking guy. If they'd had a different kind of marriage, she might have liked to see the weight. To feel they were getting older together.

But they didn't have that kind of marriage.

He dressed carefully, an Armani suit and gold Rolex. Such an eye for beauty and value, her husband. It was probably inevitable that he would decide to trade her in for a newer model.

But her inability to have children and the gambling problem didn't help.

"Are we going to be all right, Dave?"

He glanced in the mirror. "What's that supposed to mean?"

"Well . . . the fire. The business. Will we get past it?"

"You mean will you have enough of my money to burn at the slot machines?"

"That's not what I meant."

"Sure it isn't." He began to knot his tie.

"You want help with that?"

"No."

"Why are you so angry with me? I didn't do anything."

Which was such a big fat lie she could barely get it out.

But it must have sounded like business as usual to him, because he answered the same as ever. "Right, Katy. Nothing's ever your fault. Just leave Dave to take care of everything."

"You do it so well. . . ." She stood up, put her hands on his shoulders. "Listen, I know it's intense — "

"You know jackshit," he said and walked back into the bathroom. She let her arms drop to her sides. If he knew what she'd done, he'd have the right to treat her like this. But he didn't, so this just proved what a bastard he was.

When he came back out, he got the holstered gun out of the drawer.

"Is that really necessary?"

"Don't worry your pretty little head." He clipped the holster behind his back and put his suit jacket on.

"Dave," she said, going up to him. The proper wife. His friend, his lover. "I know you're under so much pressure. I just want to help you."

He looked to the ceiling. Sighed. "What do you want, Katy?"

God, she wanted to scratch his going-to-fat face. She wondered how this new one, Rebecca, was able to get herself excited for him.

"I just want to know," Kathleen said. "Are we going to be all right?"

She watched him intently. Looking for the bravado. The signal she'd come to recognize over the years, the look he apparently believed was both cunning and confident. The look that meant he was going to take another risk so the numbers would all work again.

But she didn't see it.

Instead, behind the arrogance he wore just like the Armani suit, what she saw was fear.

"You want to do something for me?" he said. "Pray the insurance company pays off. That's what I'm doing."

CHAPTER 25

The cops came back to Merchant's hospital room the next morning. Sarah expected them to dislike her from the previous day and they did. She often had that effect on people.

But by the time they left, they didn't seem to like Merchant either. He was doing well enough to speak for himself, so Sarah pretty much listened and watched.

They wanted to dig deep into an ex-DEA agent involved in what looked like a drug deal. He wanted them to focus on finding Coulter's family.

Merchant ended up telling Petronelli what he'd told Sarah about him all along: "You're incompetent."

And Merchant was normally so much more polite than she was.

The cops weren't polite at all. But they had nothing to hold him on. So the minute they slammed the door behind them, Merchant said, "Let's get out of here."

"The doctor's not going to be here until noon," she said.

The doctor, a serious Asian man in his mid-thirties, had been talking to her as if she were Jack's wife or live-in girlfriend. It felt awkward in some ways but good in others. She said, "I know he wants to talk with you before you go. Besides, they've got the formal sign-out procedure."

"Meaning roll me out in a wheelchair."

She shrugged. "Hospital policy, sweetie."

"Uh-huh." He got out of his bed and began to get dressed. The bruises on his chest and stomach were black and purple, yellowing at the edges.

"That guy got you good," she said.

"Yes, he did."

"You're pretty pissed at the cops."

"Yes, I am."

"At least they're putting someone at Coulter's door."

He pulled on his shirt. "There's that. You check on him this morning?"

"Yes. He's still in a coma."

Merchant winced as he pulled on his jeans. He said, "Think about it. No FBI involvement. Ronnie is nothing more than a 'request for an interview' to the Foster town cops. They're not even willing to hold the concept in their heads that Coulter's family could still be alive."

"Do you think they are?"

"I have no way of knowing. But you heard — the Foster cops haven't even gone back down to the marina to see if any-one saw anything the night the boat came in from the last char-ter. Maybe I could answer your question if I knew whether or not two kids were taken off McNaughton's boat that night. That'd be a good thing to know."

He sat down and leaned over to tie his shoes. She saw him catch himself on the chair arm.

"You dizzy?"

"A little."

"So running around just now won't help that. You should rest a day more. Look, I can call Alden and have him talk to the watchman. After all, the guy works for him."

"Oh, sure. Like he's going to give his full attention to that.

Better for me to go down and do it myself. See if anything else shakes loose. Maybe have a second conversation with Ronnie. Show him that hallway videotape — maybe he'll recognize 'Dr. Weir.'"

"You think the cops will just lend you the tape after the way you talked to them?"

That made him smile. "They were pissed enough that they forgot it." He walked over to the VCR and pushed the eject button. The tape slid out. "Let's get out of here before they remember it and come back."

"You're going to drive down there even though tying your shoes makes you dizzy?"

"I'll be fine."

"Oh sure you will," she said. "But how about the fourteen people you plow into along the way?"

"I'm not that bad."

"Bad enough. I'm taking you."

"C'mon, Sarah. You've been watching over me for two days straight. You've got your business to run."

"So another day won't hurt."

"Sarah . . ." He took her hands in his. Pulled her close. First she held back a little, then relaxed and put her head on his chest. He said, "You know, I'm pretty resilient. You don't have to watch over me."

"I know," she said. She kissed him. She ran her hands over his back, his sides. Feeling how in these two days he'd lost weight, how he was already different, how the plunge of a needle into flesh could have taken him from her.

"You are resilient," she said. "But I like watching over you. Let's go to your boat and you can get a change of clothes. We'll do the same at mine, and get to Foster Marina in time for the night watchman. Get a motel room down there and I'll see if I can figure out another way to make you dizzy."

That made him laugh. "Sold," he said.

CHAPTER 26

Merchant was feeling pretty much himself by that evening. The dizziness was gone, he felt hungry. It was good to be on the road with Sarah.

They got down to the town of Foster as the sun was beginning to fade.

Sarah had called ahead. Alden said he'd have the night watchman, Doug Miles, come in and they could use his office. Merchant had her thank him but asked him to call the guy and say they would come by his house. "It will be better to talk to him without his boss looking over his shoulder. We can take advantage of that later, if we need to."

It turned out his house was a mobile home. They took some twists and turns but found the trailer park just as the sun was going down. The sign at the gates of the park promised "waterfront views." When they got down to Doug's home, they saw that he indeed had waterfront views, but they included a sewage treatment facility less than a mile away.

His trailer was old and not particularly clean on the outside. By contrast, the blue Ford parked out front was waxed to perfection. It was only a few years old and appeared as if he invested every dime of his salary into making it look like a cop car. Plain looking, but set up with a heavy-duty suspension and wide tires.

Sarah and Merchant got out, and he knocked on the trailer door.

They heard footsteps inside immediately, and a young guy opened the door. He was big, looked like he'd once played football. Thick black hair brushed back, bulging chest and arm muscles over a thick belly. He was holding a can of light beer. His small blue eyes latched on to Sarah immediately. "Well, hey," he said.

Right or wrong, Merchant immediately got the impression of a guy whose high point came and went sometime around senior year in high school.

Those blue eyes came back to him, and Merchant felt the guy's appraisal and challenge. It didn't feel personal; rather the knee-jerk reaction to any man standing beside a pretty woman.

Merchant looked him in the eye and said, "How're you doing?"

Doug took a moment, sipped his beer, and then said, "You called my boss about me?"

Sarah picked up the dynamics immediately and cut in. "Not about you . . . We just asked Alden if you could help us."

"You buddies with Alden?"

"We've done business together." She handed him a business card.

"This about a repo?"

"Not exactly. But it is about one of the boats at the marina — *Isabella*."

He shrugged. "What do you want to know? She blew sky high."

Sarah smiled. "Can we come in a minute? Is it all right if I call you Doug?"

"Chick like you, call me anything, call me any time." He sipped his beer, looked at Merchant to see how he'd take this.

Merchant kept his face neutral.

Sarah smiled her most winning smile. "Oh, here we go. . . ."

They followed him into the trailer. "'Scuse the mess," he said. "Fired the cleaning lady."

He took an armful of dirty laundry off the bench seat behind the dinette table and tossed it into the bedroom. He slid the door closed and then gestured for Sarah to sit. He sat down himself in the one easy chair and sprawled his legs out. That left Merchant standing.

Doug looked at Sarah and gestured with his thumb to Merchant. "He's a big one, huh?"

"Yes, he is," she said, smiling.

"You a cop?" he said directly to Merchant.

"No. I was with the DEA."

"DEA? You do undercover?"

Merchant nodded.

"I'm gonna be a cop. And I know a lot of them here in town. Something for you to keep in mind."

"Why?" Merchant said.

"Why what?"

"Why do we have to keep that in mind? We just have some questions for you about Captain McNaughton and *Isabella*."

"Yeah, and I told the cops, the real cops, everything I could about that. Which wasn't much."

"Can you tell us?" Sarah said. "We came a long way just to see you."

"I still don't get what this has to do with a repo."

"Well, I do more than just repossessions. I do some of the preliminary investigative work for insurance companies for marine losses."

Doug took a second to think this through, and then grinned. "Oh, so you want to know if McNaughton blew himself up torching the boat, right? Shit, maybe. I don't know."

"Well, maybe you can give us an idea how busy he was," Sarah said. "Did he have much business?"

Doug lifted his shoulders. "Don't know for sure. He still

has a brother, go ask him. But it seemed to me like Mc-Naughton wasn't out that much over the past few months. The economy has been for shit lately."

"How about the week before the explosion?" Merchant said.

"Yeah, he was going out a good bit then. Had a diving charter."

"Who was that?"

"How do I know? I'm the night watchman, not his business agent."

"How do you keep awake all those hours?" Sarah interjected. "Me, I'd fall asleep."

He shrugged. "Just keep walking the docks." He pointed to a big silver thermos flask near the kitchen sink. "Pour enough high-test in there, I'm in good shape."

"So you're outside the whole night?"

"Course not." This seemed to affront him slightly. "I got the whole building to myself. The kitchen, the lounge area, everything. Not a bad place to spend the night."

"Must get lonely," Sarah said.

He winked. "Doesn't have to be."

She smiled.

"You remind me of somebody, you know that?"

"Oh, who?"

"Just a lady friend."

"Can you tell us about the night *Isabella* exploded?" Merchant said.

"Hell of a bang," Doug said. "You want more than that, talk to the fire marshal."

"Did you see Captain McNaughton down on his boat?"

"Earlier I did. Couple hours beforehand."

"Was he drinking?"

"Yuh. Had a beer in his hand."

"Did you see anybody else? He have a visitor?"

"No."

"How about the night before?"

Doug said, "Same old, same old."

"You answered that quickly," Merchant said, smiling. "Don't you have a logbook to check?"

"Course I've got a logbook. But first off, nothing much happens in my job. That's the sucky truth of it, walking around looking at a bunch of rich people's boats bob up and down all night. Besides, you think you're the first one to ask these questions? Cops already been through this after the boat blew."

Doug settled back in his chair.

"We've got another date in mind," Sarah said. "How about Saturday the twenty-fifth of July? I know you'll have to look in a logbook to remember that."

"Well, yeah." He swung around in his chair and took a black leatherette notebook from the desk. He flipped through looking for the date. Merchant could see the book was laid out by his evening rounds: Dock 1, Dock 2, Dock 3, Dock 4, Storage Shed, and so on.

"Do you have a time card you're having to use at each checkpoint?"

"Nah," Doug said. "They trust me. And Alden's too cheap to put the card reader in anyhow."

The book opened to July twenty-fifth. Merchant could see that the page was neatly filled out like the others he'd seen. But unlike the others, which had all been written in blue ink, this page was in red.

Doug studied the page, as if looking for more detail. Then he shrugged. "So, what do you want to know?"

"We want to know who got off Captain McNaughton's boat. It would probably be early morning, like five-thirty, six."

"How do I know?" Doug said. "I'm not a dock boy. I don't go down to carry their bags."

"So what did you see when they came in?"

Again with the lifted shoulders. "Big boat comes in. People gather their stuff together and leave. I'm not saying I remember anything about that morning in particular, I'm just saying that's all I'd notice. And I wouldn't write it down or be able to remember a month later who came in or not."

"Well, can you remember in general who was going out with McNaughton on his last week of charter?"

Doug shrugged his shoulders. "I don't know . . . his customer and his girlfriend or wife, whatever she was. And McNaughton's brother, as crew."

Merchant glanced at Sarah and then said to Doug, "McNaughton's brother was there? Ronnie?"

"Yeah, that's right. He almost always goes out with him."

"What did the client look like?"

"Tall guy. I don't know, I don't pay much attention to what guys look like. Blond hair, I guess."

"And how about the woman?"

"I just saw her from a distance, couple of times."

"What did she look like?"

"Like I say, she was a long ways away. Red hair, sunglasses, baseball cap. Didn't really see her face. Nice body. I can tell you that."

"And they were going diving?"

"I don't know. He had tanks in racks almost all the time so it's hard to know."

"But is it possible there were more people that morning?"

"What do you mean?"

"Is there any chance two children got off the boat that morning, too?"

He shrugged. "Hell, I'm not even saying the boat went out that night, all right? I'm just telling you what I saw in general, the last week or so. That night, that morning, I've got no idea."

"You have a VCR?" Merchant said.

The change in direction seemed to surprise him. "Yeah, sure. Why?"

"I want to show you something. See if you recognize somebody."

"The tape?" Sarah said. "I'll grab it for you."

She went out to the truck, leaving the two of them alone. That seemed to make Doug nervous. After a few moments of silence, he gestured toward the door. "You two together?"

Merchant said yes. He wondered how Sarah would have answered the question.

When she came back in, she handed the tape to Doug. He stood up, moved past Merchant, and put the tape into his combo television and VCR. He said, "Whose home movies we gonna see?"

Merchant said, "You'll see me getting my ass kicked. Tell me if you recognize the other guy."

Doug looked over his shoulder. "And this is supposed to be about an insurance scam? You guys are yanking my chain, aren't you?"

He looked at the short tape with his arms crossed. Merchant watched his face carefully, saw the tightening of his mouth and the way he backed off slightly when the blond man appeared.

When it was over he said, "Man, you started out good, but he nailed you. Don't know what else to say."

"How about you say where you saw him before."

"Don't know what you're talking about."

"I think you do."

"I don't give a shit what you think."

"Listen carefully, Doug. There's a very good chance that two kids are depending on you telling us the truth."

"I can't tell you what I don't know."

"You know more than you're telling, Doug. Now if you're scared of losing your job, don't be. Nothing you tell us has to go back to Alden."

Doug glanced over at Sarah, his face flushed. "I'm not 'scared' of shit."

"Look —"

"No, you look." Doug shoved Merchant back against the

table. "Screw you and get out of my house. I mean now. Just get out of here."

Merchant pushed Doug back. Didn't do it hard, just to give himself a little room. Doug decided to take affront and punched Merchant in the mouth.

"Damn it, cut it out," Sarah yelled. In the space of the little trailer, her voice seemed to have an effect.

Doug backed off. "Look, just get the hell out of here. Both of you."

Merchant sighed. This had been the mistake of showing the video. It was obvious Doug now thought he was a pushover. Merchant said, "Sarah, could you wait in the truck?"

He tasted blood from his lip.

"Jack, come on," she said.

"Really," he said. "I'll be right out."

"Hey, I said get the hell out," Doug said. "You want more than a fat lip, move your ass, buddy."

She walked out and slammed the door shut behind her. She looked decidedly unhappy.

Doug said, "Hey, shithead, you better follow your girl's ass —"

Merchant hit him.

It was a short blow, he twisted his fist just so. Put it right into the guy's solar plexus.

Doug staggered, then swung back. Merchant took the blow on his left arm, then came in hard with a right, left, right combination just under the man's breastbone.

Doug began to slide to the floor. Merchant helped him make it into his chair, then walked over to the little kitchenette and got the man a glass of water and a paper towel.

He waited while Doug tried to regain his breath.

"I know it hurts," Merchant said. "But just rest easy and I won't be doing it again unless you keep screwing around with me. I don't know what you're worried about . . . if you left your post and didn't see who came off the boat that morning, you just need to tell me. If you recognize this man — and I'm pretty sure you do — you need to tell me that."

"Don't hit," Doug croaked.

"No. I won't, long as you're honest."

He handed Doug the paper towel. After a moment, Doug wiped his face and mouth. He licked his lips and took a sip of water.

"I think you messed something up inside me."

"You should be all right by tomorrow. Now who was that guy?"

"I don't know his name. I really don't."

"OK. But you've seen him before?"

"Maybe. I can't be sure, that video's not clear enough. But when I first saw it, I thought he was the guy on McNaughton's boat. The customer. I just saw them going out a few times, that's all."

"Who else?"

"Huh?"

"You said, 'them.' Who else was on the boat?"

"The lady I told you about. Red hair. Like I said, she was too far away for me to tell you anything else."

"You got a name for her?"

"No."

"Who else?"

"That's it, just the two of them and McNaughton and his brother."

"Going fishing?"

"Diving, I'd guess. He had the tanks on the boat when he went out with them. Something in the cockpit, too, under a tarp. Couldn't see what it was."

"What do you think it was?"

"I really don't know, mister."

"All right. What else? How come you didn't see the boat come in on the twenty-fifth? What were you doing?"

"What's it matter to you? It's private."

"I don't give a damn what you think is private, Doug. Tell me."

"I was banging this chick."

"Who?"

Even in his condition, Doug managed to preen a little. "You find her, you tell me."

"You don't have a name?'

"Yeah, she told me some bullshit name and number, but believe me I called it and it's nothing. But I don't care. Man, we had a night."

"So this was a one-time thing. Just that night."

"The morning, actually. She came in on her boat about five in the morning. Twin engine. Docks the boat, comes up to me, and asks for a smoke. Says she can't sleep. One thing leads to another, you know?"

Merchant thought about that a bit. He said, "She by any chance the lady friend who looks a little like Sarah?"

Doug looked surprised. "Yeah. How'd you know that?"

"And was she there the night *Isabella* blew? Is that why you didn't see anyone go down there?"

Doug looked like he was considering lying. But then he just nodded. "Yeah. That night, too."

"Ah, Christ," Merchant said, and left.

CHAPTER 27

"I know you've got things to say to me, but let me concentrate first," Merchant said to Sarah when he got into the truck.

She blinked. Then said, "OK."

"Have you got a coastal chart?"

Without a word, she reached behind his seat, felt around for her chart pack on the floor behind him, then handed it to him. He turned on the dome light and flipped through the charts before finding what he needed.

She started the truck and slowly motored out of the trailer park.

"OK." He put his finger on the chart not too far from Block Island. "We know Coulter's boat went down somewhere around here about three-thirty. Say they were picked up within the hour, then the boat that picked them up dumped Matt and C.C. for whatever reason and headed back here at fifteen knots. It was capable of faster, but the wind and waves were howling that night. Yeah. Just a few hours before daybreak. And about five in the morning this dark-haired woman who looks like you suddenly arrives and takes an affinity for Mr. Charm back there in the trailer."

He told her what Doug had said. He didn't spend any time on how he got him to cooperate.

"So this woman kept the night watchman busy while Weir got Matt's kids off the boat."

"That's the way I read it."

They drove in silence for a few minutes. Finally, Sarah said, "Is Doug going to make it through the night?"

"He's going to be sore, but yes."

"I'm glad. How can you be sure?"

"Just am."

"He said he was friends with police. Don't you think he'll have you arrested for assault?"

"Not likely. He's a cop wannabe. Probably been failing the exams. But he knows if he brings me in it'll come out that he left his post on his security job. Small stuff, maybe, but it's still enough to keep him away from the force."

"And you figured that out before you hit him."

"No, I didn't know that he'd left his post, though I suspected it. I hit him because he punched me right in front of you and it pissed me off."

This did not make her any happier.

They drove in silence a few minutes more. Finally he said, "Look, I think Coulter's family is still alive. Or at least there's a good chance they were when they got off the boat."

"But Doug had nothing to do with that."

"He was getting in the way because he was worried about his job."

"Or so you thought."

"And he confirmed it."

"After you hit him."

More silence.

Then she said, "You know it's possible they were just trying to get the bodies off the boat. That's why they wanted him occupied."

"That's possible, but I don't think so. If you killed someone at sea, would you bring them back to land? Wouldn't you just weight the bodies and dump them over the rail?"

"I guess. I haven't thought about it that much. But yes."

"So if they were alive then, we've got to proceed like they are alive now."

Merchant told her about the other woman in the boat, the redhead. And that in addition to the scuba tanks, Doug had seen something under a tarp inside the cockpit.

"Huh," she said. "You got a lot out of those last five minutes in there with him. Could get addictive, beating your way to the truth."

Merchant decided not to answer that.

She was right.

"Let's go see Ronnie," he said. "You hear Doug say that he was onboard for the charter — that he lied to us?"

"Yeah, I heard that," Sarah said. "Maybe you can get him to punch you first, too."

The lights were glowing outside Ronnie's house when they got there.

Merchant walked up to the door, knocked, waited, knocked again.

Nothing.

He considered breaking in. He would have liked to spend some more time in Ronnie's office, seeing if he could track down anything about the charter. If Weir's name came up anyplace. Or anything that would lead him to the redheaded woman.

He knocked again.

Twisted the knob, ready to go, call it a night.

The door opened, and he knew someone was dead inside. The smell was there, but only faintly.

Merchant stepped into the room. The smell of death immediately became clearer. He reached into his pocket, took out his handkerchief. Wrapped it around his right hand and left the other hand down by his side, his fingertips touching his pants leg.

He checked the office first and found Ronnie's body.

Someone had stabbed him repeatedly in the upper chest and in the temple. He was lying on his back, the blood black and dried into the carpet. His eyes were wide open, and he had already begun to swell.

Merchant was breathing through his mouth now.

The place had been trashed, as if someone had swept his arm across the desktop and shoved files and records into a bag. Three file drawers were open and empty. Where there had been a computer, there was now a clean spot in the dust on the desktop.

Merchant opened the drawer where the cash had been.

Empty.

He left the office quietly, and through the open screen door he saw Sarah approaching up the walkway.

"What are you doing?" she whispered. "If he's not there, this is B and E."

He flicked off the living room light and whispered, "Hush. Go back to the truck, Sarah."

"He's here? Where?"

"Go back to the truck, Sarah. Please. Don't touch a thing."

"Oh God," she said. "Is he in there? Should I call the police?"

"We will, but not yet. Just wait for me."

He walked back down the hallway, this time passing the office and across from it a laundry room. There was a small room at the end of the hall. Merchant looked in. It was simple. Not too clean. A single bed.

There was a laptop computer underneath a small stack of newspapers.

Merchant pushed away the newspapers, and with the handkerchief still over his hand, he booted up the computer.

Once it came to life, he went into the e-mail application and saw that there were very few messages. Looked like Ronnie had been trained well at deleting them. He punched "send/receive," and the mail from the past few days came through. Altogether, thirty-three messages. Mostly spam. Penis enlargement ads, free porn photos, a job search engine, and maybe fifteen messages that were involved in gambling in some form or other: horses, dogs, casinos, and Internet gambling sites.

Merchant sat back and looked through the small pile of newspapers he'd taken off the laptop. There were three of them: *The Hartford Courant, The Boston Globe,* and the *Boston Herald.* Each was folded open to a story about a fire at a Boston jewelry store. The most detailed article was in the *Globe.* In the right-hand column someone — Ronnie, presumably — had written: "K?"

Merchant took out his pen and wrote down the date and page number of the article in the *Globe,* then went out to the truck with Sarah to call the police.

CHAPTER 28

Weir tried to force himself deeper into the black water. He was in full scuba gear, and the water that seeped into his mask didn't sting his eyes because it was fresh water, not salt. He was diving in the goddamn lake in Maine, and he hadn't even gotten to a quarter of the depth he'd have to do in the ocean and there was no way he could get himself deeper.

Weir was so frustrated, he wanted to kill somebody.

Ella.

The two brats back in the cabin.

Certainly that Jack Merchant asshole.

Kathleen for sure.

But the way things were balanced, the only one he could touch would be Merchant, and he was nowhere handy.

The pain in his right ear was just like letting someone kneel on his head and drive a spike into the ear canal.

Damn it! He checked his air supply and saw that he'd gone through three-quarters of it already. He turned himself toward the surface and slowly began to kick upward. The changing pressure squealed through his ears as he lost the hard-fought distance down. His ears and head ached.

He couldn't do what most any novice diver in the Virgin Islands could do. He couldn't dive deep. His eustachian tubes were always a problem. A few years back, he and Ella were vacationing in Eleuthera after a particularly bloody job. He had pushed the depth too far on a sport dive and ruptured his right eardrum. Instant vertigo, nausea, and severe pain. Now, even taking Benadryl and working his way down carefully, he'd managed only thirty feet.

The frustration just boiled inside.

He'd been waiting weeks for that piece of shit brother of McNaughton's to come home. He finally did, and Weir had picked him clean of the remaining cash and the chart with the coordinates.

So Weir had what he needed — if only he wasn't the pansy in the training pool crying, "My ears hurt."

When he reached the surface, he threw his mask into the boat, followed by the fins. Then climbed up the ladder, almost swamping the little fourteen-footer.

With all the screwups that had brought him to this place and time — many of them his own — he just had to think there was a way one of them back at the cabin could pay for how he was feeling.

Ella was waiting for him in the kitchen. "You make it?" she said.

He shook his head.

"Goddamn it," she said. "Have I got to do that now, too?"

He told her to shut up.

She told him if he thought she was going to stick it out here in the boonies wiping the snot noses of two kids, he could find a way to force his head deeper into the water.

Although he was in a foul enough mood himself, genuinely ready to kill a few minutes before, he began to laugh. "Sssh," he said. "The kids might hear you."

She froze. He thought for a moment she might see the humor, too. But she took two steps across the kitchen, going for the knives on the magnetic strip.

She got her hand on the midsize one, the one with the wickedly sharp blade she used for paring all those vegetables in the soups she made to pass the time.

It wasn't easy holding her down.

She was strong and had done some killing of her own.

And he didn't want to hurt her because he needed her and he came as close to loving her as it was possible for him to feel.

"Sshh," he said into her ear. "C'mon, Ella, let it go."

She jabbed him hard with her elbow, which made him gasp.

She did it again and again.

He kneed her in the small of the back and then pulled her to the floor. He put his arm around her neck in a choke hold and said into her ear, "You better find your goddamn sense of humor."

He squeezed until she slapped her hand on the floor.

Giving up.

He released the pressure a bit, and she coughed and took a deep, shaky breath. "No more," she said.

"Why?" he asked.

"Don't want to wake the kids."

He patted her on the head. "Good girl."

Ten minutes later, they were still on the kitchen floor, leaning back against the cabinets.

"What are we going to do?" she said.

"We're doing it. Step at a time."

She frowned. "This is me you're talking to. It's a hundred and forty feet down. You can't dive deep and I don't even know how. And look what a fiasco it turned into the last time we involved other people."

"Yeah, but you got a family out of it."

"Don't make me get the knife."

That made him smile. It wouldn't be funny if she didn't mean it. He changed the subject. "She said the boy looks skinny."

"Does he? I can't tell, I see him every day."

"Yeah, I think he might be. Not a handful anymore, though, is he?"

She didn't answer right away. "I don't know. He hasn't been a problem, but sometimes I see him looking at me and I'm not so sure the drugs are working."

"Seems fried enough to me."

"Maybe. Sometimes I think he's acting."

"Yeah? Maybe I should push him around a little. See what comes out."

"Oh, Dr. Weir, you wouldn't do that, would you?" she breathed. Nurse Ella now.

"I'd like to."

"Me, I'd like to put both of them on the stern of the boat with some chain and cinder blocks and see how *their* ears manage the deep water."

That made him laugh. "So cold. Even little Laurie isn't touching anything in here?" He reached over and caressed her left breast on the way up to putting his hand over her heart.

"Only you touch me there, baby," she said in her hooker's voice. But she looked away. He had seen her playing with the little girl and Ella's act was pretty damn good. The kid was cute.

The thing was, he never knew exactly what was true with Ella. But she'd been with him for over seven years, and he thought there was a good chance she loved him, too.

Close enough, anyhow.

"Listen," she said. "Sorry about before."

"It's all right."

"Yeah, I know it is." She rested her head against his shoulder. "I've just been so bored here. And the little brat's going to wake up soon and I have to be nice to her and that goes against the grain."

"You won't have to forever."

"I know. But I've got to tell you something now and you're going to get pissed. Just don't take it out on me, because if you rev me up again we might hurt each other."

Weir closed his eyes. "What?"

"He called."

"Shit. Why didn't you tell me right away?"

"We were busy. Besides, he doesn't want you to call him back. He wants to see you in New York."

"When?"

"Tomorrow at noon."

Weir groaned. "What for?"

"Progress report."

"Ah, shit." He sighed. "I should've let you stab me."

"I know, baby."

Weir drove through the early morning and boarded a nonstop flight out of Portland, Maine, just after 7:00 A.M.

One way, coach seat. He was going to drive back. Make a stop in Newport.

He took his seat by the window, and closed his eyes. God, he was tired. He tried to think through what he had to do next, put some order to his world. It was like running a business, and he couldn't claim much personal talent. There were logistics, financial problems, and personnel issues. The boat he had sunk. His own bad investment in McNaughton and his shit-for-brains brother.

He'd blown through all but eight thousand of the capital the Russian had provided. And five of that he'd just recovered from Ronnie. Which would've been fine if he was able just to take the boat out and do the dive himself, but he'd just proved in the lake that he couldn't.

Even though he wasn't the type to take blame, Weir knew

an outsider looking in might think he'd screwed up big time. Hell, never mind an outsider. The person he always felt judging him was his father. Roger VanBuren. One of New York's finest surgeons.

Weir's real name was Wes VanBuren. His father was a meticulous man, with intense views on the relationship between setting clear goals and achievement. Wes's mother had died young, and Dr. VanBuren's son was his project after he finished slicing and sewing together lives each day.

Wes had to spend hours listening to his father while he held forth in his library. He'd sit there pontificating while rolling a quarter between his fingers to maintain his dexterity. Wes wasn't just uninterested. He saw no altruism in his father's success; he saw it only as an excuse for him to preen.

But he never said that to his face.

However, away from him, Wes was quite willing to act out. Little stuff at first. Shoplifting, fights at school. But he started smartening up in his teen years and began to find ways to make money on the side. Then the police arrived at his door one day. They told his father they suspected he was selling coke in school.

His father was appalled but saw to it that Wes gave up the other dealers so his record was kept clean.

"What were you thinking?" his father said. "You involve yourself with these trash people — didn't you see how this would go wrong?"

Wes made the mistake of laughing. "You're not pissed that I did it. You're pissed that I got caught."

His father risked the well-being of his right hand by cracking his son across the face.

Then there had been another near scandal when Wes was seventeen. He slipped a girl a roofie at a party and raped her. That was the first time he'd used a drug against someone to get what he wanted, and the impact was far more profound than the sex. He marveled at his complete control of her, the fact that a pill administered at the right time took away all resistance.

The only problem was that she went to the hospital the next morning and the cops were at his door with handcuffs once again. But his father came through with a lawyer who knew how to make the girl see testifying against Wes would hurt her more than him. She dropped all charges.

With his father's name and his decent grades, Wes got into medical school. He was smart enough to do well in his studies, made it through his first and second national boards, and was officially a doctor. One of the real benefits of his medical education was his psychiatric rotation, where he was able to put a name to what he was: a sociopath. "Individuals with this disorder exhibit ten general symptoms: not learning from experience, no sense of responsibility, inability to form meaningful relationships, inability to control impulses, lack of moral sense, chronically antisocial behavior, no change in behavior after punishment, emotional immaturity, lack of guilt, self-centeredness."

He had to admit, that was him.

Knowing it clarified things.

His first murder, if anyone had known it as such, could have been construed as a mercy killing. Truth was, he was just impatient caring for an old man paralyzed by a brain tumor, and he found it expedient to triple the man's pain medication before heading off his shift.

That experience — combined with his total lack of guilt afterwards — gave him a remarkable sense of freedom. His only regret about killing the old man was that there was no money in it for him.

That opportunity didn't come for another year, when he met Ella. She was just a couple of years older than he was, the young wife of a middle-aged millionaire with a bad heart and a nasty temper. Her husband was in the hospital for only a week, but that was long enough for Ella and Wes to hook up.

They used Wes's apartment mostly but a few times went to a motel near her place. Within weeks of their being together, Ella looked carefully at him and said, "Wes, all I think about is us being together."

Wes never felt he was being tricked, more like they were both carefully interviewing each other. Because he recognized a kindred spirit in her.

The decision to kill her husband was as natural and exciting as their lovemaking. They waited patiently until her husband had a relapse, and Wes injected a huge hit of insulin into his IV bag the first chance he got to be alone with him. Insulin is naturally occurring and therefore hard to trace. Wes felt everything went well in the sense that the man died and no one accused him.

That is until a week later, when Ella's housekeeper came forward. Her sister worked as a chambermaid at a motel and had seen Ella and Wes together. Wes killed the housekeeper and her sister, which was all fine and good, but it turned out they had talked to other members of the family, and *they* talked to the police.

Ultimately, Wes decided it was an excellent time to lose the name and take off. And though common sense said that he and Ella should split up, the fact of the matter was he liked being with her. Although it went against the clinical definition of what he felt they both were, he needed her on some level, and she seemed to feel the same way.

He got them both out of town and down to a plastic surgeon in Florida. Ella was already a pretty woman, but when the surgeon was done with her she was flawless, at least to his eyes. He was more than pleased with his own face, too.

He couldn't say he loved her. He didn't think either of them was technically capable. But with her, he didn't have to act. And that was worth a lot.

Weir sighed.

He and Ella had done all sorts of things in their seven years together. With her looks, he had put her into a lot of situations where he'd help her ensnare and then blackmail wealthy married men. And the two of them had worked together on several contract murders. Most of them turned out fine, but a couple went wrong. Nothing that got them caught, but enough to give him and Ella a reputation as unreliable. Besides, there was a limit to the money they could make doing that, and the two of them burned through cash pretty fast. She was over thirty now, and while she still was a beauty, there were a lot of younger women working the same territory and it wasn't getting easier. They needed a real lump sum like this deal could deliver.

Wes had never used Ella like this to look after children. The trick was to keep her balanced long enough so that he didn't come back to the cabin one day to find she'd lost it with the brats.

Then he would have no leverage with Kathleen, and that was something he still needed. The way it was set up right now, either he got someone to do the dive on that boat or Kathleen would set him up to rip off her husband again. And his only real leverage with her was those kids.

But, Jesus, the way Ella went at him with that knife last night . . . Wes rubbed his eyes, exhausted. She'd lost it before, but never quite like that. He wouldn't want to be one of those kids living in that house.

Then again, it wasn't much fun being himself at the moment. Heading to Brooklyn to explain to a Russian fence with mob ties why he was still unable to deliver fifteen million dollars' worth of diamonds he'd promised.

The cab dropped him in front of the store.

A crowded electronics store full of cheap knockoffs. He gave his name to the clerk in the back, and after a moment, he was waved into a small kitchen area. The bodyguard, Petya, six-feet-five of muscle and bone and hellacious breath, left his tuna sub on the kitchen table and checked Weir for weapons before leading him down a dim hallway to Yegor's office.

Yegor stared at him as he came in, and Petya closed the door behind him and left.

Weir reached out over the desk to shake Yegor's hand, but the Russian just let him stand there. Yegor wasn't particularly big, but he was dense. Round shouldered, two days' growth of black beard, quiet black eyes.

"Suit yourself," Weir said and pulled up a chair and sat across from Yegor's desk.

Goddamned if he was going to remain standing. Yegor might be the gatekeeper to millions of dollars, but he looked like a taxi dispatcher. Yet his connections to the underside of the diamond world were impeccable. Mostly from moving Siberian diamonds, but he could move stones acquired by good old armed robbery, too. He tended to think he was tougher than he was because he knew some genuinely tough people and they protected him.

Yegor stared at him for a while.

Weir knew this game, felt impatient with it, but knew enough to shut up. Maybe he didn't fear a painful and ugly death, but he didn't encourage it either. He began looking around the room.

Grates on the window.

The usual office crap. Fax machine, a new computer. An electric radiator.

Finally, Yegor said, "What is your name now?"

"I'm going by Weir. Dr. Weir sometimes."

Yegor shook his head. "You like a child. You got them for me?"

"Not yet. Soon."

"You understand I have people waiting? That your failure appears to be my failure?"

"I do."

"Oh, all right," Yegor said. Playing like a nice guy. "So we understand each other."

Weir just smiled blandly.

"But I got a question for you," Yegor said.

Yegor and his questions.

Weir didn't have a weapon on him. Nothing on the flight, of course, and Petya would have found anything else. The chair Weir was sitting on was metal, pretty sturdy. That, maybe.

"My question is this," Yegor said. "Why does everything you do end up in a cluster fuck?"

Closta fock was what it sounded like. Goddamn Russian had been in the country since he was a teenager. He usually had the right words down, but the accent was for shit.

There was a metal box on the floor by the desk. Toolbox?

"You don't give me an answer?"

Weir shrugged. "I thought the question was rhetorical."

"No. I wanted an answer. How about this one: do you think I like a good story? Is that it?"

"No."

Yegor waved him off, warming to his theme. "Maybe you do. Maybe that's it. Americans love a good story. Russian Americans must too, is that it?"

Is thot it?

Yegor kept on. "I invest fifty thousand with you, and instead of the fifteen million in stones, I get stories. Stories about boats. Boats sinking, children in the water, boats exploding, people blackmailing you . . . Did you come today with more stories?"

"I came today because you requested I come — "

"I got DVD!" Yegor bellowed suddenly. He stood up behind the desk. "I want story, I go to movie. I watch TV!"

He gestured to a big old Sony on the table alongside the wall. "Look, I even got a TV in my office. I got plasma TV at home, twenty-three-thousand-dollar home entertainment center! Do I need your fucking stories?"

Focking stories.

Weir kept his eyes on Yegor but quietly lifted the lid of the toolbox with his toe. Yes. Hammer, Phillips screwdriver, but pretty small. A box cutter, but the blade was slid in.

"Answer me now!"

"Look," Weir said. "I made excellent progress this week. The captain —"

"The one who blackmail you and you blow up, yes, you tell me this story."

Weir paused.

Yegor got impatient, waved his hand. "Say it."

"All right. I told you his brother ran off with the chart and my cash. I got both back. So I know where the diamonds are now. It's just a matter of getting them."

Yegor grunted. "So why haven't you done it yet?"

"It's not that simple."

"I get boat and divers for you, help you get it."

"No, thanks."

He wasn't about to tell Yegor about his bad ear. And if Yegor sent his own people to do the recovery, Weir would be lucky to get a finder's fee. More likely he'd get a bullet in the back of the head and his own set of weights to wear to the ocean floor.

"It's not a fucking offer!"

Weir smiled. "There's not a focking chance."

Yegor went silent.

Sat there, the blood darkening his face. Then he picked up the phone and said, "Come in here."

Weir stood up and put his back to the wall. He was relieved when just Petya came through the door. Sometimes Yegor had family around, his son or his son-in-law. If Weir hurt one of them, the deal could never be salvaged. He was pretty sure Petya was expendable.

"Put his head through the TV," Yegor said to Petya. "Grind his face in good, so he gets the idea that if I want stor —"

By the time Weir bent down and got the toolbox open Petya was upon him. So he grabbed the hammer and just lifted it up, slamming Petya in the balls.

Petya screamed, blowing that bad breath right into Weir's face. Weir shoved him back with both hands, then hit him with the hammer twice. With the first blow, his aim was off and he shattered the man's front teeth. The second shot was on target, square in the middle of the forehead.

That put the big man down.

Weir spun around fast. If Yegor went into the desk drawer for a gun, he'd have to kill him.

That'd be a real shame. A *focking* shame.

But Yegor was sitting down, his hands flat on the desktop. "What did you do?" he was saying. "What did you do?"

"You know, I got your point the first time," Weir said. "I'll have the diamonds, less than a week."

Yegor nodded. He looked at Petya. "Is he dead?"

Weir looked closer. Blood flowing pretty fast from the head wound. His chest moving up and down pretty well. His front teeth pushed in.

"Won't be happy when he wakes up, but he will."

Yegor said, "One week. You'll add another fifty thousand for Petya."

"I understand," Weir said. "You can hold back the fifty you advanced me and now fifty for Petya. One hundred thousand dollars."

Yegor nodded. A little dignity restored, even with his bodyguard on the floor. "No more stories."

CHAPTER 29

Sarah had been awake for about a half hour.

She'd gotten more sleep than Jack, about five hours. She was pretty sure the cops had dropped him off at the motel around three in the morning, but she couldn't be certain.

Now it was just after seven, and tired as she was, she couldn't sleep anymore.

But that was all right. She was warm.

The curtains were parted just enough so that a single shaft of sunlight was slowly making its way up their bed.

It was now just up to Jack's arm, which lay across her. She watched it highlight the dark hair of his forearm and cross over to reveal the healed scar from the year before. When he'd been shot in the back and the bullet exited just under his collarbone.

She reached over softly, touched the scar.

His breathing didn't change.

Same easy rise and fall of his chest.

She looked closely at his face, the stubble on his chin, the bruising of his lip where Doug had hit him the day before.

He slept so solidly. Could find Ronnie's body, stabbed like that, and sleep. Could take the hours of the angry cops, yelling and posturing, and basically making up for the embarrassing fact that they had barely followed up on the Newland Police request and now the subject was dead.

Jack could take all that, and sleep solidly, while she lay awake beside him.

She could imagine resenting it, but she didn't.

He was warm beside her, and therefore, she was warm.

So she appreciated it not at all when someone started pounding at the door. Merchant awoke instantly, rolled out of bed and began pulling on his jeans. "Hold on, hold on."

He reached over, squeezed her foot through the bedclothes, and said, "Cover up, naked girl."

She groaned and slipped her head under the covers. She could hear him pushing the curtains aside to look out, then he opened the door and the room went bright. She heard someone say, "Police," but she didn't catch the name.

He stepped outside with them and closed the door.

She sighed, threw the covers back. Without him beside her, the room suddenly seemed hopelessly empty. She got out of bed, wrapped the covers around herself in case he walked in with company.

Which was exactly what happened. He opened the door. There were two uniformed cops behind him. Foster town cops.

He said, "They want us down at the station again. I said we'd go right after breakfast."

"You tell them," she said. "Order me eggs, bacon, the works."

"I'll see you down at the restaurant." He closed the door.

She went in to take a shower.

Foster cops. Not FBI. She let the water pour over her, trying to get it to wash away the weariness. Jack's contention was that as long as this stayed between local police forces, no one would take responsibility for finding the Coulters. Assuming they were anywhere to be found. Herself, she wanted out of the business. She wanted Jack and herself out of the business of finding stabbed bodies and hitting people for information.

She'd like to get back to her world. Finding boats. And maybe more sleeping in the same bed with Jack.

Feeling warm.

She turned the shower to cold. Time to wake up, face reality, and get ready for another long day talking to the police.

Luckily, breakfast was good.

Because otherwise the day just sucked.

The Foster Police Station was in a small stucco building that Sarah was fairly sure had been converted from a strip mall. She and Merchant spent most of the morning in separate rooms. One detective, a young black guy by the name of Bobby Sinclair, bounced between them. He primarily kept after them with the same questions: When did you see the cash in Ronnie's office? Did he tell you where he got it? Did he discuss his gambling situation with you? Did he mention poker? Who he played with?

And so on.

He began to warm to them somewhat in the early afternoon, when he took them out to Ronnie's house. He had them walk through carefully, tell him each and every step of their two visits. When Merchant talked with him about the Coulters, he'd listen with an expression of interest, but it seemed to her just that — an expression.

Then he brought them back to the station. As they were walking in, the other detective on the case, Kennedy, pulled up in a big Ford. Doug Miles was in the passenger seat.

Sarah looked over at Doug, and she saw Merchant do the same.

Doug avoided their eyes.

"C'mon, let's go in," Sinclair said.

"You're going to ask him about what I told you, right?" Merchant said to Sinclair. "About him being with that woman both when *Isabella* blew up and the night the Coulters' boat went down?"

"Oh, yeah. We're going to talk to him. And talk to you right after," Sinclair said. He took them into an interrogation room and asked them to wait for "just a while longer."

About an hour later, Sinclair and Kennedy came in. Kennedy was older than Sinclair, a white guy with a pockmarked face, red hair flecked with gray.

Sinclair took a chair across from the two of them. Kennedy remained standing. Sinclair said to Sarah, "Long day."

She nodded. Her patience was wearing thin and she didn't trust herself to open her mouth.

Kennedy crossed his arms. They were heavily muscled. Even though he appeared to be in his early fifties, he looked like a weight lifter.

"So what did Doug have to say?" Merchant asked.

"Well, actually, Merchant, that's really none of your goddamn business."

"What's your problem?" Merchant said.

"Not a thing," Kennedy said. He looked over at Sinclair. "You got a problem, Bobby?"

Sinclair shook his head, "Not me."

"Sinclair doesn't have a problem, I don't have a problem, what's yours?"

"We've spent the entire day here at your request," Merchant said. His voice was even, but Sarah could tell he was angry. God knew, she was. "And I'll tell you once again why we did that. Because we're trying real hard to get some official help for the Coulters."

Kennedy looked over at his partner, shook his head. "The Coulters. I called the Coast Guard, I called the Newland cops, what I hear loud and clear is that the Coulters were lost at sea a damn month ago and now you've taken up a hobby while Matt Coulter's lying in his hospital bed. Running up your bill, the way it looks to me. But what I'm looking at right here in my town is one dead Ronnie McNaughton. And I don't know who did it yet, but I'm getting a pretty good picture of why."

"Which is?"

"He was a gambler, and for a guy like him to come into twenty-five thousand in cash, it's like a junkie getting a bucket of heroin. You said yourself he went through ten thousand in Atlantic City. I got him placed in a poker game where he burned through another ten thousand in front of some very dangerous people. It wouldn't take much at all for one of them to follow him back to his house and take what little was left."

"So who did that?" Merchant said.

"It's been one day, give me a goddamn break."

"Wait a minute," Sarah said. Trying for the voice of reason. "You talked to Doug —"

"Yeah, I talked to Doug," Kennedy said.

She paused, a little confused, then continued. "So you know that this guy Weir who attacked Jack in the hospital was the same guy who was chartering Captain McNaughton's boat . . ."

She found herself talking faster because Kennedy was shaking his head.

"I don't know that," Kennedy said. "Doug said he couldn't give me a positive ID from that tape and said he told you two that. Another thing, I went out and looked at that famous bow plate you guys are telling me about, and maybe it's close to the one Matt Coulter sketched, but so are a half a dozen more I found on the Web. Everything you got hangs on that being the same piece, and maybe it's not."

Sarah said, "Look, the same guy tried to kill Matt Coulter in his bed —"

"I just told you, I got nothing to prove that it's the same guy. And that's not where our investigation's taking us. Ronnie was a gambler. A low-life piece of shit flashing cash at a poker game. This is what happens to guys like him."

"So where'd he get the cash?" Merchant said. "The twenty-five thousand."

"Inherited from his brother," Kennedy said.

"Not just inherited. He took it from his brother's safety deposit box. How did his brother get the cash?"

"Hey, maybe Captain McNaughton didn't pay his taxes, that's another department. I'm looking into a murder."

"Just barely," Sarah said.

And instantly wished she could take the words back. That damn mouth of hers.

The room went silent, and then Kennedy said, "Get the hell out of here, both of you. We've got your numbers."

Merchant shook his head. "That's not good enough. The Coulters —"

"Hey, shut up," Kennedy said. He leaned over the table, put his face in Merchant's. "If you've got a problem with that, maybe you want to take a swing at me?"

"For God's sake," Sarah said.

Merchant said, "You one of the friends on the force that Doug mentioned?"

Kennedy stood up straight, hitched his belt. "You're goddamn lucky I wasn't around."

"Dougie Miles is Kennedy's nephew," Sinclair said. "Nobody likes to hear their family's getting assaulted in the privacy of their own trailer."

"Shut up, Bobby," Kennedy said.

"Look," Merchant said, "I'm sorry about your nephew." He touched the bruise on his lip. "If it's any consolation, he got the first one in."

"It's not. For all I know, you killed Ronnie. You already admitted you fought with him once."

"Yes, I told you that yesterday," Merchant said, slowly. "We also established that I was in a hospital bed when Ronnie died. You know that."

"Bullshit, I do," Kennedy said. "What happened, you go after the cash and he come in on you? Things get out of hand?"

Merchant looked at Kennedy, then at Sinclair, and said, "What, does your partner spend the day drinking or is he just stupid?"

Faster than Sarah would've imagined possible, Kennedy reached over and took a swing at Merchant.

Merchant did nothing to stop him. Took the blow on his face. He stood up, shook his head, and wiped the blood with the back of his hand. Kennedy was breathing hard.

Merchant started around the table, and Sarah said, "Jack, no!"

Sinclair got between them. "Hey, hey, let's calm it down here."

Merchant turned around and walked to the corner of the room. Sarah immediately followed him, putting her back to Kennedy. "Don't do a thing," she whispered. "You know that's what he wants."

He nodded. "You're right."

Wiped his mouth again, then said, "C'mon, Sarah, we're going."

Kennedy shoved him.

Merchant said, "Keep it up and I'll get a lawyer in here and swear out assault charges on you."

"You asshole," Kennedy said.

Sarah got between them, her back to the cop. She said to Merchant, "Ignore him. He's useless."

Luckily, Sinclair grabbed Kennedy in time.

She hustled Merchant out of the station while she still could.

CHAPTER 30

Merchant and Sarah started back. It was midafternoon, and the traffic on Route 95 was horrendous. Merchant was at the wheel, and he felt tired, angry, and not much like talking.

He was mad at the cops. And he was a little mad at Sarah, too.

She'd gotten him into this, and if he could read her silences as well as he thought he could, she just wanted to return to her business and forget the whole mess.

He mulled on that awhile. Feeling like he had taken on Matt Coulter's role entirely, running around trying to convince people his children were alive. Which, of course, he didn't know at all.

Merchant looked over at Sarah. Yes, he was mad at her.

But mainly mad at himself.

Because he wanted out, too.

And that wasn't going to happen.

Merchant got off at Route 138 heading to Kingston, Rhode Island. He told Sarah that he'd take the train back to Boston.

"I'll drive you."

He shook his head. "No, you can go straight through Newport to New Bedford. And I can think better on the train, anyhow."

She frowned, but they didn't talk again until he pulled into the station parking lot.

"This isn't your fault," she said. "Or mine. I can feel you sitting there being pissed."

"I know." He kissed her lightly. "All the better reason for me to take the train."

That didn't seem to make her happy, but he kissed her again and got out. Best he could do in his current frame of mind.

Forty-five minutes later, the train arrived and he managed to get a window seat. He watched the passing waterfront and backyard views as the train rolled along with a slight rocking motion that made him feel sleepy.

He kept running through it all in his head. From Coulter showing up at his boat to Kennedy kicking them out of the police station. He took out his notepad, did a list. Studied it. Added to it some more.

He didn't come up with anything particularly fruitful.

So he closed his eyes and did the other thing he did well on trains.

Slept.

He didn't awake until the train was emptying out in South Station in Boston. He yawned hugely and then pulled himself together. He grabbed his bag, walked to the main station, stopped into the men's room, and washed his face. He was still not awake.

He bought a cup of coffee and decided to walk to his boat.

He started along Atlantic Avenue. The sun was low in the sky, the light golden. He was fully awake now and something was tugging at him, and he tried not to focus on it too hard. He just kept walking. And then it came to him. The jewelry store that burned down. The article Ronnie had circled in the newspapers.

The store wasn't far away.

Merchant crossed over the street into the Financial District and kept winding his way through in the direction of Government Center. Just before the Center, he found the remains of the building. The jewelry store had been on the ground level of a small red-brick building. The buildings on each side of the burned-out shell had historic plaques on the doorways. Probably the building that had burned had one, too.

Quite a loss, he thought. If he remembered correctly, the article said arson was the cause. Theft had been involved. Diamonds.

And Ronnie had found those articles interesting for some reason and written "K?" beside one of them.

Merchant finished his coffee, tossed the container into the trash barrel. Looked like he had something to do.

Once at his boat, Merchant opened up all the hatches so it could air out. He grabbed a change of clothes, walked up the dock to the showers, and let the hot water rinse away the feel of a day in the police station. He came back, threw out the food in the refrigerator that had gone bad, and heated and ate a can of stew. He opened a bottle of beer and turned on his laptop.

After hooking up his digital camera, he took a few minutes to print out pictures of the bow and anchor plate on *Isabella*, Captain McNaughton's boat. Then he logged on to *The Boston Globe* Web site and did a search for the news article that had been on Ronnie's desk about the jewelry store fire. One of the first things he realized was that Gardner's Jewelry was hardly a small operation: the Boston store was the "flagship branch" of a twenty-nine-store chain. The owner was a guy by the name of David Gardner. There was a photo of Gardner standing next to the fire marshal. His face was expressionless as his building burned to the ground.

Merchant started looking for follow-up articles and found that Gardner was seeking thirty million dollars in insurance coverage for stolen merchandise in addition to compensation for the gutted building. The security cameras had captured images of three masked men working fast inside the store. Two of them were smashing display cases and sweeping jewels into bags, the third was sloshing what was most likely gasoline on the walls. The head of the security service retained by Gardner's Jewelry was vehement in his company's defense, saying the thieves had entered the building with legitimate passwords and had known how to block the remote video access.

"Had to be an inside job," he said.

When asked by a reporter if he was suggesting David Gardner was involved, he said, "Of course not."

The fire marshal said, "We're not taking anything for granted on this one."

Merchant found another article that included a close-up of David Gardner. It had been taken about three weeks after the fire. He had a dark complexion, wavy hair, and a goatee. Handsome, but with a soft quality to his mouth. Merchant imagined him as an easy guy to dislike. He appeared to be defending himself as reporters asked pointed questions about the rapid expansion of his business, his debts, and the fire.

The article stated that the insurance carrier for Gardner's Jewelry "was researching the claim carefully" and would make no comment about whether or not they would be paying off.

Merchant kept looking at Gardner's photo.

Maybe it was just the situation he was in. The pressure of the reporters. The suspicion people were directing at him. Whatever the cause, Merchant found it interesting. And possibly worth more study.

The man looked scared.

Next, Merchant went to the on-line skip-tracing databases where Ballard Marine Liquidation had subscriptions. Long ago, Sarah had given him the PIN codes to them, and he spent the next hour and a half researching David Gardner. It was just time and keystrokes to dig into driving records, credit history, arrest searches, bankruptcy files, real estate holdings, marriage and divorce records, and a lot more. Gardner had addresses in Boston, Newport, Miami, and Lockley, Maine. He drove a Porsche, and a BMW, and owned two motorcycles. He also had a Donzi speedboat docked in Newport. His credit history was decent overall, but there were periods of time when he ran late on some of their mortgage payments.

Merchant noticed that Gardner's wife, Kathleen, held almost nothing under her name. She had a couple of credit cards, but her name didn't appear on any of the mortgages, the title for the Mercedes she drove, or really anything else he could see. He found it interesting that her first name started with a K. Could mean something, could mean nothing.

David Gardner had been married once before. Their marriage was Kathleen's first, and her maiden name was Donovan. She married Gardner when she was thirty-one. Merchant plugged her name into *The Boston Globe* site and came up with quite a few listings, which was no surprise given that she had a very common name for the Boston area.

He looked up at the clock, saw it was well past midnight. But he still wasn't tired, and he had nothing else to do at the moment. So he kept at it, punching in those keystrokes, seeking something useful in the glow of his computer screen.

CHAPTER 31

The next morning, Merchant called the *Globe* and asked for a reporter by the name of Les Pickman.

He was put through and Pickman answered on the third ring.

"I don't know if you remember me," Merchant said. "My name's Jack Merchant and — "

"DEA, that Charlestown thing," Pickman said. "Course I do."

"That's impressive," Merchant said.

"I'm an impressive guy. What's up?"

"I remember you as a guy with a big appetite," Merchant said. "Still true?"

"Yeah. But I'm also busy. You got something worth my while?"

"I see you were working on the Gardner's Jewelry fire story."

"It's getting kind of long in the tooth now, but yeah, I worked on it. The DEA involved some way?"

"I'm not with the DEA anymore."

"Yeah? How come?"

"Story for another day," Merchant said. "But I do have some questions for you and I'm buying lunch."

"Like I say, I'm a busy guy. You got something for me that'll put words on paper?"

"I don't know for sure. But would you be interested to know that a murdered man had your article cut out and circled on his desk?"

The reporter paused. Then said, "I like the words 'murdered man' connected to an article I wrote. I'd be lying if I said I didn't."

"So what do you want for lunch?" Merchant said.

Les Pickman was about four inches taller than Merchant and weighed about ten pounds less. He chose a restaurant not too far from the burned-out jewelry store, ordered a massive burger with bacon, French fries, a side salad, and a pint of beer, and told the waitress not to forget him when it came to dessert because he was fond of pie.

Merchant ordered a ham and cheese on pumpernickel and black coffee.

They chatted for a few minutes about the undercover work Merchant had done in Charlestown years back and what he'd been doing since. He gave the short version of what had happened in Miami, and Pickman, like any good reporter or cop trying to get information, kept his manner entirely nonjudgmental.

"That really sucks," he said, pushing aside his salad. "So tell me about the dead guy who likes my writing."

"Drink your beer," Merchant said. "Because I can't tell you that yet."

"You asshole," he said. He meant it, but he didn't seem terribly surprised.

"You'll be the first one to know once I can say," Merchant said.

"The only."

"All right, the only. But I'm fishing right now, and I really don't know that this murdered guy is linked to the fire in any real way other than the circled article. But if he is, it'll be a big story and you've got it."

"So what's to keep me from walking out of here right now?"

"You don't have the pie yet," Merchant said.

That got a short laugh out of Pickman. And luckily the burger arrived just then, on a plate overflowing with fries. "All right," he said. "I'm easy to buy. Exactly what're you looking for?"

"David Gardner. What do you think is going on there?"

"Read between the goddamn lines. He torched the place."

"Why?"

Pickman shrugged. "Looks like the usual. He grew that business too fast. He inherited it from his folks about twelve years ago. They'd built up three stores over three decades and he tacks on twenty-six more storefronts throughout New England in just over one. Does the term *overextended* mean anything to you?"

"Is that what his finances show?"

Pickman took a massive bite out of his burger and Merchant had to wait. When he was done, Pickman said, "Not from what I hear. They aren't publicly owned, so it's not as if I've seen their balance sheet myself. But from what the cops say, it looks decent. Which is suspicious in and of itself with that kind of growth. You understand what I'm saying?"

"Sure. Either he's just a hell of a businessman or he's got a way to funnel cash in that looks legit."

"Yep. Bread-and-butter stuff for you DEA types."

"So he's suspected of money laundering?"

"Suspected, yes. Proven, not to my sources. But this whole fire is shaky. I mean, Jesus, this is a sophisticated alarm and security system and it's all turned off with the right codes."

"And where was he when this was happening?"

"Having a late dinner in a restaurant with his finance manager, who by the way, is one pretty woman. He's going for substantial money, a good thirty million for the stuff robbed, plus the building. For a guy whose balance sheet looks decent, it's like he suddenly decided he needed a lot of cash fast. Why?"

Merchant said, "So it looks like something happened. He ran into some big debt in his personal life. Or maybe he really lost millions in jewels some other way and he wants the insurance company to foot the bill."

"Maybe," Pickman said. "He's not telling me."

"You ever talk to his wife, Kathleen?"

"Nah. She made some appearances with him right after the fire, show of support kind of thing. But that was once, maybe twice. Why?"

Merchant took out a black-and-white picture he had made on his ink-jet printer. It was from a low-resolution photo from the "Names and Faces" page about eight years back. The grain was very coarse, but it was clear that she was a beautiful woman. She was caught as she turned away laughing from an avuncular looking man at a function at the Park Plaza. The caption read, "Kathleen Donovan shares a laugh with collector Christian Winfield."

"Do you know him?" Merchant said. "His name sounds familiar."

"I don't," Pickman said. "She was a looker, though, wasn't she? Still is, really. Late thirties now, probably. Not very involved in the business, from what I can see. You might want to check out that finance manager, the chick that Gardner was having dinner with during the robbery. Rebecca D'Angelo. Blond hair, blue eyes. Plenty smart. If he's laundering money, he'd have to go through her. Which I suspect he's doing, too."

"So who do you think he's laundering for?"

"You tell me, Mr. Ex-DEA."

"Any reason to think it's drugs?"

"Not that I've been able to find. But when it comes to laundering drug money by buying large amounts of diamonds, you know there's quite a bit of precedent. But I've got other stories to chase, and this one is just a fire. Not murder or something really cool. Unless you've got that to hand me."

"Can't say I do." Merchant sipped his coffee. Thinking about whether he should try to convince Les to put the public spotlight back on the Coulters. Between Weir's attack on Matt in the hospital and his possible link to Ronnie and Greg McNaughton, there was probably enough for an article.

"You sure?" Pickman said. The burger gone, he was all business now.

"Not yet," Merchant said. "First, I'd like to figure out why David Gardner suddenly needed thirty million dollars in insurance money."

"Yeah, I guess," Pickman said. "Could make it juicier." He waved the waitress over and ordered that piece of pie.

CHAPTER 32

As Merchant was leaving the restaurant, his cell phone rang. It was Sarah.

She said, "Listen, I've got some good news. Ben Pryor just called looking for you. He's at the hospital and Matt is responsive now."

"Damn, that is good news." Merchant had pretty much given up on the idea of Coulter recovering. "He's conscious?"

"*Responsive* is the word he used. I'm not sure if Matt will be up for a chat, but it's worth a try. And, Jack?"

"Yeah?"

"You still blaming me for getting you into all this?"

"Hey, I was feeling sorry for myself, shoot me."

"Believe me, I considered it," she said. "Call me after you talk with Matt."

When he got up to Coulter's room, there was a police officer outside his door. The door was open, and Merchant could see Ben Pryor standing beside Coulter's bed, talking with a doctor. Coulter didn't look alert.

"Just a minute, sir," the cop said. He was a young black man with humorless eyes. "Let me see some ID please."

Pryor saw him outside the door and said, "Be right with you, Merchant."

He continued talking with the doctor quietly, and then they both came to the door. The doctor, a short, potbellied man with curly black hair, said, "The good news is that he was coherent. Sometimes recovery is linear. But more often it's spotty progress like this."

He shook Pryor's hand, nodded at Merchant, and left.

Pryor's face was grim. He said to the officer, "I called him to join us."

The cop nodded, took his time looking at Merchant's driver's license, and then wrote his name down on a clipboard. "Go ahead, sir."

Pryor and Merchant went back to Coulter's bedside. His head was cocked at an angle, and he was breathing deeply. There were monitor wires leading to his chest, his head, and he had an IV tube in his arm. He looked as if he had shrunk.

"Jesus Christ," Pryor said. "He talked to me. I've been coming at lunch most every day, just talking to him. This time, he opened his eyes, said my name. Reached his hand up and took mine. He asked for you. I got on the phone looking for you while the doctor and nurse tested his responses. By the time I came back, he was gone again."

"Did he say anything about the suicide attempt?"

"No. We didn't even get there."

Pryor said nothing more for almost a minute. Just watching his friend lying there.

Then he looked over at Merchant. "Would you have had anything to tell him?"

"Yes. There's been a lot going on. And there's a lot I had to ask him."

"Yeah? I've been bugging the cops and seen squat other than them keeping a guy on the door."

"That's worth a lot. There's a guy down in Connecticut

who was just killed — I think by the same guy who tried to kill Matt."

"You think, but the cops don't?"

"That's about right."

Pryor looked at his watch. "I'd like to hear about this. I've got to take a call back at the office, but it won't take long. Can you come back and join me?"

"Sure," Merchant said.

Pryor took Coulter's hand and squeezed hard. "C'mon, Matt," he said. "Enough of this shit, huh?"

Pryor led the way up his office steps, two at a time. He gestured to the conference room, said, "Make yourself at home," and then said to his secretary, "That conference call up yet?"

"Two minutes," she said.

"Good." He turned back to Merchant and said, "Hey, the cops returned Matt's computer to me. I looked at that suicide note he was supposed to have written. I've been looking at his writing for years, and there's no damn way he wrote that pathetic thing, even for a suicide note. Jeanne, give Merchant the computer, let him check it out."

The phone rang as he said this, and she picked up the line, listened, and said, "He'll be right on."

Pryor went into his office, and Merchant could hear his voice booming as he apparently tried to convince someone to buy advertising space in his journals.

Merchant waited in the conference room, looking through the photos he'd printed out on his ink-jet the night before. The bow plate on *Isabella,* the pictures of David and Kathleen Gardner, the news articles and photos about the explosion of *Isabella,* and the articles about Ronnie McNaughton's murder.

And then Jeanne came in with the laptop computer. "Here, Ben was saying you might want to look at this."

"Sure. Do you know what the file is listed as?"

"Gee, I don't," she said. "Here, let's see if I can help you find it." She opened up the computer, turned it on, and said, "Do you remember the date that Matt tried to . . . well, whatever it was that happened. Whether he really jumped or not?"

Merchant thought about it, said, "I guess that would be the twenty-fifth."

"OK." She opened the Search program and looked for files that had been created or modified that day.

Two popped up.

One simply said, "Note."

And when Merchant opened that, it was the suicide note.

He closed that file. And looked at the title of the second file. It was "Letterhead." It was time-stamped as having been modified at the same time as the suicide note. A minute after, in fact.

"What's this?" Merchant said.

She opened the file. It was the company letterhead formatted on the computer screen. "Well, you know, if we want to send someone an e-mail with an attached Word doc that looks like a letter, we just have the letterhead ready like this on the computers."

"I got that," he said. "But what was Matt doing modifying it one minute after writing a suicide note?"

She shrugged. "I've got no idea."

Pryor came in about ten minutes later. "Sorry to hold you up. It feels crazy doing business at times like this, but we've got to keep making a living. So what have you learned?"

Merchant hesitated.

Pryor wasn't his client.

But his friendship with Coulter felt real to Merchant. And that would have to do under the circumstances.

Merchant filled Pryor in on what had been happening, laying out the photographs and articles as he went: finding the anchor plate on the remains of *Isabella*; the likelihood that Weir had been chartering *Isabella* at the same time Coulter's family was lost at sea; Greg and Ronnie McNaughton's deaths. "It comes down to this: there's one point where we know that *Isabella* was at sea about the same time *Seagull* went down. We know that when *Isabella* came in, the night watchman was being occupied with a woman who might be linked to Weir. So the kids might have been taken off the boat then."

"My God," Pryor said. He sat back in his chair. "So you think there's a chance Matt's kids are still alive?"

"I don't know," Merchant said. "I've got this string of *mights* that may add up to something. But I don't have any evidence they're alive or dead. There's a fair amount of evidence something's going on down in Foster that involves this guy Weir, who tried to kill Matt in his bed. But I haven't had any luck getting the police to pay serious attention. I'm trying to build enough of a case to get the FBI involved."

"Jesus. I got to tell you, I thought you were just scamming Matt for money when I first met you. And you were attacked yourself by this guy."

"Did you see the security tape?"

"Yes. The cops showed it to me. I'd never seen the guy before."

"How about this — do you recognize either of these two people?" He laid down the pictures he'd taken off the Web of David Gardner and his wife, Kathleen. He had folded the paper so that the captions and their names were hidden.

Pryor studied them carefully, then shook his head. "They look vaguely familiar, but I don't know why. Who are they?"

Merchant unfolded the paper, showed him the full captions. He told him about finding the newspaper articles in Ronnie's bedroom.

"Huh," Pryor said. "That sounds like a pretty thin connection, but I guess you know your business. Of course, now that you say it, I know of Gardner's Jewelry, and I do remember hearing about a fire."

"Is there any particular reason that you think Matt might know them? As advertisers for your publications maybe?"

"Nah. I'd be the guy to know that. I'm the publisher, but that means glorified space salesman for trade books like these. And none of our books involves the jewelry trade, at least not directly."

"How about indirectly?"

He frowned. "Well, I suppose *Retail Display Monthly* would be the closest. Display cases are certainly an important part of the jewelry business, and so our advertisers would consider a chain like Gardner's Jewelry to be an important client."

"So how would Matt run into the Gardners?"

"Don't know if he would. But he was editorial, so he'd be out there doing industry stories and going to trade shows. Might've run into them there."

"Any way we can check that?'

Pryor said, "You really think it might help?"

"I don't know. But it could."

Pryor glanced at his watch. "OK, then." He got up, went to the conference room door, and called Jeanne over. When she came he said, "Have Tommy join us, and ask him to bring the complete set of *Retail Display Monthly*."

"The complete set?"

"That's right. Eight years' worth. He doesn't need to break his back, just start with the first year and keep bringing in a case at a time. And I'd like you to do a couple of name searches on the trade show mailing lists we've compiled for the magazine."

"What year?"

"All of them. From the beginning."

Her eyes widened. "What names?"

He looked over at Merchant, and he gave her David and Kathleen Gardner's names. "You should also look for her under her maiden name, Kathleen Donovan."

"Got it," Jeanne said. "This is to help Matt?"

"Yep," Pryor said.

She smiled. "Happy to do it, then. Want a pot of coffee?"

It took them just under two hours. Tommy, the young editor of the trade publication, found the article. "This them?"

He flipped open the magazine and splayed it out on the middle of the table. It was a quarter-page article about the Gardner's Jewelry display case redesign.

"This is six years back," Pryor said. "Before your time, Tommy. Matt would have been editing this himself, and probably did most of the interviews and writing."

David and Kathleen Gardner were photographed behind the counter. The caption read, "David Gardner turns to his wife's good taste and Pennella Display to create a stunning new look for his ever-expanding chain of jewelry stores."

The article went on to tout the virtues of the case, but Merchant didn't read that until later. He was struck by the photograph of Kathleen Gardner. The color photograph. He had only seen her picture in black and white before.

She was a redhead.

CHAPTER 33

After Merchant left Pryor's office, he went to the Boston Public Library. He went through the entrance on Boylston Street and waited a few minutes for an available computer monitor. He spent a little while on *The Boston Globe* Web site trying to make a fragmentary memory become something real.

It was about Christian Winfield, the man who had been in the news photo with Kathleen way back when her last name was Donovan.

Merchant did a name search against that and came up with a couple of hits. One of those hits led to a link where a woman was singing the praises of "this wonderful estate jewelry dealer that I met . . ." She included a link to Christian Winfield's Web site.

It was a very simple site, including a photograph of Winfield and pieces of estate jewelry with little stories under each. The effect Winfield was trying to achieve was that he was reselling pieces either from estates or from "dear friends with means."

The tone of the page brought the memory to life. Back when Merchant was doing the work in Charlestown, Winfield's name had come up. It was a small thing: a dealer who was beginning to expand his base came in wearing a Rolex that he bought "off this class-act guy on Commonwealth."

The dealer had long since been incarcerated, but now that Merchant had the name pegged, he could remember the guy playing with the name, rolling the blue-blood sound of it off his tongue: Christian Winfield. Christian Winfield.

At the time, Merchant had checked with a Boston Police detective who told him that Winfield had a good act and did some legitimate business but also had tenuous mob connections and a record for trafficking in stolen goods.

Merchant jotted down Winfield's Commonwealth Avenue address and closed out of his Web site. He figured he'd just walk over and meet the famous Christian Winfield himself. But then he found three more hits. And one of them was a two-week-old news article about Christian Winfield's suicide.

Merchant left the library, walked two blocks toward the Charles River and three more blocks along tree-lined Commonwealth Avenue until he got to Winfield's building.

He looked at the listing of apartments; Winfield's was number eight. Merchant started by pushing the button for the building supervisor but got no response. Next, he tried apartment seven. Nothing there either. He kept pushing buttons until he reached apartment four. A woman's voice said, "Yes?"

"I'm looking for Christian Winfield," he said.

"Ahh . . . you've got the wrong apartment," she said.

"I've been calling him for a couple of weeks," Merchant said. "Any idea how I can get through to him?"

The woman was silent for a moment.

Then she said, "I'll come down."

She was an attractive woman in her early thirties with short brown hair and paint on her T-shirt and shorts. She joined Merchant on the steps.

He reached out to shake her hand, but she pulled back.

"Wet paint," she said. "My daughter is at day care and I'm doing her room over."

"Thanks for coming down," Merchant said. "I hate to bother you, but I talked to Mr. Winfield a few weeks ago, and I haven't been able to get a call back from him since."

"How long ago was this?"

"Oh, I don't know, maybe as much as three, maybe four weeks. I'm from out of town, and I'm back in Boston now for a couple of days."

"I see." The woman frowned. "Were you close to him?"

"No, friend of a friend. I talked to him on the phone, and I'm trying to get in touch with a woman I used to know." Merchant smiled, acted a little embarrassed. "It's sort of a high school romance thing. My family moved to D.C. when I was seventeen. Since then I've gotten married, now I'm divorced. I checked her name out on the Web, and I saw this photo. . . ." Merchant pulled out the news article that showed Winfield with Kathleen Donovan. "He said he could probably put me in touch with her but he had to check with her first because she'd gotten married since —"

The woman put up her paint-spattered hand. "I'm sorry, but I've got to tell you that Christian's dead."

"Dead? How? I know he was an older guy, but he seemed strong on the phone."

"I know, it was shocking for all of us. But I don't think things have gone well for him in recent years. And I think he had a drinking problem. And that's maybe all that happened."

"Why? Is that how he died?"

"Well, yes. Pills and drinking. I don't know all the details, obviously. He was found in his room after a couple days, and it's all pretty horrific for us here in the building. I'm sorry, but I've got to get back to work."

She started to push open the door.

"Ma'am. I am sorry to hear about Mr. Winfield." He held up the photo. "But any chance you saw Katy Donovan? He told me he was going to invite her up to his place to talk about me. Truth is, we were both pretty broken up when my parents moved me, and Mr. Winfield said he wasn't sure she would want to see me again."

The woman looked sympathetic but wary. "Well, I don't know you, so I can't really be of help."

"You don't have to do anything. If you can just tell me if she came by here to see Christian. If she did, and I haven't heard from her, then maybe it means she doesn't want to. I'd just like to know."

He could see the woman was torn. She didn't want to be mean; she didn't want to help some stalker. Finally, she said, "I'm sorry. I did happen to see her come by a few weeks ago. I have no idea what it means that she didn't call you."

"Thank you," Merchant said. Keeping his tone and expression sorrowful but feeling a solid click inside. "That's all I needed to know."

CHAPTER 34

Sarah was waving good-bye to a young couple who had just bought a twenty-four-foot inboard-outboard.

"See you later," she said, as they towed the boat out of the lot.

Lenny came up behind her. "See you later," he mimicked in falsetto, "in about six months when I take it back."

"Jerk," she said. But he was right. She'd tried to push them to a twenty-footer with a practically new Mercury outboard, but the husband had been dead set on the biggest boat he could possibly buy.

Lenny handed her the portable phone. "Speaking of jerks," he said, "here's your boyfriend."

"Hey," she said to Merchant. "Tell me something intelligent and cleanse my palate of this idiot I've got answering my phone."

Lenny smiled and gave her the finger. He began walking back to the office slowly, dawdling in the sunshine.

"You sound like you're in a good mood," Merchant said.

"I am. Just sold a boat. Got a decent stack of paper on boats that I need to repo. My business is cooking. Tell me how Matt's doing."

"Not so good." He told her what he had learned at Ben Pryor's office and at Winfield's apartment.

"Interesting," she said. "So you think Kathleen Gardner is the redhead that our friend Doug Miles saw on *Isabella* with Weir?"

"I don't know. Like you say, it's interesting. Doug said he saw her from a distance, wearing sunglasses and a baseball cap. That he really didn't see her face. From any legal standpoint, that's not an ID. But it's certainly enough to make me want to talk with her."

"When you going to do that?"

"Probably tomorrow morning. I was hoping you'd chase something for me this evening, too."

"Jack, I'm awfully busy right now."

"I know. The good news is that we're back to being paid."

"We?"

"Yeah. Pryor asked how I was set for money, and I told him Ballard Marine Liquidation had gone way past the first three days of pay."

"So this is a BML job now?"

"You said it was from the very beginning. Remember?"

"Vaguely," she said. But, of course, she did. "You expect me to spend more time on this myself, huh?"

"That's right. He's sending you a check for seventy-five hundred dollars."

"Whoopee," she said. "I can make better money running my real business."

"True. But we both know you're a sucker for being paid at all. And if you play your cards right, we can meet for dinner. Maybe even stay together tonight."

"Double whoopee," she said. But she was smiling. "So what do you want me to do?"

She was on the phone all afternoon calling marinas looking for a Black Watch powerboat whose owner was apparently trying to stash it even though he was seven months behind on payments.

She considered trying to follow up Jack's request over the phone, too. She knew the manager of the particular marina in Newport pretty well, but she decided it was best to see what she could learn face-to-face.

Plus there was the part about meeting Jack.

So around six, she got in her truck and started for Newport.

It took her a little over an hour before she was driving down America's Cup Avenue on Newport's waterfront. It was still hot, but she felt good with the windows and sunroof open. She pulled into the parking lot, locked the truck, and headed down toward the docks.

The early evening sun bathed the waterfront in warm, raking light. On a hunch, she continued past the office and went down the ramp to the fuel dock. The dock moved slightly under her feet, and the smell of salt water was sharp and pleasant. Nice time of day to work on the water. Sure enough, she found Walter down on the diesel dock, pumping fuel himself and chatting with the owner of a big Bertram.

"Uh-oh," Walter said when he saw Sarah. "Who're you coming for now? This guy?"

The boat owner was about Walter's age, in his late fifties, with a big gut. He said, "I can only hope you're looking for me."

"You don't want her," Walter said. "Repo woman. Yank the boat right out from under you, leave you swimming."

The guy clutched his heart. "RepoWoman!"

They both found this very amusing.

Sarah tilted her sunglasses, letting the sun reflect just so. "Oh, I've got my eye on you," she said. "You'll never know when or where."

More laughter.

The best way to get things done around the boys.

Walter finished topping off the tanks, and Sarah helped untie the boat. The guy roared off, leaving a big wake behind. Making like he was escaping from the repo woman.

"What a putz," Walter said. "But he tips well. So, who are you really here for?"

"I just came to chat with you, Walter."

"Uh-huh. I ain't got a boat, Sarah, so you can't take it."

"Well, I'll have to settle for some information, then. I understand David Gardner keeps his boat here. The Donzi."

"He did. Hasn't for a while now. He not paying his bills?"

"Just trying to track it down," she said. She didn't want to lie to Walter if she could avoid it.

"It hasn't been here for almost a month."

"He tell you why he moved it?"

"Nope. Didn't tell me shit. No one does."

"Were you here when he took off?"

"No. You need to know exactly when he left?"

"That'd be helpful."

"Well, you know me. Always helpful, never helped. Come on up to the office."

She walked along with him up the ramp. He breathed the salt air in deeply and said, "I tell you, I never get tired of this." He waved at the boats. "All these guys spending millions of dollars on these toys and they're too busy earning the money to hang out. I make a crappy forty-five thousand a year but I'm on the water all day. Who's smarter?"

"You, Walter, you."

"Always a pleasure to have you around, Sarah."

She followed him into his office, and he pulled out a file of receipts. "He keeps an account with us, so let's see the last time he got gas."

He put on a pair of half-glasses and thumbed through the yellow receipts until he found what he was looking for. "Uh-huh. Here you go. Bought eighty bucks' worth of gas just under a month back." He showed her the date.

"Good," she said. "Do you know who was at the pump?"

"Yep. See the initials there? That'd be Russ. You want to talk with him?"

"Sure do."

"Make his day," Walter said. "A real repo woman."

Russ was a skinny teenager with a surprisingly deep voice. He looked a bit trapped when Walter called him up to the office and said, "Talk to this lady. She knows what you've done."

Walter winked at Sarah and pointed toward the door.

"Bye," she said.

"Always a pleasure."

Outside the office, Russ said, "I don't know what he meant."

"He was just teasing you," she said. "Doesn't he do that all the time?"

"Yeah," Russ said. "And I don't know what he means all the time, too."

Sarah laughed.

Russ smiled back. "So, what can I tell you?" They began walking slowly down the dock. She could see him trying to relax, walking along with a woman.

"I'm just trying to track down a boat." She showed him the receipt. "I know this was a while back. . . ."

"Oh, yeah. Mr. Gardner's Donzi. Sweet."

"So you remember."

"Yeah, well, he's a good tipper."

"Is he a nice guy?"

Russ shrugged. Then said, "He's a good tipper."

"Like that, huh? Well, if not one, it's good to be the other. Do you remember the night he took off on the boat?"

"Yeah, actually I do."

"Good memory."

"Well, this was a little different. He came down just around ten in a big hurry. He wanted me to fill the boat up, which I did. But that's not why I remember it. It's because of later."

"What about it?"

"Well, he took off in the boat. You know, ten at night. People do it, but not that often. So I remember thinking it was kind of cool, you know, heading off in a fast boat like that in the dark. But seeing him later. That was the thing."

"He brought the boat back?"

"No. I saw him walking."

"I thought you saw him taking off in the boat."

"I did. But then I saw him in the parking lot as I was leaving. Just around eleven. He was getting into his car."

"So he brought the boat someplace and then came back for the car."

"I guess. But that's not what was weird."

"And what was that?"

"He was wet. His hair was plastered down. It was dark, but I think his clothes were soaked."

"And he didn't say why?"

"He didn't look in the mood to talk. Just got into his BMW and peeled out."

"And you haven't seen the boat since?"

"Nope. Not since that night."

She smiled, and that made him blush all over again. She put out her hand and said, "Russ, you've been a big help."

CHAPTER 35

Sean had known the moment he woke up that he had better do it that day and four o'clock would be his best shot. It wasn't that he felt ready. It was just that soon he wouldn't be able to do anything. The drugs, no real food. He kept getting weaker.

That morning he ate breakfast with his head down, not saying a word to Ella or Laurie. He did the dishes the way Ella told him, and managed to palm a spoon so he could crush the pills into powder.

Lunch came and went. He saw a chance when she made up a can of tomato soup for herself and the chicken and noodle for him and Laurie. But he was afraid Laurie might want the tomato soup, too. She loved it.

Best to wait until four o'clock.

"Making your shake?" Laurie said about ten minutes before four.

"Thinking about it," Ella said.

"Can I have some?"

Sean tried to act normal, but couldn't help but hold his breath. They were all in the living room. He was reading a

Sports Illustrated for the tenth time, and Ella and Laurie were on the floor playing a game.

"Sure, honey," Ella said. "Full of stuff that's good for you. Soy milk, bananas, and a protein mix. You want one glass or two?"

"Zero!" Laurie said and pealed with laughter. "I want zero glasses!"

This was part of their routine.

"You got it," Ella said, touching Laurie's nose. "One for me, zero for you. Now remember, this is my private time, right? No interruptions for a half hour, OK?"

"OK."

At times like this it could seem to Sean like Ella was a friend of his mother and she was just watching them for the day. Except the doors were padlocked from the inside and the keys hung from Ella's belt loop.

Ella stood, stretched, picked up her magazine from the coffee table, and went into the kitchen to make up her shake in the blender. Sean sat planted in his chair. The magazine lay open in front of him, but he didn't even see it. All his energy was focused on listening. He heard the clink of the blender. Heard her open the refrigerator. The pouring of liquid. That would be the soy milk. He'd put half the ground pills into that. He didn't know how much she was giving to him. He'd tasted the soy milk, and the medicine taste didn't seem bad, no worse than his soup.

He hoped it was enough to kill her.

His heart pounded.

He kept trying to read the magazine. An article about the Boston Bruins that he knew by heart.

Maybe ten minutes passed with him staring at the same page. It seemed like an hour and ten minutes.

Laurie worked on her game. It was called Jenga, and it involved stacking little pieces of wood into a tower, then carefully removing one piece at a time. The loser was the one who made the tower fall.

Sean hoped Laurie would stay put. He didn't want her interrupting Ella with her drink.

And for another fifteen minutes or so, that was what she did. She built the tower up and took it down a piece at a time until it crashed. She did it twice by herself.

Then she began to look bored. She turned to look at the doorway to the kitchen and frowned.

He knew she was afraid of Ella, too. Not the same way he was, but she took Ella's order about private time seriously.

She set up the game again. She whispered to him, "Sean, how long's it been?"

"Not yet," he said and knelt down beside her. "Hey, can I play?"

She looked at him doubtfully. He hadn't asked to do that in a while.

But she shrugged. "OK. Me first."

She took her piece out and beamed triumphantly.

His turn. And he realized his mistake. His hand was shaking so badly he almost knocked the tower over.

"Sean, what's the matter?" Laurie said.

"Just tired," he said.

"You're always tired. You're like an old man now."

"Yeah." He breathed out. Tried to relax. Steadied his hand against his knee and pulled out a piece near the middle.

Her turn. With her little finger, she pushed a piece near the bottom out. Success.

She began to chant, "Your turn, Shaky Sean, Shaky Sean, Shaky Sean, it's your turn —"

There was a crashing sound in the kitchen. Glass.

Laurie's head whipped around. "Ella, did you drop something? Ella?"

She stood up.

Sean grabbed her hand. "Wait."

It sounded like Ella was throwing up.

"Let go!" Laurie tried to tug away.

He got to his feet, pulled her back. "Wait." Then he called out in what he hoped was a normal voice, "Ella, are you all right?"

And she came around the corner.

Her face was stark white. She was breathing fast. And she held a long knife in her hand. "You little bastard," she whispered. "I know what you did."

Laurie screamed.

She backed up against Sean, and he pulled her to the corner and said, "Stay there!"

Sean knew there were very few things in the room that could be used as weapons. Ella and Weir had taken care of that. Yet Sean had spent a lot of his time trying to figure what he *could* use. When he turned and saw Ella advancing on him, though, his mind went blank.

She wasn't moving well. She stumbled and used the back of the hand holding the knife to brush the hair from her face. She looked over at Laurie and said, "Go to your room."

"Ella, don't," Laurie said. "Leave us alone."

"Go to your room," she said.

"No, Ella!"

Sean looked at Laurie, saw the ashtray on the shelf behind her. A heavy glass ashtray filled with pennies.

"I tried, honey," Ella said. And raised the knife.

Sean moved beside his sister, got the ashtray in both hands, and flung the pennies into Ella's face. She covered up, stumbling when she did. He brought the ashtray down on her head. She fell to one knee and slashed out with the blade. But her aim was off and she hit his leg with her hand. He hit her again, and she clutched at her head. He tried to peel the knife out of her hand, but her grip was too strong. So he reached down and grabbed the key ring. He yanked as hard as he could and ripped the belt loop.

He stood up, breathing hard. She was still clutching her head. He knew he should keep hitting her until there was no chance of her getting up. But that was one of those things she could do that he couldn't.

He grabbed Laurie by the hand. "We're going," he said. He hustled her into the kitchen. She was crying hard now, so hard she couldn't catch her breath.

"Stop it," he said. "Just stop crying." There were six keys on the ring. One was a car key. One a regular key for the kitchen and front doors. Four of them little padlock keys for his room, Laurie's, and the padlocks that they'd put inside the kitchen and front doors. He slid the first padlock key in. His hands were slippery with sweat, and it took him too long to realize the first key slid in but it wasn't going to work. Same with the second.

"Sean!" Laurie screamed.

He turned. Ella was in the kitchen. But without a word, she stumbled down toward her own room, holding the walls for support.

He slid the third key in. Twisted, it stuck, he tried it even harder. He pulled it out, then put the fourth key in.

"Sean, hurry, she's coming!"

He turned, saw she was coming down the hall. And she had a gun.

He twisted the key, and this one worked.

The door window beside him shattered, blowing glass into his face. He screamed and so did his sister, but he kept moving. He yanked her away from the door and ran outside.

He ran around the corner to the van.

He had never driven a car, but he thought he knew how to do it. They could run into the woods, but even drugged like she was, Ella might be able to go faster than Laurie.

So he ran around to the driver's side, opened the door, and shoved Laurie in. She had to climb, but she was scared and moving as fast as she could. She climbed over to the passenger seat and screamed, "Sean, she's here!"

He put the key in the ignition. Twisted it, and the engine turned, caught. He slid down on the edge of the seat to put his foot on the brake. He knew you had to put the brake on to shift. And then he tried to push the gearshift on the column down — but it wouldn't give.

The windshield cracked in front of him. She was walking toward them, shooting.

He yanked at the gearshift, yelling, "Come on!"

This time it worked because yanking at it pulled it slightly forward. He didn't know you needed to do that. He put it in D and stepped on the gas, but something was wrong. The van moved, but it shuddered and there was a red light under the speedometer that read: "Brake."

But he didn't have his foot on the brake.

He gave the van more gas.

And it stalled.

He looked over and saw that Ella was too close to miss. He shoved Laurie to the floor and tried to yell something to Ella that would make her stop.

But she shot him anyhow.

CHAPTER 36

Kathleen was nearly asleep when Dave slipped into bed.

She started to move away, then came to consciousness just enough to realize this was progress, and she'd better capitalize on it.

She eased back against him and made a sound deep in her throat, half fake and half real, when she felt his rigid erection pressed against her.

But when she reached back to grasp his thigh, she truly came awake and screamed.

He wasn't her husband, but she knew who he was.

She scrambled for the edge of the bed, but then he was on top of her. He put his hand over her mouth and entered her savagely from behind.

She tried to elbow him, but he was ready for that. After that, she fought briefly, then simply buried her face in the pillow.

When he was done, she got into the bathtub and washed herself. She was shaking so hard she just sat in the tub crying, her arms crossed about herself.

He had never done this before.

She looked up to see him standing in the doorway.

She immediately stood and covered herself with a towel. "You raped me." Her voice was flat.

He rolled his eyes and said, "By my count, that's more than the tenth time we've done it. And every other time, you were tackling me." He looked at himself in the mirror, checking his neck. As if she'd been at him there. He'd hammered into her from behind with her arms pinned across her chest, and now the bastard was looking for marks. His silver blond hair, the body, the way he must have worked out to make himself that hard . . . She wondered if he was gay and if he'd just given her HIV.

She took her robe off the bathroom door hook and wrapped it around herself. "Why did you do that?"

"Because you needed a wake-up call."

"What's that mean?" A tear streaked down her face. She couldn't run to the police. Couldn't tell her husband. Couldn't do a damn thing about it. She couldn't believe how deeply she'd let herself in.

"It means we're done waiting."

"Did you bring a tape of the children?"

"No. We're not doing that anymore. You want to see them make it through this, just do your part."

"I — Did she hurt them?"

He looked away.

Kathleen felt like she'd been punched in the stomach. He didn't look guilty — she doubted he could feel such an emotion. But it was evasive. "Are they all right?" she said.

"They won't be, you don't set up something soon. You can count on that."

"Look, I'm trying to get closer, but there's no way he's telling me what you need. You've got to find that boat."

"I'm working that end. You work yours."

She turned from him and went back into the bedroom. She sat down on the edge of the bed.

He began to get dressed.

In spite of everything — the rape, the children he was holding hostage — she felt exasperation. She'd told him how to rob her husband of fifteen million dollars' worth of diamonds and he'd botched it. Now he wanted her to set up the same thing all over again. She said, "You just don't know what you're asking."

"Hey, make it happen. It was your idea in the first place."

She closed her eyes, wanting to scream.

Because he was right.

The element of every good con is to make the other people think they are conning you. She knew that. She had thought maybe when she got married to Dave she would never have to think that way again. But she had started thinking that way again when it became clear that he was cheating on her.

She knew the way he thought: he probably would have put up with her fading looks if she could bear him children. He'd just have his girls on the side, and he'd let Kathleen maintain the home and grow matronly over time. And that would have been fine with her. But after her miscarriages and the gambling problem became a little too obvious, she knew that he would want to trade her in.

This she'd figured out in the abstract.

Then she began to gather evidence. The bright blond strands of hair in the shower stall of their Back Bay condo. Kathleen knew how much her husband liked screwing under the hot streaming water. She'd done that with him herself back when he was cheating on his first. Then there were the averted eyes of the Boston store employees one afternoon when she stopped by unexpectedly. She waited forty-five minutes before he came back from lunch with the new finance manager, Rebecca. She was hanging on to his arm and his every word. Both of them looked flushed, somewhat guilty, and very alive.

Then Kathleen hired the private detective. Got proof in the form of a sheaf of unmistakable photos that Dave was cheating and that Rebecca was indeed a glossier, more nubile model. But the truly troubling photos were those of him meeting with a prominent downtown divorce attorney.

Kathleen had spent exactly one day on tears and fantasies of confronting him. Then she talked to her lawyer and got the bad news on the prenuptial. Even with Dave's philandering, the contract was solid. She'd get five hundred thousand at best. And the lawyer would walk away with a hunk of that.

So she started to plan. Back in her twenties and early thirties, Kathleen had been stunning enough that sometimes men gave her gifts — jewels, cars even. And she sometimes found it more expedient to break things off at a time when the gifts were still worth a good deal. Her friend Christian would help her dispose of those gifts and convert them to cash.

Christian was a gentleman. He always made it feel like he was doing her a favor rather than that she was doing something tawdry like taking her jewels to a pawnshop. She would arrive at his beautiful apartment, have tea, talk about life and the jewelry she was designing those days. She'd shrug off the fur, say she hated it now that she was no longer dating the man. . . . And he'd offer to "take care of it" for her. Later, there would be an envelope of cash. As time went on she began to specialize more in jewelry, diamond jewelry in particular.

That was how she met Dave, when she was shopping in advance and he shuffled aside the salesman to wait on her himself.

Even after she married Dave, Christian would help her from time to time. Dave gave her a generous allowance by any standard, but in the early days of her marriage she tried to hide her gambling problem from him and would occasionally sell some of her less-used jewelry. At these times Christian would suggest that if she ever "needed anything bigger" she should call him.

Which was exactly what she did after seeing her lawyer. Christian told her his condo was being painted, so they met at the Ritz for lunch. He looked older, less vital than she remembered, which only made sense. She hadn't seen him in several years: more settled in her marriage, she simply pressed Dave for more money, and he reluctantly gave in.

Christian had to be pushing seventy-five. At lunch he wore one of his Brooks Brothers suits and bow ties to go with his lean frame, gray hair, and bright blue eyes. He listened carefully to her story, held her hand, and said, "Kathleen, if you and I put our heads together, I'm confident we'll be able to devise a substantially better exit strategy than your lawyer suggested. Now, knowing you as I do, I suspect you already have something in mind?"

So she told him. How her husband didn't own the fastest growing chain of jewelry stores in New England on price and selection alone.

"Money laundering," she said. "The jewelry business is perfect for it, and Dave never has been one to pass up an opportunity."

Christian smiled. "He sells legitimate diamonds in exchange for large amounts of, let's say, drug money . . . and what? A bushel basket full of cash receipts?"

"That's right. And they can resell the diamonds or ship them out. Highly portable, easy to smuggle."

Christian said, "How much are we talking?"

"I don't know for sure. But when we first got married, we went up to our vacation place in Maine for a long weekend and he got stinking drunk. He had just bought the place because I wanted it, and then he started whining about the risk he'd taken to get it. Mainly blowing off steam, because it scares him when he pulls these things off. They put millions of dollars' worth of diamonds together and receive millions in cash back. All done late at night, at different drop points. Scary stuff with scary people."

"These are drug people?"

"That's what he said. Colombians."

"And he knows that you know about this business?"

"No. He was really drunk that night, and the next morning I just told him he passed out early. He's never talked about it since, but I'm pretty sure I can read when he's about to do it. He gets nervous as a cat, and spends a lot of time talking on the phone out of his office at home. Very guarded. Then it blows over, and he's flush again, and no expense is too much."

"You think he's going to be setting up another one soon, then?"

"Oh yeah. All the signs are there. And if he's going to divorce me, I better get this done now or I'll never be close enough again."

"Mmmmm," Christian said, thinking.

"But this is the thing," she said. "I don't want Dave getting hurt. He's a creep, but he doesn't deserve that."

"Of course not." He sipped his tea. "And if the cash is taken, the Colombians will kill him."

He spent a few more moments in silence, then said, "Well, your exit plan seems clear. We arrange to take the diamonds just before the swap. The Colombians keep their cash. I put together the sale of the diamonds for you, and after your divorce you wait a reasonable time before you move far away from your ex-husband and begin to enjoy your financial freedom."

"Can you still put that all together?" She never would have asked him that before, but now he looked so old.

He laughed. "Don't worry about a thing, Kathleen. This is what I do. And I've got just the young man in mind to handle the logistics."

And so Weir had appeared on the scene two nights later. It was exciting to have the plan under way, and he was handsome and attentive. She thought it would be safest to keep him close, so she took him to her bed that very night and told him everything she knew.

In the coming weeks, she got him into both of Dave's cars,

the BMW and the Porsche. He could tape just Dave's side of the conversation in the cars, but with the phone taps in the Newport and Back Bay home offices, he could get both sides.

Weir and Kathleen would meet at a motel or down at the Newport home at night and they'd listen to the tapes together. He made her feel so much better on nights when the tapes held conversations between Rebecca and Dave about what they'd done in the hotel room that day. It became obvious that Rebecca was more than just her husband's lover. As the finance manager for all the stores, she was actively involved in the money laundering. The receipts ostensibly came from any number of the twenty-nine store locations.

Bit by bit, Kathleen and Weir were able to piece together the plan for the next drop. It was to be a rendezvous on the water, at the mouth of Narragansett Bay. Dave was to take the diamonds on his Donzi speedboat and receive fifteen million in cash in exchange for them. Each diamond would have the appropriate paperwork and cash receipts attached.

Weir had assured her that no one would get hurt. He showed her the Taser gun, told her he had a plan for pulling Dave's car over in Jamestown with a Ford outfitted with a dashboard light, like an unmarked state cruiser. "The Colombians will come and go to the rendezvous point, they'll never be involved. And, hey, Dave might even be able to file an insurance claim for the stolen diamonds. Life goes on."

Kathleen had relied on him for the details and trusted Christian's word that "he knows what he's doing."

The way it actually turned out, however, was different. Weir hadn't exactly shared all the details with her. But the upshot of it was that he didn't rob her husband on the road, but had hidden in the small cabin of the Donzi. Most likely he had intended to try to rip off the Colombians, too, but Dave messed things up by going down below just outside Newport Harbor. They fought briefly, but Dave surprised Weir by jumping overboard the first chance he got.

Kathleen could have told him. Her husband was not a brave man.

Weir could probably have killed him, but it was pitch dark and the wind was coming up, making the waves break. He couldn't find the flashlight on the boat, and even though he circled looking for Dave, he couldn't find him. Mainly, he had no particular reason to care if Dave lived or not. He simply took off in the boat for a rendezvous point of his own on Block Island, where he had his girlfriend waiting for him in another boat. Apparently, he was planning to go to New York and use another fence to sell the diamonds — cutting Kathleen and Christian out of the deal.

But he hit something along the way. Pounding through the waves in the dark. Hit a partially submerged log, a telephone pole maybe. Or a cargo box. Just a part of the ocean's drifting trash. Ripped the bottom right out of the boat. Pure bad luck he called it. Could happen to anyone.

She suspected Weir had said that many times in his life. Either way, the boat went down fast with the diamonds aboard, and he was left calling his girlfriend for help on the cell phone. He grabbed a seat cushion and drifted for hours until she found him just after dawn, half dead from exposure. They had only the vaguest idea of where the Donzi had gone down.

Kathleen didn't hear from him for a week, until he came back telling her she had to help him "intercept another shipment." She told him that it was impossible and they'd better damn well get the diamonds he'd lost at sea. And since she no longer trusted him, she arranged for the boat and diver. She got Ronnie McNaughton to introduce her to his brother, who she knew needed the money and was tough enough to keep Weir in line. She told them both she would be going out with them during the search.

She also called Christian, but he didn't return her calls. Finally she went to his building and buzzed every apartment except his.

Eventually someone buzzed her through, and she went up to his door, knocked quietly, and waited for Christian to let her in.

The old man who opened the door was Christian, but he bore little resemblance to the dapper man at the Ritz-Carlton. He was unshaven, dressed in a T-shirt and an old pair of suit pants. He was clearly drunk.

He didn't recognize her at first.

And then he did, and he looked frightened, then began shaking his head in abject apology.

"Kathleen," he said. "Kathleen, I'm sorry. I just don't have the resources or the contacts I once had. I know he was a mistake, I know."

He talked for a long time after that, his words slurring together. Telling her how disappointed he was. That he was getting old and "this was to be my retirement fund."

But she didn't really listen.

"Shut up," she said, finally. She reached over and shook him.

That stopped his blather for a moment.

"If I get them back, can you still move them?" she said.

"I thought I could, but I'm not sure. I'm not sure of anything anymore."

She just stood there in the lonely old man's apartment, realizing for the first time what a small-timer the designer of her "exit strategy" had become.

Perhaps had always been.

She turned and left him alone. Two weeks later, she read that he had committed suicide. She didn't go to his funeral, she told herself she didn't care.

But still, the night that he was buried, she did something she hadn't done since she was a little girl. She cried herself to sleep.

Now Kathleen just felt so damn tired. Probably to recoup his loss, it looked like Dave had torched his Boston store, taking the whole building to the ground. He was trying hard to get the insurance company to pay for it, but they were balking.

All in all, the safest bet for Kathleen would be to use the photos she had of Dave and Rebecca and file for divorce. Go for the five hundred thousand and cut her losses.

That would be the safest plan.

But with Weir around her neck, that was no longer an option.

He bent down so his face was right in hers. He said, "Those kids are depending upon you to set me up again. What are you going to do?"

She said again, "You just don't know what you're asking."

He raised his hand to hit her and she snapped, "Dave will see the bruise, you idiot!"

That made him pause.

She stood up, went to her nightstand, opened the drawer, and took out a pack of cigarettes and a lighter. She tried not to smoke, but sometimes she needed them.

Her hands were shaking. She was aware of him right behind her, aware that he could break loose at any moment. She was also very aware that six inches deeper into the drawer was a revolver Dave had bought years ago. She'd been going to a firing range in East Greenwich twice a week since Weir had come back into her life. Before this was over, she knew she was going to have to use it. And maybe now was the time. She could tell the police he had broken in, she had been raped.

But those kids. And Ella.

They'd talk.

Even though she wanted the children safe, she wanted to get through this thing without going to prison. So she kept her back to him and closed the drawer. She gestured to the table and two chairs she had under the window. "Let's talk."

Not surprisingly, he sat down.

He was a dangerous, self-obsessed screwup. But he was

still just as willing as the next guy to have Mommy make everything better. She tried to keep her voice calm and practical. "Look," she said. "Let's think this through. Have you had any luck finding the chart?"

"Yeah. Ronnie came home. He had it with him."

She paused. "Is he all right?"

The man was a loser, but nevertheless she had brought him and his brother into this, so she felt somewhat responsible.

"Couldn't be better," Weir said.

"Meaning you killed him?"

"That's right."

"Jesus." She put her head in her hands. Everything he touched . . . First the Coulters, then Captain McNaughton, now Ronnie. She really should have shot Weir a few minutes ago, when she had the chance.

"C'mon, stick with me," he said. "McNaughton brought this on himself and his brother by blackmailing me."

There was an element of truth in that, and for the sake of her own conscience, she latched on to it. McNaughton and Ronnie had found the Donzi with the sonar towfish on their own and had dropped a marker over it. McNaughton marked the coordinates on a chart, and after the problem with the Coulters, he told Weir he would hold on to the $25,000 deposit and wanted another $25,000 and proof that the children were home safe before he'd take Weir to the site and do the dive.

Apparently, he thought he could have his cake and eat it, too.

So, in a way, he did deserve it.

You just had to spend a little time with Weir to know that his impulse control was not good. He lost his temper, killed the captain with a choke hold, and blew up *Isabella* to cover.

She raised her head and said, dully, "So you've got the chart. What's the problem? Just dive down and get the briefcase."

"It's not that easy. A dive to a hundred and forty feet is complicated." He went on to talk about nitrogen narcosis, about decompression time, and a lot of other nonsense.

She wasn't sure if she was hearing right. *This* was the problem?

But she kept her tone reasonable. "OK, we've got to consider which is the bigger problem. I've worked on Dave, I've listened carefully, I've got nothing, *nothing* that suggests he's going to do another setup with the Colombians anytime soon. He's scared witless."

"That's not up to him. It's up to them."

"And have you heard him say anything on the telephone or car tapes that suggests they are putting something together?"

"No. But you're his wife, damn it. Find out."

"I have. The answer is no, he's not doing it."

He took out his cell phone. "All right. So I call Ella and tell her the baby-sitting gig is over. Do what she wants to do."

"Goddamn it," Kathleen said. "I can't make Dave launder more cash just because you want me to. Even you can understand that, can't you?"

"What I understand is that you owe me a way to get fifteen million in diamonds. Whether I rip hubby off again, or you get me into one of his stores with the security system off, I don't care. He did it in Boston, we can do it."

"For Christ's sakes, you think he comes home and says, 'By the way, honey, you want the security code to the Lexington store?'" She took a deep breath. Tried for that calm tone again. "Look, the only way it's going to happen is that boat. That's our shot. Get somebody else to do the dive if you can't."

"I told you it's not that easy."

He was getting angry.

But she kept after him awhile longer. Gently, trying to be his partner instead of the woman he had just raped. Before long, he was complaining to her like she was his big sister. It made her want to spit at him, to scratch his eyes out. He whined for a while about things she already knew, Mc-Naughton's blackmail, the cash Ronnie gambled away, Ella being on the verge of totally losing it.

One problem after another, all stemming from his own lack of self-control and poor judgment.

But she kept her voice calm. "I've got enough cash to rent a boat and hire another diver," she said.

"Yeah, but that's just somebody else I have to kill," he said. "Every time I do that, the risk of getting caught goes up."

She forced herself to take his hand. "Tell me the real reason why you don't want to do the dive yourself," she said.

So he did.

It was his ears. He couldn't equalize the pressure in his ears to get to that kind of depth.

With that last bit, she suddenly felt the urge to laugh. His ears. His goddamn ears, and people's lives were hanging in the balance. It truly would be funny if her life wasn't one of them.

Hers and the lives of those two children who had just happened to be in the wrong place at the wrong time.

CHAPTER 37

After a late breakfast at an expensive little restaurant over-looking Newport Harbor, Merchant and Sarah drove out of the center and went to the former jai alai courts.

They parked the truck and walked in just far enough apart that they didn't look like they were together. There were two guards at the front lobby, both men. Sarah had the packet of photographs in hand. She said, "Hi, guys. I'm hoping you can help me," while Merchant kept going straight through the double doors into the slot machine rooms.

Over the next fifteen minutes or so, he walked slowly through each room. He had been there once years ago, when the place still had live jai alai. Gambling had always been the heart of the sport, but at least then there had been some sweat involved.

Now the only athletes at ten in the morning were chain smokers frittering through their cash as fast as they could. The sheer number of slot machines was hard to comprehend, well into the hundreds. He took an escalator to the next floor and found a simulcast room where not only could you watch dif-ferent sports playing across a bank of more than a dozen televisions but each chair in front of the bank had its own personal monitor and betting station.

Even though there was nothing overtly sexual about the place except a few graphics on some of the machines, the feel was similar to that of a porn theater and about as uplifting.

He was glad to leave.

Sarah was waiting in the truck behind the wheel. "Thought I lost you to the slots," she said.

"Not for me. How about for anyone else we know?"

"They didn't recognize David Gardner or Greg McNaughton. Ronnie, one of them said he was pretty sure he recognized him. The other one said, 'He looks like every other mutt we see here, so how do you know?' They also pointed out that they paid very little attention to guys unless they cause trouble. Kathleen, on the other hand, she's a different story."

"Definitely remember her?"

"Oh yeah. She had a decent win a little while back and tipped the tall one to walk her to her Mercedes. He's seen her plenty of times before. She's got the itch."

"Good job, Sarah."

She started the engine. "What do you expect, with my looks, my charm?"

"How much did you tip them?"

"Only twenty apiece."

"Practically irresistible," he said.

The Gardners' house was a little way past the Fort Adams State Park entrance. It was a large cape with natural gray shingles and a spectacular view of Narragansett Bay and the Newport Bridge.

They parked in the crushed shell driveway, Merchant took his backpack out of the backseat, and they walked up to the front door. Merchant rang the doorbell. They waited a few minutes, hearing someone moving inside the house. Then Kathleen Gardner opened the door.

She was probably pretty most of the time, but right now she looked as if she'd spent a rough night. Dark circles under her eyes, and her light skin was so pale that it seemed almost translucent.

"Yes, what?" She raised her hand against the sunlight.

"Mrs. Gardner?"

"Yes?"

Merchant introduced himself and Sarah. "I'm sorry to bother you, but it'd be a great help if we could talk to you for a few minutes."

"I'm sorry, I just woke up. . . . What's this about?"

"Can we come in and talk with you about that?"

"Well . . . who are you again?"

He reintroduced them. He had the feeling she was acting more distracted than she really was. It was after ten-thirty and she was fully dressed in jeans and a mannish white shirt. She didn't look like someone who had just woken up but like someone who hadn't slept at all.

On an impulse, he said, "Are you all right, Mrs. Gardner?"

Her head jerked back slightly.

Then she smiled. He could see how pretty she could be. "I'm fine, thank you, but I still don't know why you're here."

"Can I show you something?" Merchant said. He reached into his backpack and pulled out the hospital security videotape.

"What now?" she said. "Blackmail before breakfast?"

"Nothing like that, ma'am," Merchant said, smiling as if her joke didn't ring false. "We're just hoping you can help identify someone for us."

"Who?"

"Well, that's what we'd like to know. Can I show you?"

When she hesitated, Sarah said, "Mrs. Gardner, we'll be very quick."

"Can I see some ID?"

They gave her their business cards and driver's licenses.

"Marine repossession," she said. "Does this have to do with Dave's boat? Because if it does, you'll have to call him."

"Did something happen to his boat?" Merchant said.

"Not that I know of . . . Again, why are you here?"

"To help identify someone. If I could show you the tape . . ."

She glanced over her shoulder, then sighed. "You're persistent. I suppose you can come in for a few minutes."

They followed her in. The house was simply but expensively furnished. She led them to the kitchen and pointed to a television and VCR combination on a shelf at the end of the room.

Merchant turned on the unit and pushed the tape in.

She took a step forward and watched. Her face remained blank. Carefully so, in Merchant's opinion.

After a moment, she said, "Is that you?"

"That's right."

"Well, that's a terrible thing to see. Again, I'm perplexed as to why you're showing me."

"Do you know who he is?" Merchant said, pointing to Weir running down the stairs.

"No idea," she said. She waved her hand in the direction of the hallway. "Listen, I think I've been generous with my time, but I really don't have anything to tell you."

He met her eyes and said, "We're here for Sean and Laurie Coulter."

And waited.

There was something. A slight pulling back of her head. Her eyes widened ever so slightly. A stiffening of her whole body.

Then she said, "Who? What do you mean?"

Merchant laid their pictures on the counter. "You know who I mean."

The photos rattled her. "I have no idea what you're talking about!"

"Yeah, you do," he said. "We even know how you first met Matt." He laid the article from *Retail Display Monthly* on the counter. "He interviewed you."

"That was years ago — I barely remember that!"

"Can you help us find them?" Sarah said.

"I don't know who you're talking about," she said.

"Are they alive?" Merchant said.

She looked over to Sarah. "You two are talking nonsense to me — a man I met I don't know how many years ago and I'm supposed to know something about his family —"

"Please, Mrs. Gardner," Sarah said. "We just want to find them. Help us."

She hesitated.

Then shook her head. "Listen, I was crazy to let you in here. Two strangers. It's time for you to go."

"Mrs. Gardner, there are witnesses," Merchant said.

That stopped her.

"Witnesses to what?"

"You," he said. "You and the man on the tape. Going out on Captain McNaughton's boat. Ronnie's brother. So why are you lying to us?"

"Lying to you? Who do think you are?"

"We know that you're friends with Ronnie McNaughton, Mrs. Gardner. We know about the gambling. We've got witnesses that put you together with him, too."

She put her hand up. "Stop. Stop right there."

"It's not stopping here," Merchant said. "We want this family back."

"I have no idea what you're talking about."

"Tell us about your relationship with Ronnie Mc-Naughton."

She crossed her arms over her breasts. "Listen, you've got some little crumb of something and you're blowing this all out of proportion."

"The crumb being you know Ronnie."

"No. Well, maybe, I've met lots of people at jai alai, I don't remember names, they're just people around — "

"Then explain to us," Sarah said. "And while you're at it, explain to us what happened to your husband's boat."

Mrs. Gardner looked at them. Walked back to her kitchen counter and picked up their business cards. Seemed to gather herself. She looked at them carefully. "Is that what this is about? His goddamn boat?"

"Among other things," Merchant said.

"Salvage, that kind of thing? Is that what you do?"

Merchant said, "Right now I'm looking for answers."

"Ultimately, you're looking for what? Money?" she said. "You're trying to shake me down for something?"

"Answers," Merchant said. "Tell me about Ronnie. Tell me about Weir."

She fingered the cards, looked at each of them. Something harder than the rich lady of the house emerged. She said, "I've got nothing to say to either of you. You're fishing. I don't know why you came to me to do so, but that's what you're doing. Now get out of my house."

They kept asking questions, but she stopped answering.

After just a minute or two of that, they left.

CHAPTER 38

Weir stepped into the kitchen.

Kathleen was sitting at the counter, her head in her hands. Feeling sorry for herself, he supposed.

"You screwed up," he said. "You admitted to knowing Ronnie."

He looked through the venetian blinds at Merchant and the girl getting into their truck.

He said, "What's her name again?"

"Sarah Ballard," Kathleen said.

"Give me their cards."

She did.

"Marine repossession," he said. "That was good, though, you asking if they did salvage. Smart."

"Yeah," Kathleen said. "I'm smart."

"I'll give you that, Katy. Any time." He looked back at her and smiled. She was still striking, but her looks had definitely begun to fade in the time he'd known her. Strange how fast some women lost it.

"It's been rough," he said. "But you stick with me like you have and you'll get your cut. And we'll get those kids settled in a foster home someplace. It'll all work out."

She said, "You better get going."

He headed out just after Merchant and the girl drove off.

Weir had left the Ford van he'd rented in New York a couple of blocks away and jogged to it as soon as their truck turned the corner. He took off fairly fast, pushing the Ford along until he got the truck back in sight. Then he eased off, putting a reasonable distance between them.

Weir reached into his overnight bag, rummaging until he found a baseball hat and some sunglasses. Not much, but he knew he'd have to get closer once they got into Newport center or he'd lose them at a stoplight.

Sure enough, once they were in the town, he was able to keep only a couple of cars between them. They pulled into a parking lot behind one of the B and B's on America's Cup Avenue, and Merchant got out. He had his bag over his shoulder, and he walked around to the driver's side and talked to the woman for a few minutes, kissed her, then got into a beat-looking Saab.

Decision time, Weir thought. Follow him, follow her?

But then he got a good look at Sarah's face as she pulled back into traffic.

Quite the looker. Reminded him of Ella. And that gave him a sense of ownership.

He swung in a few cars behind her.

Even though he had a lot to do, he was content for the time being with following a pretty woman home.

He followed her off Route 195 for the New Bedford exit. He had never been there before, and after a slow ride past run-down houses and shops, they entered a surprisingly pretty and historic town. She went down by the waterfront and then over a bridge, where she took an immediate left down the driveway of a marina. He waited a bit there, then drove into the parking lot of the marina to see her walking down to a boat.

She climbed aboard a good-size trawler, forty feet or more. Nice-looking boat. Not fast but well made. Boom off the stern. Once the girl was down below, he got out of the van and walked to the edge of the parking lot. Playing the tourist, looking at the pretty boats.

He kept walking until he could get a clear view of the stern of her boat. Swim ladder. And in the slip beside it was a good-size Mako with twin outboards. It was custom painted with the same trim as the trawler. Had to be hers.

Interesting.

He walked back to the van, got binoculars from his bag, and came back to take a closer look at the Mako.

Very interesting.

There were dive tanks attached to brackets just aft of the console.

He stretched his neck, moving side to side. Thinking. Feeling himself heat up. Knowing that if he just followed his instincts, he'd come up with a good excuse as to why he needed to go after that girl right now.

And here she might be the answer to his problems in one complete package.

So it was almost a relief when the girl came out and he no longer had the option of surprising her on the boat. She had a blue backpack slung over her shoulder, and she stepped off her trawler and began heading back to the ramp.

He got into his van and took off before she got to the parking lot. He let her pass him on the way out, then followed her back over the bridge and along the town coastline. She pulled into a boat lot full of used power and sailboats. She got out and walked over to two big guys who were power-washing a big Bayliner.

Just from the body language, the way they stopped to talk to her, Weir could tell she was the boss. Whether or not they really did salvage work, this girl had a yard full of boats. Plus two back at the dock. One big enough to accommodate lots of people, handle a tow, and with a swim deck for divers. The other, a fast dive boat with four tanks ready and waiting.

Just like his father had always tried to tell him, sometimes it pays to have a little patience.

CHAPTER 39

Merchant headed back to Boston and was downtown just before one o'clock. He parked in the garage underneath Boston Common, took his backpack, and climbed up the stairs into the bright sunlight. He walked over the bridge in the Garden back to Newbury Street. It was a warm afternoon, pleasant.

Nice time of day to go sling a little mud on the Gardners' marriage.

Merchant used his cell phone to call their home, and a man answered. "Gardner," he said. "What's up?"

Faintly in the background, Merchant could hear a woman say, "Dave . . ." and then what sounded like Gardner snapping his fingers.

"Who's there?" Gardner said, impatiently.

Merchant ended the call.

Their building was in the second block of Newbury Street, just down from the corner of Berkeley Street. It was on the right side. He went into the foyer and saw that there were only five buttons. It looked as if each tenant had a floor, and the Gardners had the penthouse. Merchant went to the café across the street, got a cup of coffee and a fresh blueberry muffin, and settled in to wait for Gardner's woman guest to leave.

He had to wait only a half hour before Gardner came down to the front door with a young woman with long blond hair. They didn't kiss; perhaps that was his idea of being discreet. But Gardner watched her walk away, and she gave him a look and smile over her shoulder that anyone watching would have been able to read.

As it was, Merchant was fairly certain he was the only one looking. He was halfway across the street as Gardner started to close the door.

"Just a moment, Mr. Gardner," he said. He didn't speak loudly, and he looked to his left to see if the woman noticed.

She didn't.

Gardner noticed Merchant looking, though, and it seemed to worry him. "Are you are reporter?" he said.

"Not even close." Merchant climbed the steps quickly to the landing beside Gardner. He was a good-size guy, heavier than Merchant would have assumed from the photos. Carefully trimmed black goatee, hair gelled back in place. Ready for an ad in GQ. Except he looked tired.

Another similarity with his wife.

"A cop?" Gardner asked.

"No."

Gardner flashed a quick smile. "You sure about that? You look like one."

Merchant shook his head. "That's in the past." He handed Gardner one of his Ballard Marine Liquidation cards.

Gardner glanced at the card, apparently saw nothing worth his time, and turned to the door. Over his shoulder he said, "I'll check with my accountant. If I'm behind on boat payments, I'll take care of it."

"Be a shame to be making payments on a boat you're not even using," Merchant said.

That slowed Gardner a bit. He looked over his shoulder and said, "Least of my worries."

"I'd guess not. After talking with your wife this morning, I confirmed that your boat has been gone for a little more than a month now. In fact, it went missing the night before your fire here in Boston."

That stopped Gardner. He turned around. "You're talking to my wife? About my goddamn boat?"

"About a lot of things, Mr. Gardner. And I'd like to talk with you. Can we go upstairs?"

Gardner stared at him, his hands on his hips. "What the hell does my wife have to do with anything?"

He seemed to mean it.

Merchant said, "That's an attitude that can get you in trouble."

"Who says I'm in trouble?"

"Anyone who can read a newspaper."

"Yeah, well that's not a good enough qualification to come up to my condo."

"How about a discussion of what your wife's been doing."

That gave Gardner pause.

Merchant continued, "A discussion that hasn't made it to the newspapers yet."

"So you *are* a reporter."

"No. But I know a few. And all your story needs is a little boost to bring it back to life — that missing boat will do just the trick."

Gardner seemed to take that in. Then slid his key into the lock and said, "What goddamned next? All right, come on up."

As Merchant followed Gardner into the small elevator, he saw the elegant line of his sport jacket was broken by what looked to be the grip of a handgun in the small of his back.

It wasn't uncommon for jewelers to carry them but not

what Merchant would have expected of someone at Gardner's level.

Merchant considered disarming him but decided against it. Whatever chance they had at a conversation would cease if he manhandled the guy.

Once out of the elevator, Gardner opened the door.

Like the home in the Newport, the condo was expensively furnished, but it felt more masculine. As if the condo was his and the Newport home was Kathleen's. There was the faint smell of perfume in the air and a half-full bottle of wine on the kitchen island.

Gardner pulled up a stool at the island and indicated that Merchant should sit on the other side. "So who are you exactly, and what have you got to tell me about Kathleen?"

"First, let me ask you this, Mr. Gardner. . . ." Merchant took out the packet of the Coulters' photos. "Do you know any of these people?" He laid them on the granite countertop. He pointed to Matt in the family picture. "How about him?"

Gardner barely looked. "No," he said.

"Please look carefully."

Gardner sighed, looked over the photos with exaggerated patience, then paused looking at the family photo. Maybe Merchant saw some hesitation there. But he couldn't be sure.

Gardner said, "So, typical American family. Who are they?"

"The Coulters. Do you know Matt Coulter? Cecilia Coulter?"

"Can't say I do. And I'm going to ask you again — who are you and what have you got to say about Kathleen?"

"I was once a cop — DEA. I'm not anymore. But I'm working on something I care about quite a bit. And either my work can hurt you or you can help me and I'll leave you to go about your business."

"Selling jewelry is my business."

"Well, sometimes home life intrudes on business life, Mr. Gardner. Do you know your wife has been included as part of a murder investigation?"

"What?"

"You ever hear of Captain Greg McNaughton? Or his brother, Ronnie?"

"No."

"So it'd surprise you to find that your wife was going out on Captain McNaughton's boat?"

"Was this a charter boat?"

"A dive boat."

"Well, nothing surprises me with Kathleen. I didn't know of her diving, but she and I go our own ways, Merchant. And she has lots of time on her hands, so she's always doing whale watches and nature walks and all that kind of crap. Diving wouldn't surprise me. This Captain McNaughton is dead?"

"Yes. And his brother, Ronnie."

"How were they killed? And when?"

Merchant told him about the explosion on McNaughton's boat and finding Ronnie's body.

"And how does that tie in to Kathleen?"

"She knew Ronnie through Newport jai alai. And a witness has her going on their boat."

Neither point was actually solid, but Merchant was willing to lie for the time being. He could apologize later, if need be.

Gardner raised his hands and dropped them on the counter. "Gambling. Yeah, she's got a problem. I guess running into lowlifes is one of them. But the fact she hires this Ronnie's brother to go out on a cruise or a dive, I don't see how that's an issue. Lots of people have probably hired them, why don't you go talk to them?"

"Because there's another guy she knows that's more of a problem. You know of a guy by the name of Weir? Sometimes calls himself Dr. Weir?"

"Never heard of him."

Merchant took opened his backpack and pointed to the VCR in the corner of the kitchen. "May I?"

"Knock yourself out."

Merchant played the tape. Pretty much watching Gardner as he watched the screen. And he saw a reaction when Weir appeared. Much the way his wife's had, Gardner's eyes widened slightly and his face went carefully blank.

When the tape was over, he said, "So, you got your ass kicked. What is it you expect me to tell you?"

"You know who he is?"

"No."

"Ever see him before?"

"Never."

"Not even the night your boat got stolen?"

"Who said it got stolen? It's just being repaired."

"Not what I heard."

"Yeah, what'd you hear?"

"That you took off in your boat just fine. But you came walking back later, clothes still soaking."

"Yeah, so I slipped off my boat, big deal. I was helping the repair guys load it onto the trailer and I fell."

"Tell me the name of the shop," Merchant said. "And what's the repair?"

"None of your goddamn business. Look, Merchant, you come to me with some coincidences. I'll talk to my wife maybe, but that's between me and her. So if you've got nothing else, I've got other things to do."

Merchant said, "Unless you give me something useful, I'm going to the reporters who've been covering your fire and tell them there may be some interesting new angles."

"You've got nothing!"

"Really?" Merchant began to check off points on his fingers. "How about I put it to them like this: one, your wife has been seen accompanying a man who tried to kill a wounded father of two in his hospital bed. Two, she's been going out on a hired dive boat with the assailant. Three, both the dive boat's skipper and his brother, Ronnie McNaughton, have been killed violently. Four, your wife gambled with Ronnie at the Newport jai alai courts, which was how she probably met him. Five, your boat was stolen just a week before she started going out on the dive boat — "

"I told you it's in for repairs — "

Merchant rolled on. "Six, the night after your boat was stolen your store suddenly bursts into flames, and seven, you are now looking for your insurance company to compensate you for thirty million dollars' worth of stolen diamonds."

Gardner's face had drained of color.

"I need to know where your boat is, Gardner, and I need to know right now. And when I asked you to tell me if you know these people, I saw something in your face. Now give it up to me right now, or I'll let the *Globe,* the *Herald,* and a bunch of cops ask the same questions in public."

Gardner's chest was rising and falling rapidly. He swore softly under his breath, then leaned against the counter. "My goddamn wife. She's got nothing to do but enjoy the life I provide her, I don't ask a frigging thing . . . and now you come around. You've got maybes and half ideas, but you've got no proof. But you can screw up my business, and you can certainly screw up my insurance payout."

"That's true, Gardner. So what's it going to be?"

"What are you looking for, Merchant? Money? I'm pretty tapped out right now, but I can probably put enough cash together to take care of a nuisance thing. That's all you are to me."

"I'm not interested in that. I've got questions and you've got answers."

Gardner sat there, thinking. Clearly trying to control his anger and come up with an answer that'd get Merchant out of his face. Finally he said, "OK. The boat, I don't know where it is. It probably was stolen. But there was no way I was going to make an insurance claim against it at the same time I was making one for the fire."

"C'mon," Merchant said. "That doesn't make sense. That has to be a fifty-thousand-dollar boat."

"Doesn't mean a damn thing. I'm looking at millions on the diamonds, and there was enough pressure on this without me tacking on a stolen boat. Which was just plain coincidence."

Merchant made a face. "This is bull."

"That's what happened." Gardner put his hand up to stop Merchant's next question. "Look, you're working for these people, right? This Coulter guy, right?"

"What have you got to tell me?"

"Just this . . . the name's familiar. The face is familiar." He tapped on the family photo at Matt. "You asked for something and I'll tell you. I know this guy, or at least recognize him. Something to do with the business, but I can't say what. Retail supplier or something. I've seen him, heard the name. Met him at a trade show or something like that."

"I know about that already. *Retail Display Monthly*. He did an interview with you and your wife several years ago."

"Yeah, OK. That's it, I knew the name was familiar."

"So your wife would know him, too."

"I suppose. She might recognize him, might not. Why?"

Merchant slid the photos of the Coulters closer to Gardner. "Just so you understand. Coulter's wife is dead. His two children are gone. Disappeared."

"I don't know what you're talking about."

Merchant told him about Coulter appearing at his dock, about the search for his family. "He's the guy that Weir tried to kill in the hospital."

Gardner seemed genuinely bewildered. "Look, my wife's not a saint, but she wouldn't do anything to hurt kids. She's just not that kind of person."

"Well, she's hooked up with someone who'd do anything.

This guy Weir. When I put it all together, I see your boat disappearing, your wife out there with Weir soon after . . . and then the Coulters' sailboat sinks right about the same time."

"You think they picked them up or something?"

"It seems likely from what Coulter told me."

"Did they or didn't they?"

"He can't be sure."

"Why not?"

Merchant told him about Coulter's amnesia.

"For Christ's sakes, you're threatening my business, my reputation, and your guy's got amnesia."

"That's the direction my investigation has gone," Merchant said. "So your business problems don't add up to a lot for me. Whatever your part is, I don't really care —"

"What do you mean, my part?"

"Money laundering. Arson. I'm ex-DEA, so I tend to see drugs everywhere. Maybe it's something else, but the cops latched on to it and I'm beginning to see it their way. You laundering money for the Colombians, Gardner?"

Merchant was fishing with the last bit, but it got a reaction. "That bitch! Did she say that?"

Merchant waved that away. "I don't care, Gardner. I want to know what happened. Did your wife and Weir get together and decide to rip you off? Is that why you torched the place, to recover jewels that were stolen from you?"

"Who've you talked to about this?" Gardner said.

"Don't worry about that. Just answer my question."

"I need to know." His voice was quavering. Going for indignation, but it sounded to Merchant like he'd hit the mark.

"Is that why your boat is gone?" he said. "Did he rob you on your boat?"

Merchant heard something.

It was out in the hallway, the elevator.

Gardner took his hand from his lap and put his cell phone on the counter. The light was glowing on the screen. It was on.

Someone had been listening to their conversation.

"You brought this on yourself, buddy," he said and switched the phone off.

Gardner was on the living room side of the counter, and he turned and was halfway to the door before Merchant caught up with him.

Merchant wrapped his left arm around Gardner's neck and hauled him back, reaching for Gardner's handgun at the same time.

"Jesus —"

Gardner fought briefly, trying to elbow Merchant, but he was too close for it to matter much. And he stopped entirely when Merchant put his gun to his head.

The door opened, and a Hispanic man Merchant had never seen before came in holding a revolver.

Merchant started to tell the man to put the gun down, but without a word, the guy shot Gardner.

Gardner clutched his chest and began to sag, and Merchant turned his gun on the Hispanic man.

The guy's gun went off again, and Merchant felt a burn along his right ear.

Merchant fired three times. He missed once but caught the gunman in the chest twice. The rounds blew him back against the open doorway, and he slid down against the jamb to a sitting position. He tried to say something, couldn't, then coughed blood. He looked down at the blood all over his white shirt and dark pants, looked at Merchant, and then his eyes went still.

Merchant knelt beside Gardner, but he was no longer even trying to cover his wound. The bullet wound was right over his heart. Merchant felt for a pulse, but he already knew from the slackness in Gardner's face that there was none to find.

He was dead, too.

40

Merchant did nothing for a few seconds.

That was probably all it was, seconds, but it felt like minutes. Standing there, seeing the blood on the walls. His ears still ringing, the smell of cordite almost overpowering in the condo.

He thought quite a few things during those seconds: that it was the middle of the day and there was a good chance the other owners of the condos were at work. That if he called the police, he would probably never get past it all. An ex-DEA agent shooting a Colombian.

Most of all, he thought about the conversation the people who'd sent the gunman had been listening in on. If they had decided Gardner was too much trouble to keep around, who else would they consider expendable?

Certainly Gardner's wife, Kathleen.

Accurately or not, Merchant had pretty much put her at the center of Gardner's troubles. If he was right, she was the best link he knew for finding Matt Coulter's children. If he wasn't, she was dead for no reason other than him laying out his hypothesis.

Merchant stopped thinking so much and began moving.

He went to the Colombian, touched his neck for a pulse. Found none. The guy's right pants leg had ridden up, revealing a small snub-nosed revolver in an ankle holster. Merchant unstrapped it quickly and shoved the gun and holster behind his belt.

Then he checked Gardner's body. There was just the wound in his chest.

Merchant went into the kitchen, took a dry cloth from a hook over the sink, and wiped the granite countertop down where he'd been resting his hands. Did the same with the butt of Gardner's gun. He stepped over the Colombian's body and wiped the doorknob he knew he'd touched.

And then he came back into the room and knelt down beside Gardner's body.

Holding the gun with the cloth, he put Gardner's hand around the butt and fitted his finger inside the trigger guard. He aimed just to the right of the door and squeezed the trigger. The round punched a hole in the wall.

Gardner gets two rounds into the Colombian as he comes in the doorway. The Colombian shoots him once in the chest. As Gardner falls to the floor, his finger twitches one more time and he puts a hole in the wall.

Gardner's hand has cordite on it. His prints on the gun.

Merchant knew it was far from perfect.

But it was the best he could do under the circumstances.

He took the dish towel, left the door open, and got into the elevator. He rubbed every surface down that he could remember touching. Once he got to the lobby, he used the cloth to open the front door.

He stepped out into the brilliant midday sun, expecting to find a small crowd gathered. But even though there were plenty of people on the street, the only ones that seemed to be paying any attention to him were two men double-parked in a dark blue Lexus.

They didn't look like cops, they looked like family to the man he'd just shot upstairs.

But they must have taken him for a downstairs neighbor, because though they looked him over carefully as he walked by, they didn't follow him.

Merchant went straight to his car.

CHAPTER 41

Kathleen had managed to sleep after Weir left, and now she was up. Even though she wasn't hungry, she decided she should eat. She began making a salad, noticing that her hands were still trembling a bit as she sliced cold chicken. As she so often did, she wondered what was happening with the two children. She took a handful of walnuts from the bag over her refrigerator and dropped them onto the cutting board.

She didn't remotely consider herself the maternal type, but she frequently harbored the simple fantasy of driving up to Maine, telling that bitch Ella "I'll take them now," and that would be the end of it. The kids would come back and live with her for a while until she found the right kind of home for them.

She would feel so much better about herself if she could just do that. But, of course, it wasn't possible.

A car roared into her driveway.

She stood there, stunned. The knife poised over the walnuts. A beautiful, sunny afternoon in her home, and the blue Lexus skidded right in front of her eyes, the heavy sound of its tires on the crushed shells a precursor of violence.

Two men got out immediately, walking fast toward her door.

She saw one of them reach across his waist, pull out a handgun, and hold it alongside his leg.

They moved out of her line of vision, but she heard them hit the front door once, then twice, and she heard wood splintering.

She turned and ran for her bedroom and the gun she kept in the nightstand.

They didn't say a word, and neither did she.

God knows, she thought about it.

She thought about screaming that she was calling the police. That she had a gun.

But she knew it would all be over in a few seconds one way or another and there was no sense making it easier for them.

She slammed the bedroom door shut behind her, locked it.

Ran to the nightstand and got out the gun.

She knew it was loaded, she didn't worry about that. She was thinking about knocking over her wooden table, bracing herself behind that, but they kicked the bedroom door in before she could do it.

A big, dark guy.

Her knees buckled under her, which was OK, because she fell forward against the bed, and his first shot went over her head. She aimed at his body and pulled the trigger. She didn't account for the kick like she should have; the bullet went high and a black dot appeared just under his right eye.

The guy behind him was sprayed with blood and brain matter. She got a shot in at him, too, but missed altogether. He pulled back into the hallway.

She was screaming by then, didn't realize it was her doing it, and she still didn't seem to have the use of her legs, although she didn't think she was hurt.

She knelt beside the bed, just staring at the doorway,

waiting for him to come back through. Not knowing if she could do what she needed to do again, but certain she couldn't stand this waiting much longer.

"Get in here," she screamed. "Get in here, you bastard."

But then she heard someone else's voice, heard a man say, "Drop it!"

And guns went off again, this time in the hallway.

When the second man — the one she'd showered with blood before — came back in the room he was clutching his neck. He was backing away from whoever had shot him.

He seemed to remember her at the last second and swung the gun around to her. But by then she had braced herself on the bed, squeezed the trigger the way they had taught her at the range, and this time she controlled the kick better.

Still, she hit him in the face, too. So that must've been where she was aiming. She turned the gun back to the doorway and waited for whoever was next.

CHAPTER 42

Merchant put his back against the wall in the hallway. He had seen the man he'd shot take the second hit, and he had no interest in taking one himself or being forced to shoot her.

"Kathleen," he said loudly. "It's me, Jack Merchant. I was here to see you this morning."

She didn't answer.

"Do you understand me?" he said again. "Are you all right? Are you hit?"

Still no answer.

He moved along the hallway slowly. "I want to come in," he said. "I just need to talk with you."

Then she spoke. "What do you want?" she said.

Her voice was surprisingly calm. Conversational, almost.

"What I said before. I'm trying to find Matt Coulter's children."

She was silent.

He put his head back against the wall. Suddenly afraid of what she was going to say next. That she truly didn't know what he was talking about. Or that she did, and Sean and Laurie were both long dead.

But instead she said, "All right."

"Good," he said. "I'm going to slide my gun onto the floor so you know you don't have to worry. I want you to do the same for me."

"You first."

"Here goes." He slid the revolver on the polished wooden floor into the bedroom. It bounced off the heel of the man he'd shot.

A moment later, he saw her gun slide into view.

He took a deep breath and walked to the end of the hallway — then stepped into the room.

She was kneeling beside the bed. Her face was stark white. She said, "Tell me I did the right thing trusting you."

He let out his breath. "Are they alive? The children?"

"I can't know for sure. I've been doing everything I could to keep them alive."

"Where are they?"

"Maine."

"Your property there?"

"Not our house. On the same lake, though."

"What happened?"

She stared at him and said, "I don't . . . You mean what happened that night? On the boat?"

"That's right. To their parents."

She stood up, lifted her shoulders. "Crazy thing. But it didn't have to turn into this. We were asleep."

"You and Weir?"

"That's right. We headed out so early in the morning that Weir and I fell asleep in the bow and the captain was at the wheel. He got a Mayday signal and he didn't ask us, he and Ronnie just went and picked them up. He was like that. And the guy recognized me."

"Matt?"

"That's right. He interviewed me and Dave for some stupid little feature in a trade magazine years ago, and he recognizes me. Still, it didn't have to turn out like it did, but he went nuts."

"You mean Weir."

"I mean Weir, yes. Matt Coulter recognizes me and Weir was already freaked out that Greg had picked the family up. And he just reacted. Hit Coulter with a baseball bat that Greg used when they hauled in big fish. Then his wife screamed and tried to get in the way and he hit her, too. Killed her on the spot. The children were down below, and he was ready to go down and do the same to them, but Greg and I stopped him."

"How?"

"Greg and Ronnie had found my husband's sunken boat with a sonar towfish, and Greg knew the exact coordinates, but Weir didn't. Greg was supposed to do the dive first thing in the morning, as soon as the weather cleared. But he told Weir he'd never do the dive, never give up the coordinates if the children were hurt.

"And I sort of guaranteed it, saying if anything went wrong, I'd help him get more diamonds from Dave. Weir needed both of us, and so he left the kids alone. So we went down below and told the kids there had been an accident. We just made it up as we went along. We said *Isabella* had come down on the raft. I don't think Sean believed us for a minute, but Laurie was young enough —"

Merchant held up his hand. "I want to hear it all, but we've got to get the cops into this now."

"I'm going to prison," she said.

Probably, Merchant thought. But he saw no point in agreeing just then. "Just do the right thing helping get the children back," he said as he picked up the phone.

"I tried to help them," she said. "I've been the only one keeping them alive."

"You just need to keep telling the truth," he said. "That's going to make a difference."

"Not enough," a man's voice said behind them.

Merchant turned to find Weir standing in the doorway holding a gun on him. Weir bent down, picked up one of the guns with his left hand, and aimed it at Kathleen. "Have a seat on the floor, Merchant. We've got a little time to kill until it gets dark."

CHAPTER 43

It was after nine when Sarah got to her marina. Once onboard her boat, she cracked open a beer, turned the shower on, and let the steam build for a minute before she stepped in. She stood under the needle-sharp spray until she was feeling alive again, then adjusted the knob to let big fat drops pour over her. Occasionally she reached out for the beer, and the cold inside her was a very nice counterpoint to the liquid heat on her skin.

She felt like a cleaner, nicer person when she'd left the shower, dried off, and pulled on a pair of cutoffs and a T-shirt.

She walked back up to the main cabin, toweling her hair.

So relaxed was she that she stood flat-footed when she realized there was a man in her cabin, a smiling blond man who looked just like the man she'd been seeing on that security videotape — Weir.

He was pointing a strange-looking gun at her, and before she could even register a complaint he pulled the trigger and twin barbs shot out pulling wires. She dropped to the floor as electricity coursed through her body.

It wasn't so much that she woke up. Because she was conscious. But her muscles had contracted so hard she couldn't do a damn thing. It was like being paralyzed except that she was moving the whole time, her muscles vibrating like plucked bowstrings.

He rolled her over, pulled her hands behind her back, and wrapped tape around her wrists. Then he turned her back over and straddled her hips. He took his time tearing off a piece of tape, then put it across her mouth.

"Christ," he said, running his fingers along the line of her jaw. "I'd like to play with you, but I've got people waiting in my van." He stood up, hauled her down the companionway to the aft cabin, and shoved her onto the bed. She lay there, exhausted and disoriented, slowly trying to shake off the effects of being shocked. Her head still wasn't clear when he came back a few minutes later with Kathleen Gardner. He had a gun at her back. He had her lay on the bed beside Sarah and bound her, too.

After that, he was gone for maybe ten minutes and then came onboard with Merchant.

Merchant said to Sarah, "Are you all right?"

She nodded.

Weir had draped a sport jacket over Merchant's shoulders, apparently to hide that his hands were bound behind him. Weir took it off and pushed Merchant between the two women. "Lucky you," he said.

For the next forty minutes or so, she could hear Weir putter about the boat quietly. She could hear him whistling tunelessly to himself, and at one point he started both engines, let them run for a while, then shut them down. She heard him do the same with her Mako. She could also hear the brief hiss of escaping air, as if he was checking the scuba tanks.

Basically, he seemed to be familiarizing himself with the boat, and she could only imagine if he took them off bound like this what he intended to do.

It was hard to breathe as it was, and it was just too easy to see him bringing her up to the rail of her own boat and pushing. She'd be bound, unable to keep herself afloat. Just dropping to the bottom with her hands behind her back.

There were a lot of ways she didn't want to die, but at the moment, that was at the top of her list.

CHAPTER 44

They had been on the road for a couple hours at least, and Sean had to pee. He and Laurie were sitting in the third-row seat in the back of the van, as far from Ella as she could put them.

There were no side windows, but he could look ahead through the windshield to the cars on the road. When they stopped for tolls it was excruciating to be so close to another person. The toll collectors at the first two stops said nothing, but the third was friendly and said, "There you go," to Ella when she handed her change.

But he and Laurie weren't in a position to call for help.

Their hands were tied, their ankles tied to the seat posts, tape across their mouths. There were curtains on the back window. Laurie was squirming, and he knew she must have to go to the bathroom, too.

His forehead itched under the bandage. Ella's bullet had put a big scar along his forehead, but the headache was pretty much gone now. She had put the bandage on his head the first time and let him change it twice himself. Ever since they'd tried to escape, Ella had dropped the last of whatever act she'd been playing. She didn't pretend that she was a nurse or someone who cared about Laurie. No more games, no meals together.

She was their guard; they were her prisoners, and nothing else.

He kept thinking about the time he had her down and he didn't hit her again. How he thought that was something he just couldn't do.

He could do it now.

Somehow, he fell asleep.

It wasn't pleasant. The pressure in his bladder came and went. It was an element in nightmarish dreams that he couldn't quite remember when he awoke to Ella shaking him roughly.

"Wake up, goddamn it," she said.

She had a knife out, and she let him see it.

"Now listen to me," she said quietly. "I'm taking the tape off your mouth, and then I'm going to walk you down a dock to a boat. It's late, there's no one around to hear you. If you decide to check that out, however, I will cut you. If you try to run, I will cut you. If you make me mad in any way, shape, or form, I will cut you, and then I will come back and do the same to her. Do you understand me, Sean?"

He stared at her.

He didn't doubt she'd do what she said, it was just that he was tired of being scared.

"Do you understand?" she said again.

He nodded.

She pulled the tape away, and he breathed deeply. Licked his lips.

"I've got to pee," he said.

"You can do it on the boat," she said.

"Whose is it?"

"Nice people," she said. "You'll like them. Now shut up and walk."

* * *

Dr. Weir was waiting on the boat. It was a big trawler. Sean had never seen it before. "Ella," Weir said and kissed her. He ruffled Sean's hair like they were old friends. "Good to see you."

Ella said, "Take him. I'm sick of him."

"Sure." Weir took Sean by the arm, pulled him toward the aft cabin. He had to step down two stairs, and there in front of him were three people on the bed. He pulled back for a moment, thinking they were dead. But they were tied up, like he was. A big man and a woman with black hair that he had never seen before. And the redheaded woman who had been on the boat that had rescued him and Laurie. The one who had been nice to them.

"Pretty cozy in here, isn't it," Weir said.

"I've got to go to the bathroom," Sean said.

Weir waved toward the head.

Sean went into a surprisingly large bathroom with a tub. He turned to see that Weir was waiting outside the open door. "I've got to sit down," Sean said. He could feel his face flush, but there it was.

"Jesus Christ," Weir said. But he took a knife from his pocket, sliced the tape behind Sean's hands, and closed the door.

Sean opened the medicine cabinet. Saw aspirin and some other pills, deodorant, creams, nothing that he could see as a weapon. He looked in the cabinet below. Brush, a blow dryer, soap, shampoo, cold cream, nothing that he could use. He looked in the right and left drawers. The razor was one of those kind with three blades, he couldn't see cutting anything with that.

The best he could find was a small pair of scissors. Tiny, just a couple of inches long, with curved blades, for cutting fingernails.

He sat down on the toilet and did his business while shoving the little scissors into his shoe. They weren't much, but maybe he could use them to hurt Ella or Weir somehow. Maybe cut one of them in the face.

That'd be worth something.

CHAPTER 45

Weir had never actually run a boat this big himself before. He'd taken the wheel of *Isabella* upon occasion while they were searching for Gardner's boat, but backing a boat like this big fat trawler out of a dock was a long way from taking the helm for twenty minutes in the open sea.

Not that he cared if he damaged the boat or dock. But he was sure there were people sleeping on the other boats, and he didn't want to call any attention to himself. Plus, the boat had to work for at least another five hours.

That was how long he calculated it would take to reach the dive spot at the glacial ten-knot cruising speed of a trawler. Probably more like eight knots with the Mako in tow. He looked down at Ella in the Mako. It looked tiny from his height on the flybridge. He gave her the thumbs-up, and she started the outboards, turned on the running lights, and backed the boat out. She puttered slowly into the harbor and waited for him.

He started both engines, climbed down the ladder, and walked around the boat, releasing lines. The wind began to shift the boat against the dock, but he decided not to worry about it. He climbed back up the ladder, pulled the shift levers for both engines back, and nudged the throttles forward.

It was too much. The boat powered back hard, and the hull screeched along the dock. He ignored the sound and spun the wheel over once the bow was clear of the pilings so the boat would back in toward shore.

But it barely responded. The wind kept pushing the boat sideways. He felt his stomach lurch. The whole thing was going to fall apart right here because he couldn't get the frigging boat away from the dock. And then he remembered that boats this size pretty much had to be steered with their engines at slow speeds. So he shoved the port shift lever forward, forgetting to adjust the throttle. The transmission slammed into forward gear. The engine almost stalled but didn't. The boat began to turn. He reversed the starboard engine, this time remembering to ease the throttle.

The boat turned even faster. Then he shifted the starboard engine forward, and the boat began moving slowly out of the dock area to where Ella, the closest thing to the love of his life, was waiting.

He laughed.

He kept his voice low. Didn't want to wake anyone who might look out and wonder why he was running the boat instead of Sarah. But, still, he was laughing with relief. They weren't there yet, but he could see an end to all this.

He could see a time when he could take what he needed from the ocean floor and send everything that troubled him right back down.

CHAPTER 46

Merchant's hands felt like wood.

The tape around his wrists was tight, almost cutting off his circulation. Sarah must have felt the same way, but still she kept working.

Sarah and he had their backs to each other. She had succeeded in pulling some of the tape away from his fingers but had so far made no headway against the tight roll around his wrists. He had been face-to-face with Kathleen, and though she had looked at him with hope for a while, she eventually turned her head away.

Weir and the woman he'd called Ella were up on the flybridge. They'd left the lights on low in the cabin and put the children on the floor at the foot of the bed. About an hour after they left the harbor, the boat began to roll on ocean swells.

Merchant had never been seasick in his life, but he was considering it now. The cabin was plenty big under most circumstances. But with five people in it, the smell of their fear and diesel fumes, and the heat and noise of the engines below them, he was beginning to feel nauseated.

Sweat trickled off his forehead into his eyes. He wasn't too worried for himself, because he didn't feel that bad. But he was worried for the others, the children particularly. With the tape over their mouths, they might choke to death if they vomited. He figured maybe his hands were free enough to help them with that.

He rolled over. Sarah did the same, and they lay still for a minute or so, their foreheads touching.

Then he turned onto his back, drew his legs up and rocked forward and then back, then did it once more so he was sitting up at the foot of the bed. Sean was on the floor to his left, leaning against the wall. Laurie to his right.

Merchant looked at Sean, then at Laurie. It was impossible to tell their color in the poor light streaming from the open bathroom. But Laurie's face was slick with sweat, and so was her brother's. Merchant slid off the edge of the bed and on his knees worked his way backward to the little girl. He reached back for the tape on her face but couldn't seem to get to her. She made a noise, and when he looked back at her, she had turned her face away.

The boy made a sound. His sister looked over at him, and he nodded his head and pushed his face forward, miming for her to do the same.

He looked at Merchant, and if Merchant could read his eyes right, he was imploring him to try again.

Merchant reached back, and this time his fingers brushed the girl's cheek and he fumbled for the edge of the tape, lightly scraping his fingernail underneath, then he pulled enough away so she could talk.

He could hear her breathe, and she said, "Sean, I'm going to be sick!"

She spoke too loudly. The boy made an impatient sound, and she seemed to get it. Merchant backed over to him, he leaned forward, and Merchant was able to pull the tape partially off.

The boy said, "I'll do yours."

The boy rolled to his knees and then leaned his head

against the wall and got to his feet. He backed over to Merchant, fumbled for the tape, and then pulled it away.

Merchant took a deep breath. "Thanks," he said. "You need to be able to put it back on if they come back, you understand? Rub your face against the wall or against your knee to push the tape on."

Sean nodded. "I get it. Who are you?"

Merchant gave him his name. And said, "Your father hired me and Sarah to find you."

The boy stared at him, frozen.

Then said, "He's alive? My dad's still alive?"

"Yes, he is. He's hurt but alive." Merchant knew the next question, made a decision, and when the boy asked about his mother, he lied. "She's OK, too," he said.

The girl and boy started to cry.

CHAPTER 47

Sarah heard footsteps on the cabin roof. She sat up, and Merchant saw her and immediately bent down to help the boy put the tape back over his mouth. But Sean shook his head and turned around.

Sarah felt a hand clutch at her heart, she wanted to yell at the boy. But it seemed he had other plans, and she realized just as Merchant did that the boy was trying to give him something.

Merchant turned, took whatever it was, and then crawled back onto the bed between her and Kathleen. Sean knelt beside his sister, and together they rubbed the tape back onto their faces on the edge of the bed.

They settled down to their former spots just as the door slid open. Ella stood there.

Sarah had a sense of what it had been like wherever Sean and Laurie had been. The boy running everything he could behind Ella's back.

She stood on the steps, the revolver in her hand. It was hard to believe Ronnie McNaughton thought Sarah and Ella looked the same.

This woman was scary.

She sat down on the stairway, looked carefully at the boy and girl. Sarah was sure she was going to check the tape around their mouths, but then Ella did something that gave Sarah a quick touch of hope.

She yawned.

Sarah awoke when the sound of the engines changed. He'd cut the throttle, and they were just puttering along.

The cabin was light. Morning.

She looked at Ella. She was still awake. Haggard, yes, but her eyes were open, her gun still in hand.

Sarah could hear Weir walking on the deck and the sound of the anchor dropping.

Minutes later, he came into the cabin.

He was smiling. "All right, then. Moment I've been looking forward to. . . ." He leaned over the bed, took Sarah by the arm, and hauled her into a sitting position. He pulled the tape from her mouth.

"I looked in earlier and saw you were sleeping," he said. "That's good. You're going to need your rest for this morning."

Merchant sat up and leaned against the headboard.

Ella moved forward with the gun, but Weir put up his hand. "That's all right." He leaned over and ripped the tape from Merchant's mouth. "Might as well get his two cents in."

Weir stepped back and said in a phony boardroom address, "You're probably all wondering why I brought you here today. . . ." He smiled at his own humor, then said, "All right, it's pretty simple. I lost something and you're going to go get it." He pointed to Sarah.

"What?" Merchant said. "Diamonds? Or drugs?"

"Just diamonds," Weir said. "In Dave Gardner's boat."

"How deep?" Sarah said.

"A hundred and forty feet."

She blanched. "I've never gone to that depth before."

"Well, you will today."

"Do you know what you're asking?" Merchant said.

Weir touched the gun tucked under his belt. "Does it look like I'm asking?"

"Those tanks are just filled with air," Jack said. "At that depth you should be using a helium mixture or nitrogen narcosis is a real problem. And the time it'll take, she'll need to decompress. There's a lot to go wrong."

"She refuses, she'll get a bullet in the head," Weir said. "That's a problem too, right?"

"You're going to kill me anyhow," she said.

"I'm willing," he said. "But there's really no need. You don't know my real name, or Ella's. Once we get the diamonds, we'll have enough cash to never even set foot in New England again. We take off on your Mako and you putter home on this barge. Everyone's happy. You refuse, I start with Kathleen, work my way through the kids and eventually to your boyfriend — and then you. Have you got the stomach for that?"

"I'll go," Merchant said. "I've done those kinds of depths before."

"That's not an option," Weir said. "I like you right where you are, a nice thick roll of tape around your hands."

Sarah stared at Weir. His pale blue eyes, his too-handsome face. She believed him. The part about the killing, not about letting them go.

But her diving would give Jack time, maybe opportunity.

"Let me go with her," Merchant said.

"So you two can swim away? Not a chance."

"We wouldn't leave them." Merchant nodded to the children.

"Don't waste your breath," Weir said.

"No, Jack," Sarah said. "You stay here. I'll do it."

"Good girl," Weir said. He looked at Ella. "She thinks her boyfriend will figure out how to save the day before she gets back up."

"I bet she does," Ella said. For the first time, Sarah saw her smile.

Ella took her to the forward cabin to get into her wet suit.

"Can I have some privacy?" Sarah asked.

"No, you can't," Ella said. She stood in the open doorway and kept the gun pointed directly at Sarah.

After Sarah started putting on her suit, Ella said, "You and I look a lot alike. Has he gone after you?"

"Weir?"

"That's right."

"No, Ella. Other than shooting me with a Taser gun and threatening to kill me, he's been a perfect gentleman."

If Sarah read the woman's face right, the news actually pleased her. She added, "You goddamned *freak*."

That brought another one of Ella's smiles. "You've got no idea. Hurry up and get into that wet suit."

Once dressed, Sarah went back into the main cabin and said, "I'm going to see Jack before I go."

"No," Ella said. "He's waiting for you." She pointed through the window to Weir standing alongside the rail.

"Yeah, well shoot me in the back," Sarah said. She kept moving down into the aft cabin. She could feel between her shoulder blades where the bullet would come, but being scared made her angry. And they needed her healthy to do the dive, so screw them.

Merchant and Kathleen were sitting back to back. Sarah slowed down, just long for them to separate so Ella wouldn't see them.

Merchant's face was drawn tight, Sarah could see how afraid he was for her. That made her stomach drop even more.

She knelt down in front of him and wrapped her arms around him. "Hey," she said. "You'll have this all straightened out when I come back, right?"

"You bet," he said. They kissed.

"Come on," Ella said.

He pulled back and kissed Sarah's cheek. She felt the rasp of his morning beard and wondered if that was the very last time she would. His kissed her neck, and then whispered, "You swim away. Use your compass and head toward Block Island. Stay at twenty feet, with two tanks you can do an hour and a half."

She pulled away. Put both hands on his face, looked at him straight on, and shook her head ever so slightly. "I'll be seeing you real soon," she said. "And after that, I'm going to make a point to be in my office when you come to visit, we're going to sleep together more often, and I'm even going to tell you that I love you from time to time. That sound like a plan?"

"That sounds like a very good plan."

She kissed him lightly and stood.

On impulse, she touched Kathleen's leg. "Good luck," she said. She took a moment to kneel before the boy and girl. They had moved beside each other against the bulwark. "Hey," she said, touching their cheeks. "I'm Sarah."

She recognized the look of hope in their eyes. She also realized that from the moment Matt Coulter had walked into her office, she had never believed they were still alive. And yet, here they were.

Maybe Jack would be able to look at her that way tomorrow, the day after, and in years to come.

Because right now, she could feel him looking at her as if he'd never see her again.

CHAPTER 48

Weir was impatient, and his instincts dictated that he should go below and haul Sarah out on deck with the gun in her face. Maybe shoot one of the others to make his point.

But he also knew that his instincts were often faulty.

That Sarah needed her head on straight to make this dive. So he waited.

And when she at last made it up on deck, he said, "Beautiful day for a dive."

"Shove it," she said.

He smiled blandly. Whatever got her down to pick up his diamonds. After that, she'd pay.

He put his set of double tanks on her, and she staggered under the weight.

"You're not going to have much bottom time at that depth. Even with both tanks, from here and back you've got about fifteen minutes," he said. "See that float right there?"

She put her hands over her eyes to block out the glare and said, "Yeah."

"You follow that line down."

"Who put that there?"

"Captain McNaughton."

"So did he dive on this boat already?"

"No. We found it with a sonar towfish. The weather was rough, so we were going to wait out the night and dive on it the next morning, but we got interrupted."

"So why haven't you gone down and gotten it yourself? You afraid of the depth?"

"Just do what you're told," he said. He didn't feel like going into his damaged eardrums with her. "You're going to follow that line down. When you get to the bottom, put this line on the anchor and swim in a circle around the anchor holding the line. Even if you have to do a full revolution, you should hit the wreck."

"And what am I looking for?"

"A briefcase. About this big." He held his hands apart. "You'll have to go down into the cabin. There's a cabinet along the starboard side. Slide that open, find the briefcase. It should be that simple."

He handed her a dive light. "It'll be dark inside the boat."

"That simple," she repeated. "So why didn't you do it?"

He felt his face flush. Ridiculous, really, considering he was planning to kill her later. But he felt embarrassed.

"I tried," he said. "Had a burst eardrum a few years back and I can't go deep now."

She just looked at him, and he felt the urge to hit her but kept it to himself. She said, "There's a decompression chart in my bag. Grab it for me."

He almost told her not to waste his time. What was a case of the bends when he was planning a bullet for her? But he supposed he had to keep up the act for the time being. He dug through her bag, found the chart, and she took it from him. She looked at it and said, "I'll need to take another tank down. I'm going to want to put in at least twenty minutes of decompression time at fifteen feet."

He hesitated.

There was plenty of air, she had four singles on the Mako.

"No problem," he said, pulling out his spare regulator. "I'll put this on one of your tanks and you can take it down."

Just like he was concerned about her welfare.

He doubted she believed him, but she didn't argue anymore. He helped her down the ladder. Her face was white and her lips were pressed together tightly. If he was a different type of man he would have felt bad about what he was doing. He pulled the Mako closer, climbed aboard, and put the regulator on the spare tank. He turned the valve, checked the pressure, and then pulled the boat close again.

He waited for her to get ready.

She sat on the edge of the platform and put her fins on. She put the mask on, checked her air pressure, and then without a word or a look at him, she rolled into the water. He handed the tank down to her, and she slipped below the surface. He could see the bright yellow of her tanks for a short while as she angled toward the float.

Then she began her descent and was gone.

CHAPTER 49

The water was cold.

Never mind that it was late summer, that she knew she'd be warm in a few minutes. Right then, the water seeped in at her neck, her wrists, and her ankles, and it was cold.

Fifteen feet down, she looked over her shoulder and saw her boat, impossibly large above her. She turned back and kept kicking in the direction of the float.

She hesitated at the line. She held the spare tank in her right hand and the line in her left. The water was reasonably clear for New England, which meant she could see for about fifteen feet below her, and then the line disappeared into murkiness that gradually changed to an inky blackness.

She'd been diving for about six years and had never gone by herself. She was a recreational diver, not a pro. She'd never gone below a hundred feet. Never dove on a wreck, never dealt with the possibility of nitrogen narcosis — never even had to deal with a decompression dive.

She let some air out of her buoyancy compensator vest, and the lead weights about her waist started to pull her down.

Her ears immediately began to feel the pressure. She swallowed, there was a reassuring click in both ears, and she continued down. She kept doing that, feeling herself sink, watching the depth gauge show her move down, thirty, forty, fifty feet. As she went deeper, the pressure on her face mask felt tighter. She looked up and watched the silvery bubbles rise along the line to the surface. She knew the deeper she went, the faster she used the air. A tank that would last an hour at fifteen feet was good for only about an eighth of that at the depth she was going . . . which meant the two tanks on her back would barely be adequate; she would definitely need the spare to make the dive and decompress.

Around eighty feet, the line began to bow out and she felt the pull of a deep-water current. Her breath began to rush a little faster, and she went back up a dozen feet and decided she would leave the spare tank there. She wanted both hands for the line if the current was going to pull her.

It was awkward tying the straps around the line and getting it to stay in place. She wasted a couple of precious minutes doing it and started cursing Weir for not planning this through.

Not that she believed he intended to let her live, but somehow the difference between shooting her and letting her drown seemed significant.

She continued down, pulling herself hand over hand against the current. The water was far colder and darker now. She paused to switch on the light.

She gasped when she did, something large passed just outside the periphery of her beam. A big fish of some kind. She played the light around her, saw it reflect back again.

A six-foot shark swam into the range of her light, glided by, then switched back a little closer. She cried out and kicked at it, and it twitched once and then was gone.

Her heart was pounding. And she swore into her mouthpiece. If it came back, she had nothing to defend herself. No shark stick, no speargun, not even a knife strapped to her ankle. All she owned was the knife, and Weir didn't consider it part of her necessary equipment for this dive.

She continued down.

At a hundred and ten feet, she paused to swallow a few more times. She had been working to clear her ears all along, but now she had no more moisture in her mouth to swallow. She took the mouthpiece out a bit and let a little of the salt water swish in her mouth. She spit the water out and noticed as she did that she felt rather calm.

It was comforting, realizing that she was getting used to even this. The boat and her troubles on the surface seemed another world away. She started letting herself drop further. Her weight was quite negative now, it had been some time since she'd put any compensating air into her vest. But that was all right — she headed down anyway.

The cold was kind of interesting, too. A while back she'd started shivering, and if she paid attention, she'd realize she still was. But she didn't feel cold. She felt comfortable.

One hundred and twenty feet.

Hell, she felt *good*.

One thirty. A fish like something she'd never seen before swam by. The second it was gone she couldn't remember exactly what it was like, just that it was remarkable.

One forty and she realized that the muck below was close to solid. In fact, when she played her light down the line, she saw that it reflected back in something man-made — the anchor.

The anchor for the float, the anchor for the line she was holding in her left hand.

She was on the bottom.

Sarah stayed there for a moment, contemplating what that meant. Then remembered a man a million years ago had said something to her about using the loop of line attached to her vest. She thought about it, feeling really stupid about it, really drunk, actually, and the idea pierced through her fog and she thought, *Narcosis.*

"Jesus Christ," she said aloud, but with regulator piece in

her mouth, her words were just an alien sound in this very alien world.

She knew she was drunk with the nitrogen the way a drunk driver might suddenly realize that he'd had a few too many — she recognized it, but it didn't seem too important.

She forced herself to concentrate on that line on her vest, then remembered Weir saying she had to tether that down and do wide circles to find her way to the sunken boat.

If she concentrated, she could understand the concept. But it seemed impossibly hard to do.

Behind all of the fog, though, an urgency that had been in her before started to come back. An urgency about Jack on that boat, about Weir. About those children.

How much air do I have left? Sarah thought with sudden clarity.

She looked at her dive computer and saw that she was already halfway through her air. She hadn't even found the boat yet.

Sarah took the loop of line off her vest, carefully snapped the clip at the end to the ring on top of the anchor shaft. And then she slowly swam backward, watching the bright yellow line straighten out in her flash beam until she was at the end of the line.

Then, holding the line in her left hand and putting the flashlight in her right, she began kicking in a broad circle around the anchor. The current wasn't as strong as it had been around eighty feet, but still she had to strain against it part of the way around the circuit, then it became easier. She played the light left and right, looking for the boat.

It wasn't until she noticed a star-shaped rock a second time that she realized she had circled the anchor twice.

Her breath began to rush.

She closed her eyes and talked to herself.

Forced her drunken mind to *think*.

The boat couldn't be inside the circumference.

Had to be outside. She began kicking slowly again. This time she pointed the flashlight beam so it played outside as far as it would go. And this time she saw a glow.

She stopped and immediately kicked up a cloud of black silt, which the current swept away.

She went up a half dozen feet and played the beam in the same direction. And saw, just faintly, the glow again. She played the beam right and left and saw the glow was the reflected light off a white fiberglass boat.

She had found it.

But she was also at the end of her rope, literally. The rope leading her back to the float anchor, which led to her spare air tank, which led back to her boat and Jack.

And Weir.

He'd shoot them all if she came back without the diamonds. That much Sarah knew even in the state she was in.

She looked at her compass, saw that straight ahead to the boat would be 170 degrees, so going back to the anchor should be . . . She shook her head. This was simple. She stared at the compass, aware of each breath taking her preciously low air.

Three hundred and forty degrees.

She let go of the rope.

She drifted with the current right up to the hull.

And saw it clearly for the first time.

If she hadn't been so out of it with the narcosis, she probably would have started crying. As it was, she just felt stupid. She held herself against the slick hull, trying not to let the current sweep her away.

The hull was upside down.

CHAPTER 50

Sean didn't have to fake the need to go to the bathroom. Ella was taking Laurie in right now.

Sean saw Jack and the red-haired woman move their backs to each other. She was probably using the little scissors, trying to cut him free.

This was the first chance they'd gotten. Ella had been with them the entire time, sitting on the stairs holding the gun.

He listened to Laurie in the bathroom, sobbing, saying to Ella, "Please don't tape me again, you don't have to. Please, Ella, I'll be quiet."

He hated the way his sister's voice sounded, but it was good that she was being noisy. Part of him wanted her to cry, to scream, so that Jack and the red-haired woman could work faster, not have to worry about being overheard.

The bathroom door opened, and Ella came out with Laurie. "Sit down," she said.

"Please . . ." Laurie said.

Ella bent from the waist so her face was right in Laurie's. "Shut up," she said.

Sean got a sudden jolt. It wasn't the word, or even the inflection, but the deadness in her eyes when she looked at his little sister. Whatever act she'd put on before, it was just that.

Laurie got it, too. She sat down and didn't say another word as Ella used the roll of tape to bind her hands and cover her mouth.

Sean swallowed hard. If Ella let Laurie go to the bathroom, it wasn't to be nice, but probably because she didn't want the cabin to smell while she was sitting there guarding them.

So she might let him go, too.

Sean made a sound his throat. Ella looked over at him. He nodded toward the bathroom, tried to say "Please" through the tape.

Irritation flashed across her face, and he thought she was going to come over and kick him. But she reached into her pocket, pulled out a knife, and sliced the tape from his ankles. "All right, get up," she said.

It was hard to do with his arms tied behind his back, and she stepped around him and said, "Hold still." She put the gun barrel to his head and then used her left hand to cut the tape from his hands.

"Move," she said. "You give me the slightest reason, I'll finish up with you right here and now."

She followed him into the bathroom and stood behind him with the gun pressed against his spine. It was hard to pee at first, he felt too nervous.

But once he finally started, he went as slow as he could. Thinking how crazy it was, he might live or die depending upon how long he could pee. If this gave Jack time enough to get free.

She put the gun up to the back of his neck. "You're done," she said. "Put your hands behind your back."

He hesitated, thinking this was still maybe his best chance.

She shoved him hard, so he stumbled against the sink. "Right now!" She jammed the gun just behind his ear, making it hurt.

He put his hands behind his back.

Then he moved when she told him. They both backed into the bedroom. He saw Jack and the red-haired woman. Both of them looking at him, but he couldn't tell if Jack was free.

He'd have to guess not.

Because Jack didn't stop her from tying Sean up again. This time, tighter than ever.

CHAPTER 51

The good thing about the narcosis was that Sarah didn't feel particularly scared.

So while it took her some time to gather her thoughts and see that the front of the boat was partially supported on a rock, it didn't frighten her unduly when she realized there might be a possibility of crawling under the rail into the cockpit. When she knelt beside the boat, she could see about a two-foot space between the mucky bottom and the top of the boat's gunwale. She leaned into the space and shined the light into the cockpit. The light reflected off the white fiberglass, and she could see clearly enough that the cabinway door was open. Beyond that, the cabin was in darkness.

A part of her brain was still sharp enough to start a beat.

Telling her that she might get stuck. That a space like this was like a cave, and any number of creatures might have taken residence.

She tried to move forward anyhow.

Just do it. She tried to squirm underneath.

And she felt a solid clang of her tanks against the side of the boat.

She felt over her head to the valve, looked at the space

again — and realized there was no way. She couldn't get in there wearing all the gear. Wearing the tanks, anyhow.

She took a look at her computer, and *that* registered. More than two-thirds of her air was gone.

She forced herself to put it all together:

She was 140 feet deep.

Her reactions, thoughts, and movements were clouded.

Her options were to give up, return to the surface empty-handed, and just deal with whatever Weir was going to do. Or take her tanks off, crawl into a dark underwater hole, and hope she'd be able to find her way back.

Either way, he'd probably kill her.

Still, foggy as her head was, she had the sense of something that she could do. It was too vague to be called a plan, but she knew she needed the case of diamonds in her hand. Without them, she had nothing. With them, she had some power.

Sarah knelt in front of the boat and began to take off her tanks.

It wasn't easy. The tunnel vision of the mask made it hard to see the buckles, but she got free and slid the tanks up next to the hull. With the tanks off, the regulator mouthpiece wanted to twist away, and she had to hold her hand against it so she could keep breathing.

She held on tight to the hull, thinking that if she got swept away from the tanks, she'd be dead in minutes. The idea should have been terrifying, but it wasn't. She began to breathe deep, purposely hyperventilating so she'd have a little more time. And then she dropped the mouthpiece and pulled herself through the narrow opening into the upside-down cockpit.

Whatever nitrogen-induced sense of calm she'd felt before vanished. She was surrounded by thick fiberglass on all sides, and she had no air. She put the beam of light into the cabin and started in — just as an eel about as long as she was tall came out.

She cried out and scrambled back deeper into the cockpit.

She hit her head, and water rushed into her mask. Water was in her mouth and throat from crying out, and she couldn't seem to stop her body from reacting. . . .

Until she did.

She froze. Grabbed the light and looked around the cockpit. Her mask was half full of water, so she could barely see.

But she thought the eel was gone.

She pushed herself over to the opening to where her tanks were lying and got close enough to grab the regulator hose. Lying in the muck, she pressed the purge valve. A blessed rush of air bubbled about her face, and she took in the mouthpiece and breathed deep. Her heart was pounding. She cleared her mask of water and lay there trying to gather her thoughts.

The eel was probably a conger. She'd seen them before in shallower waters. They had vicious sets of teeth but would tend to leave you alone if you left them alone. But swimming into one's home was pretty much the opposite of leaving it alone.

I was lucky, she thought, and suddenly that seemed hysterically funny to her. Lying under a boat 140 feet down sucking on her last bit of air and she was lucky.

Abruptly, she dropped the mouthpiece, turned around, and swam into the small cabin.

Might as well do it while she was in a good mood.

In a way, she *was* lucky. The sliding cabinet door was easy to find. And it slid open. And there was a briefcase, which she was able to get out easily enough. She turned around and swam back to the opening, where she lay for a minute, breathing that wonderful air. And then she crawled out and wedged the briefcase under the hull while she donned the tanks again.

She checked her air.

A little less than a quarter of it was left. She had to get back to that spare tank.

She looked back at where she thought the anchored line was and could see nothing but dark gloom. She looked at her compass, turned herself until she was facing 340 degrees, and began kicking against the current.

She swung the beam of light along the bottom, hoping to catch the bright yellow line she had used to circle the anchor. She'd attached it to a rock, so it shouldn't have floated away.

But still she didn't find it.

She knew the current was pushing her, she'd had to compensate to try and hold the 340 course. Maybe she'd compensated too much, maybe not enough.

But she didn't know where that anchor was. She hadn't even realized before how cold the water had become at this depth, but now she was shivering so hard that she was clutching herself for warmth.

She looked up to the surface. It was just a light above her. The visibility didn't allow for anything so simple as seeing the silhouette of her big fat tub of a boat. Not at this depth.

She looked at her air pressure and knew that she didn't have a choice. Without finding her way back to the anchor and line, she wasn't going to get to the spare tank — and, without that, her time to decompress. She'd be lucky just to make it to the surface without running out of air. The nitrogen bubbles in her system would expand into her joints, and she'd be in excruciating pain or worse not long after reaching the surface.

Assuming Weir let her live that long.

She started up.

CHAPTER 52

Weir was not a happy man.

He was up on the flybridge, holding the binoculars to his eyes. Looking for that woman. That *bitch*.

He had anchored the boat close enough to the buoy, both bow and stern, so that he could stay close at all times. And for a short time the bubbles from her tank came to the surface just fine.

Which meant she was where she was supposed to be, doing what she was supposed to be doing.

But for too long now, the bubbles had not been breaking on the surface.

Which could mean nothing. He supposed there could be a current down below that was sweeping away her exhausted air. But there was another possibility, and that was that she had just left them all high and dry, so to speak, and swum off on her own.

Truth was, she could get quite some distance if she stayed shallow with two tanks. Now that the wind was coming up and the surface was choppy, she'd be hard to see once she surfaced.

He cursed her again and thought about hauling up one of

those kids, or maybe Merchant, and making an example out of one of them.

It was a satisfying idea, but it wouldn't do much good if she wasn't around to see it.

He forced himself to calm down. He'd been resisting the urge to call Ella up to help him look. He wanted her down there keeping an eye on Merchant.

"Shit," he said.

He leaned on the console and tried to make himself focus. But the frustration bubbled and popped inside him, and he knew it wouldn't take much for the rage to come on.

Once that happened, he'd have a boat full of dead people and no diamonds to show for it. Nothing wrong with the former, but everything was wrong with the latter.

He looked at his watch. At that depth, she should've emptied the double tanks by now. And maybe she was hanging on to the float line at fifteen feet doing her precious decompression, but he was sure he'd see the bubbles breaking if she were doing that, *sure* of it.

He raised his binoculars again, looked carefully at the float to see if it was moving at all. But it bobbed along serenely on the surface. Nothing to suggest Sarah was using it to guide her back to the boat.

He then methodically began to train the binoculars off the bow in ever expanding sweeps. His hands were shaking slightly with the anger coming on again, and forcing method upon himself only infuriated him more.

And then he saw her.

The yellow tanks burst to the surface about a quarter mile away.

And she turned in the direction of the boat and waved her hand.

He drew his breath in sharply and steadied himself against the console. It was hard to keep her image stable through the binoculars from his vantage on the flybridge. Every movement of the boat felt exaggerated, and she seemed to move in and out of his view with infuriating regularity.

But he saw it.

She had the briefcase. And she was waving for him to come pick her up.

"I'll be damned," he said. It must not have been as hard to do as he thought. She'd just gone down and gotten the briefcase. He still felt a little embarrassed that she'd accomplished what he couldn't, but it wasn't as if she was going to be around to tell anyone.

He yelled down to Ella. "She's up. Come help me with the anchors!"

He started the engines and hurried down the ladder to the stern. Ella came out on deck.

"She got them?"

"Looks like it," he said. Acting calm, although he didn't feel it. He leaned forward, kissed Ella on the lips. "It's taken us some time, but it looks like we've done it."

"Seven years," she said, smiling. Teasing him.

"Hey, the first millions are always the hardest."

She looked over her shoulder at Sarah. Then back at him. Her smile faded. "We don't have them yet. What do you want to do here?"

He shrugged. "I'll get the stern anchor. You wait by the bow. When I get back at the wheel, I'll give you the word and you push the button to raise the anchor. I'll motor up to her, and you go down to the swim ladder and get the diamonds from her."

Ella lifted her gun, showing him. "Any reason for her to get onboard?"

He thought about it. "Yeah, I suppose so. We'll put her in the cabin with the rest of them, lock them down tight, and sink the boat. That way no bodies floating free. So, yeah, bring her onboard."

She started to turn, and he said, "Ella?"

She looked back. "What?"

"You know we can't keep the little girl," he said. "She might talk someday."

Ella looked at him. She seemed genuinely startled. "Keep her? Why would I want to do that?"

He looked at her carefully.

He supposed he knew her better than anyone in the world and he still didn't know what she was thinking sometimes. "Okay, then," he said.

She stepped back, kissed him, and said, "You're all I need, baby. Just you."

He kissed her back. "Goes both ways."

And he wasn't lying. He couldn't be sure about her, but as long as he could screw around once in a while, she really was all he needed.

He hurried to the stern and started hauling up the small anchor he'd taken from the Mako. As he did so, he glanced back and realized the portholes to the aft cabin were open.

Which meant that Merchant, Kathleen, and both children had most likely heard everything he and Ella just said.

Oh well.

It wasn't as if they were going to tell anyone either.

CHAPTER 53

Merchant's hands were free.

He sat up and used the little scissors to cut the tape around his ankles and thought about what he'd heard.

What they had all heard.

And while listening to Ella and Weir had made the children's faces turn white beneath the tape, Merchant felt pretty damn good.

Sarah was alive.

And they weren't planning to shoot her before she got on the boat.

He turned back to Kathleen, pulled the tape from her mouth.

"Listen," he whispered. "I've got to trust you."

"You can."

"I can't, but I have to. You know they plan to kill you, right?"

She nodded.

He knelt on the bed behind her and cut the tape binding her hands. Once they were free, he gave her the scissors and walked halfway up the open stairway to the main cabin. He looked around carefully and didn't see Ella nearby. He assumed Weir was the one running the boat up on the flybridge over the main cabin. He went back into the cabin and raised a finger to his lips when he saw Kathleen pulling the tape from Sean's mouth. The boy nodded.

Merchant knelt on the bed and looked through one of the aft portholes to the rear deck.

He didn't see anything but the fiberglass of the gunwale in front of him, and then Ella walked past. That close, he could see her only from the knees down, but then he saw her bend to open the gate that led to the swim ladder. She called up to Weir, "OK, that's close enough — she's about fifteen feet away." Then she said, presumably to Sarah, "C'mon, you can swim the rest."

Merchant could hear Sarah say something, but her voice was low — weak — and he couldn't make out the words. It didn't sound like she was on the swim platform yet, though.

She must have asked for help. And apparently Ella was too eager for the diamonds to refuse because she started down the ladder to the swim deck, facing backward — keeping an eye on Sarah, perhaps, maybe afraid of being pulled in.

"Has she got them?" Weir called. "You can see the case, right?" Merchant could hear him overhead, getting off the flybridge and hurrying down on the cabin roof to the stern.

Leaving the engine in neutral and the flybridge unoccupied.

Merchant walked quickly back into the main cabin to the steering wheel and gearshifts. This console pretty much matched the one up on the flybridge — and if Weir wasn't running the boat, he would.

Merchant shoved both engines into gear and slammed the throttles down.

CHAPTER 54

Sarah was a few feet from the stern of her boat when suddenly the engines roared and the props frothed the water white.

The wash roiled around her legs, and she cried out, kicking away from the boat, thinking that her legs would get caught in the propellers.

Ella was just about to step off the ladder onto the swim platform when the boat took off, and she too cried out — and fell into the water. She came to the surface as the towed Mako was almost upon her. She put her hands up and the boat went right over her.

But the outboard motors were tilted up, and she apparently rolled under the boat relatively unscathed.

After the Mako swept by Sarah, Ella surfaced about ten feet away. If she was dazed, she didn't show it. She started treading water, and then she saw Sarah. She reached down, came up with the gun above water, and aimed it at Sarah. "Get over here," she said.

Sarah didn't say anything. Ella was treading water furiously to keep the gun above water, and there was no way she could do it for long. Of course, the gun might still fire underwater. Sarah was pretty sure it could.

"Give me that vest," Ella said. "Right now."

Sarah took out her mouthpiece. "It's not that simple," she said. "It's attached to the tank."

"Then inflate it all the way and I'll hold on to you," she said. "I know how it works." The woman's head dipped below the water, and she came up spitting. "Now!"

"I've got a better idea," Sarah said. "You hold on to the diamonds." She kicked her fins hard so that her body raised out of the water to her chest and she heaved the waterlogged case toward Ella.

It didn't go more than a few feet away, but she didn't care. The effort of going up sent her right back underwater a couple of feet. She jackknifed cleanly and kicked downward, pressing the release valve on her buoyancy compensator to let out the air inside her vest.

She saw streaks of bubbles in the water as Ella apparently fired at her, but the bullets missed her by several feet.

She kept going down. There was less than a hundred PSI left in the tanks, worth a minute or two. She turned and looked up.

Ella was struggling on the surface.

She had one hand on the bag, the other on the gun.

From below, Sarah watched the woman. She was apparently afraid of Sarah coming up underneath her because she treaded water in a circle, firing bullets straight down until there was none left.

Then she dropped the gun. It spun quickly as it descended into the dark water, then disappeared.

Sarah watched the woman fight to hold up the bag until her head started appearing below the surface. She'd kick and presumably scream for Weir on the boat.

But Sarah didn't have to be on the surface to know the boat was still headed away. She could hear the screws turning and knew that, whatever was happening on the boat, neither Jack nor Weir was on his way back for her or Ella just yet.

All in all, Sarah felt just fine fifteen feet below the surface watching Ella drown. The only problem was she could feel that familiar tightness in the last couple of breaths that meant she was out of air.

Just as Sarah started for the surface, Ella let go of the briefcase.

It drifted within Sarah's reach as she swam up, and given that it was easy to grab and that she'd worked damn hard to get it, Sarah reached out and took hold.

CHAPTER 55

When the boat had taken off, Weir lost his balance along with Ella. The difference was that he wasn't on the swim platform, but on the aft deck. He just had to grab the rail.

He turned immediately, expecting Merchant to come out the port side doorway.

But he didn't.

A part of Weir lost it right then. The part of him that was conscious about how far they'd come. The part that was aware Sarah had the case in hand, he'd seen it. He was practically *done*.

The other part of him kept cool. He knelt down on the deck and aimed his gun at the doorway.

But Merchant wasn't coming out.

Weir caught a flicker of color in his right peripheral vision, and there was Merchant coming over the top of the aft cabin. He held the wooden tabletop from the main cabin like a shield in front of him. Weir fired twice, thinking the bullet could pierce the tabletop, but apparently not. Merchant kept on coming.

As Weir got to his feet, Merchant threw the tabletop.

Weir had to duck, but even so, the edge of the table caught

him in the right shoulder and side of his head. He stumbled, fell against the rail, and tried to swing the gun back.

But Merchant was there. He got both hands around Weir's gun hand.

Weir tried to butt him with his head, but Merchant shifted and took the blow to his shoulder.

Weir tried kneeing him.

Same kind of thing, Merchant took it on his thigh.

Weir wasn't exactly frightened, but he was surprised. He was used to having speed and strength on his side. He shifted quickly to try to roll Merchant over his hip against the rail.

But Merchant moved with him and kept up the pressure on his right wrist.

Weir suddenly pulled the trigger three times. The rounds went off less than six inches from Merchant's face, and then Weir yanked back on the gun with all his might.

Merchant moved with him but still held tight to his gun hand. Not frightened of the noise and flash. He bent Weir's wrist against the rail and twisted hard, and Weir suddenly decided, *Screw this,* and dropped the gun into the water.

That got Merchant to relax his grip, and Weir yanked his hand away and then just piled into Merchant.

The lump of frustration that had been in his chest ever since he'd lost the diamonds burst and provided fuel for his arms and fists. He butted Merchant again and this time got him back on his heels. He followed through with a series of blows to Merchant's body.

Merchant tried to cover himself, and Weir put an elbow into his face, sending him reeling. Already Weir could feel the victory coming, could feel it the way he had in that stairwell. He was going to get this interfering bastard on the deck and then he would kick him until every bone in his body was broken, and then he was going to lash an anchor to him and drown him.

Weir could see it all, right down to the anchor chain he'd use.

His breath was coming hard. But that didn't matter, because he was certain Merchant didn't have anything left.

And then Merchant hit him back.

He came out of his protective posture and hit Weir three consecutive blows in the ribs, knocking the breath out of him. Weir dropped his hands and stumbled back. Merchant broke his nose.

Blood poured down Weir's chest. He swung a looping right hook that Merchant blocked with his left arm. Merchant put a hard fist right into Weir's mouth. The pain was excruciating, and he spit out two broken teeth.

I'm losing, he thought.

That was something that had never even occurred to him before. Setbacks, yes. Mistakes, all the goddamn time. But losing?

He evaded Merchant's last blow and jumped onto the aft cabin roof. He ran for the stairway to the flybridge. Merchant tried to grab him, but Weir kicked him away and crawled desperately the rest of the way up.

He knew there was one of those heavy flashlights the cops used under the console. It'd be a whole lot better than nothing.

He scrambled on his hands and knees to the console, opened the cabinet door, got his right hand around the flashlight, and Merchant was right behind him.

He whirled around and tried to hit Merchant in the knees, but the guy wasn't only stronger than Weir had realized but faster, too. He moved away, then stepped in and kicked Weir in the face.

That put Weir down, but he still had the flashlight, and he sat up and threw it as hard as he could. It went end over end and punched Merchant in the chest. That knocked Merchant back, and Weir took advantage of the rolling motion of the boat to come to his feet. Merchant looked a little stunned by the blow, but Weir kept his distance. He knew now that there was no way he was going to beat Merchant in a straight fight.

Weir took two steps, vaulted over the console, and began to slide down the windshields to the foredeck. He could see the plan simply enough. Get down into the main cabin, get hold of one of the knives in the galley. Put that knife to one of the kids, cut him or her to prove he truly meant it, and then hold the other one for hostage. If he did it right, he could get Merchant locked back in the aft cabin, trying to minister to whichever kid Weir made bleed.

As he landed on the foredeck, Weir was already confident it would work. There would be no hesitation in him if he got into the cabin.

When he turned around, he saw through the windshield that Kathleen and the boy were at the wheel.

Fine, then. It'd be the boy he'd cut, and the girl he'd hold hostage. He started to the starboard side door, which opened right where Kathleen and the boy were running the boat.

Keep it simple, he told himself. *Yank Kathleen out, backhand her, shove her toward the rail. Haul the boy down into the galley and grab a knife. . . .*

But Merchant dropped down in front of Weir.

Just dropped in from the flybridge.

Weir swung a left and right combination that Merchant took on his arms. Merchant shoved him back. And then Merchant hit him with a fast series of blows: body, face, and neck. Weir stumbled back. Blood was pouring out of his mouth and nose. His arms were like lead from trying to fend Merchant off.

He backed up all the way to the bow and braced himself on the edge of the low wooden rail. From this angle, he was cornered, but he could kick out at Merchant if he got any closer.

The boat was rolling so much, it was hard just to keep his footwork, but if Merchant tried to take him, he would have to deal with Weir like a cornered rat.

Braced and ready as he was for Merchant's attack, he wasn't ready for the change in the boat.

Suddenly it was out of gear, and there was a huge racing noise and a crash of gears. They'd thrown the trawler into reverse.

Poised as he was on the edge of the rail, he lost his balance.

He swung his arms wildly, tried to catch at the rail, but he was over it and falling into the water before he knew what was happening.

Then he was spluttering to the surface as the big trawler hull continued forward, the engines not yet able to restrain its momentum. He put his hands up over his head, and he was under the boat, rolling along the bottom of the hull.

The twin screws were coming closer, throwing up a torrent of water in reverse.

If he'd never been truly afraid before, he was now. He hit the slick fiberglass ceiling as he rolled and tumbled. Choking on seawater, he begged Kathleen and the boy to put the engines in neutral, to let him live. Even in that circumstance, a part of him remained clearheaded enough to know that they couldn't hear him, and even if they could, he was begging for a favor he'd never have given them.

Still, he hoped. Right up to the instant the spinning starboard prop was less than a foot away from his face.

He thought, *Not like this*.

But it was just like that.

CHAPTER 56

Kathleen felt the shudder in the wheel, saw the starboard engine tachometer dip, and knew what had happened.

The boy saw it, too.

They went through the starboard doorway and hurried back to the aft rail. The water immediately behind the boat blossomed red briefly, and she could see something that looked like a large bundle of rags floating in the wake.

She felt some revulsion, but not much. Mainly what she thought was, *Good.*

If Sean was feeling anything different than she was, he didn't say so. She put her arm around him, and he let her hold him for a moment. Then he looked at her directly and said, "You were with him," and shrugged her arm off.

He turned to go back into the cabin, presumably to let his sister free. And Merchant was already up on the flybridge, turning the boat around. Hurrying back to pick up Sarah.

Kathleen wanted only to cry, but that wasn't going to do her any good. She stood by the rail until they passed Weir's body. This time the revulsion was hard to ignore — most of his face was gone.

Nevertheless, some of the weakness in her knees was relief.

She closed her eyes and tried to savor that freedom. But being who she was, she couldn't stop her brain from ticking over.

She was still in a spot. Kidnapping charges probably.

Maybe worse.

She thought for a moment, then walked around to the ladder to the flybridge and climbed up to join Merchant.

"See them yet?" she said.

He shook his head. "We didn't go far, but the boat was all over the place." He pointed to the GPS. "I'm headed back to the last waypoint he had entered, the float over the wreck. But we should be able to see them by now."

She knelt on the cushioned seat to his left, took the binoculars, and carefully swept back and forth. She came across the orange float, then methodically swung out to the left and then the right of that.

She saw a flash of yellow, came back, and saw Sarah on the surface. She was holding on to Ella by the back of the shirt.

"Right there," Kathleen said, pointing them out.

Merchant turned the boat to them immediately. "Is she alive?"

"She sure is."

Kathleen had made men feel happy before. Briefly, anyhow. But never anything like what she saw on Merchant's face.

It didn't seem fair.

She waited on the aft deck while Merchant went down to the swim platform. He tossed up the briefcase that Sarah was holding as if it meant nothing. Then he came back and said, "All right, Ella, climb up."

While Sarah stayed in the water, Ella slowly climbed the ladder. Her face was white, and her lips were blue with the cold. She was shivering visibly.

"Where is he?" she said.

"He's dead," Merchant said. "Now kneel down and put your hands behind your back."

She looked at him, and Kathleen steeled herself, thinking that Ella would lash out at him. But she didn't. She seemed to cave inside. And she knelt down and didn't fight him when he tugged her arms behind her back and used his belt to bind her arms behind her.

Kathleen couldn't be certain because Ella was drenched — but it looked as though she was crying.

"You're crying for him?" she said.

Ella said, "You don't know anything."

Privately, Kathleen had to agree.

The Mako drifted up beside the swim platform, and Merchant pushed it away as he knelt to talk with Sarah. Kathleen could see that Sarah's face was bluish from the cold. But the way she was cradling her left arm and trying to move the fingers in her hand it was obvious she was in a lot of pain. Merchant looked more than concerned — he looked scared.

He helped Sarah climb up the ladder onto the swim platform and unstrap the double tanks.

"All right, you sit here," he said to her. "Just hold on tight."

He shoved the empty double tanks up to the aft deck, and Kathleen pulled them out of the way. She couldn't believe how heavy they were.

He climbed the ladder quickly to the aft cabin. "Sean," he called. "Get up to the bow!"

Merchant hurried up the ladder to the flybridge and started the trawler's engines. Kathleen followed him to the flybridge. She saw Sean go to the bow, and Merchant yelled, "In a minute I'm going to want you to drop the anchor. See where the power up and power down buttons are?"

The boy knelt by the electric winch, then waved.

Kathleen said, "What's the matter?"

"Sarah's got the bends. She had to come up too quickly. It can paralyze her, even kill her. I've got to get her back down deep enough and give her that time."

He put the boat in gear and slowly headed back in the direction of the orange float about a half mile away. He picked up the radio handset and began calling, "Mayday, Mayday."

A moment later, the Coast Guard responded and they switched to another channel. Merchant said, "I've got an emergency. I've got one person dead and a diver suffering from the bends."

He went on to give their position and requested a helicopter for support.

He turned to Kathleen. "They've got to come from Otis Air Force Base on the Cape. We could be looking at an hour, and then they'll still have to airlift her to Providence. We can't wait that long. I've got to get her back into the water to decompress. You want to help, go back and make sure that I'm not going too fast, that Sarah's OK on the swim platform."

"Sure."

Kathleen went back down to the aft deck. Sarah was sitting on the platform, holding on to the chrome ladder up to the deck.

"Are you all right?" Kathleen yelled over the engine noise.

Sarah looked up. Her face was very pale, but she nodded.

"You think this is going to make a difference?" Ella said.

Kathleen turned. Ella had managed to prop herself up against the gunwale. She said, "You think you help them right now that means you won't go to jail with me? For kidnapping, for murder?"

"Shut up," Kathleen said.

"I'm not your friend," Ella said. "But they're not either. You think they're going to thank you? Tell the cops to forget what you've done? It doesn't work that way."

Kathleen ignored her and went back to look down at Sarah. Her eyes were closed, and she leaned her head against the transom of the boat.

Ella said, "You better think fast. Because when help comes for them, we go to jail. It's that simple, but it doesn't have to be."

Kathleen jumped slightly as the engine pitch changed suddenly when Merchant put the boat into reverse. There was the rattle of chain up at the bow as Sean apparently began lowering the anchor.

The engines died altogether, and Merchant came hurrying back down the ladder from the flybridge. He climbed onto the swim ladder and said, "Hold on, Sarah. I've got to get these tanks set and we'll get you right down."

He pulled the Mako close, climbed onboard, and quickly began to hook regulators and the packs with the orange vests up to two individual scuba tanks. He kicked off his shoes and stripped off his shirt. He put one of the tanks on himself, grabbed fins, a mask, and the tank for Sarah, and pulled the Mako close again so he could step onto the swim platform. He helped Sarah up and held the tank for her to put on.

Sean came back to stand beside Kathleen at the rail. His sister was behind him, and she seemed frightened when she saw Ella.

"It's all right," Kathleen said, reaching out to comfort her.

But the little girl shrank from her.

"What should I do?" Sean said to Merchant.

"Just stay on the radio with the Coast Guard," he said. "I gave them our position, but you know how to read the GPS?"

"Yeah, sure."

"Good. If they ask again, just repeat that and tell them I've gone down with Sarah."

"All right," Sean said. He took his sister by the hand. "C'mon. We'll wait in the cabin."

"And, Kathleen," Merchant said. "Just so you know" — he tapped his pants pocket — "I've got the keys to the boat with me. Just keep doing what you've been doing, trying to help those kids. I'll speak up for you when the time comes."

"I'll be here," she said.

He and Sarah put their hands over their face masks and stepped into the water.

Ella said, "That means at your parole hearing. Maybe ten, fifteen years from now. That's when anything that he has to say might matter. Or you can listen to me now and still have a life."

Kathleen stood looking down at the water until they were out of sight. And then she turned to hear what Ella had to say.

"He took the keys to this tub," Ella said. "But I've got the keys to the fast boat." She nodded to the Mako. "I pulled the boat from the docks in Newport, remember? I've still got the keys in my pocket."

Kathleen looked down to the front of Ella's pants and, indeed, she could see the edge of a key fob in the right pocket. She reached over and tugged it free. The fob had the Mako insignia.

"Listen," Ella said. "Do they have a helicopter on the way?"

Kathleen didn't answer.

"Do they or don't they?" Ella snapped. "Answer me!"

Kathleen inclined her head.

"All right, we don't have much time. If you set me free and we run for shore, I'll show you how we can lose ourselves in a crowd. We take the diamonds to a fence I know. There's a Russian in New York that's waiting for them to come through. We take off right now, we split the money fifty-fifty, we go our separate ways. You want, I'll even introduce you to a surgeon down in Miami who can change your face, and I can arrange for different papers — Wes and I did it, I can do it with you, too —"

Ella stopped talking.

Kathleen turned.

Sean stood there. His breath was coming fast, and he was holding a knife. A big knife from the galley probably, and though he looked frightened, he also looked like he was going to follow through on what he thought he had to do.

"Move," he said, his voice breaking. "I should have done it before. I should have kicked her head in. If you set her free, she'll kill us."

"I won't," Ella said. "I promise I won't. Sean, I kept you alive all this time!"

Kathleen stood up between the two of them. "You don't need to do this, Sean."

"Move!"

"No." She shook her head. "I'm not going anywhere with her. We're waiting for the Coast Guard, then the police."

She handed him the boat keys.

He looked startled. As much by the tone of her voice as by her handing him the keys, she'd guess.

Because he recognized the truth when he heard it.

She wasn't sure what she would have done if he hadn't appeared, ready to kill to protect himself and his sister. Only twelve years old, and Kathleen had played a part — a big part — in bringing him to that point.

"You're not going to set her free?" he said.

"No, I'm not," she said. "She and I are going to prison. You're going home. That's what's going to happen."

Behind her, Ella began to cry.

Sean looked at Kathleen closely, and after a moment, she could tell that he believed her. He lowered the knife. Which gave her a small but solid piece of satisfaction.

Because Kathleen had always known she was better than this.

EPILOGUE

TWO MONTHS LATER

It was nearly the end of October, and though it had been warm most of the day there was a hint of coolness in the air now.

Merchant and Sarah were up on the flybridge of her boat, and Matt Coulter and his two children were sitting below them on the forward cabin roof. They had put on light jackets and Matt had his arms around both of them. Ben Pryor and his wife and son were inside the cabin preparing a meal for when they reached Newport in about a half hour. After that, Sarah and Merchant would stay on the boat overnight and then take it back to New Bedford in the morning.

"Emotional day," Sarah said.

"Hard not to be."

The day trip was so that the Coulter family could honor C.C. Though she was buried in Newland, Matt had asked Sarah and Merchant if they could take them out to where *Seagull* had gone down.

Matt had led his children in halting prayer to their mother. He had been out of the hospital for only a few weeks and was frail and gray-faced. But he told his wife that they were all together again and that they had come back to this point with the help of old friends and new, and from here they would be starting fresh.

Sean and Laurie had been quietly friendly with Sarah for the trip out but kept their distance with Merchant. He was fairly certain it was because he'd lied to them about their mother still being alive.

It had seemed like the right thing to do at the time.

Still did, as a matter of fact.

Sarah said, "You think you're free and clear?"

"Of shooting the Colombian? I think so. I don't know if the cops believed Dave Gardner shot him or not, but I cleaned up well enough that they haven't come after me. And I had a major piece of luck with that handgun."

"Didn't feel like it at the time," she said.

"I'd guess not."

The gun that Ella had tried to use on Sarah in the water had been the revolver Merchant had taken from the Colombian's ankle holster. If the police had recovered it and matched prints from the dead Colombian along with Merchant's, it would've been hard to say he'd never been in Gardner's apartment. Since it was now at the bottom of the ocean, there wasn't much chance of anyone finding it and making trouble.

"Has Kathleen's lawyer been in touch with you?"

"Yeah, I went in to see him on Tuesday. I'll say what I can for her. Put it this way, I don't think those two children would be alive today without her. That's got to count for something, but there's not much doubt she'll do time. He says that if she's convicted, he'll also want me to be available for the sentencing hearing to help him make a case for leniency. I'm going to talk to Matt about her too, but not today."

"No, not today," Sarah said. "And how about Ella?"

"Just what you'd expect. The D.A. is driving hard against her. Once they ran her prints, they found links to over five murders from here to Florida. Kathleen looks like Pollyanna beside her."

Sarah shivered suddenly. "God, I just got a touch of being back in that water again. I've never been as cold in my life as that decompression dive."

"Yeah, the temperature's dropping fast now." Merchant took a backpack from under the console and pulled out sweatshirts for both of them. He held the wheel while Sarah put hers on. Once she took the wheel back, he reached over, took the thickness of her black hair trapped in her sweatshirt, and pulled it free. Instantly the breeze whipped it around her face, and she smiled. He leaned over and kissed her.

Months ago, she would have hesitated, maybe even evaded his kiss. Now she relaxed into him, and her closeness just about filled him.

He said, "You honor your promises rather well, Ms. Ballard."

"Hey, a deal's a deal," she said. "You've been finding me more available?"

"I have."

"Sleeping with you more?"

"I believe I've noticed that."

She slapped his chest with the back of her hand. "You damn well better have noticed it."

"And that last thing?"

"Oh, you mean that *love* word?"

"Uh-huh."

"Yeah, I don't bat that around too easily," she said. "You can't expect everything."

"I can, actually," he said.

"Well, you know I do," she said. "You just know it."

Not really looking at him as she said it.

He put his arm around her, OK with where they were. Much better than in the past. Feeling just a touch melancholy that she couldn't let go entirely.

But he could live with that.

Eidson, Bill.
The mayday

		DATE DUE	